Other books by Janice Walker

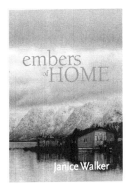

Embers of Home
ISBN: 978-0-9928232-1-4

Forever Home
ISBN: 978-0-9928232-2-1

The Lights of Home

Janice Walker

Author: Janice Walker

First published in 2014 by Erin Rose Publishing

Text and illustration copyright © 2014 Erin Rose Publishing

Design: Julie Anson

ISBN: 978-0-9928232-0-7

A CIP record for this book is available from the British Library.

An Erin Rose Publication

All Rights Reserved.

This novel is a work of fiction. Names and characters are the product of the author's imagination and any resemblance to actual persons, living or dead, is entirely coincidental.

No part of this publication may be reproduced, stored in a retrieval system or transmitted by any form or by any means, electronic, recording or otherwise without the prior permission in writing from the publishers.

Unauthorised reproduction of any part of this publication by any means including photocopying is an infringement of copyright.

*Dedicated to my son Jasper,
for your endless inspiration and humor.*

1

"What have I got myself into?"

After weeks of thumb twiddling, and a strong push from Giselle, I've finally taken the plunge into the unknown and joined an online dating site. Tonight is a milestone. It's my first blind date.

"I knew you would be having second thoughts. That's why I phoned. Go for it, Tara. Just think of it as practice. You have nothing to lose. He certainly looks your type," encourages Giselle.

"Giselle, he could also be a lunatic. I don't know how my love life became such a desert that I've resorted to this. But like you say, I've nothing to lose."

"I can smell the chloroform from here," quips Giselle.

"Don't joke. It might be me using that on him if this drought goes on any longer. Anyway I'd better go."

"OK, let me know how it goes. And don't forget the code," she reminds me, although there's no need.

I pull on a pair of jeans and a smart black jacket. Thankfully I can wear high heels tonight. The guy I'm going to meet 'says' he is 6' 2", so at least I won't tower over him.

Being tall means I can get away with eating what I want. The drawback is that so many of the guys on the dating site are below average height, and I want a man I can look up to. I've a habit of going for men who play it cool, and if a guy shows interest in me I automatically think there's something wrong with them. But it's only recently that insight into my self–worth has surfaced. Now I'm aware of it, I can do something about it. That's why I'm trying something different.

I check myself in the mirror for the last time. With full make-up I don't see the school geek in the mirror, the one who was told she was 'so ugly.' Admittedly my looks have improved since then, mostly down to puberty, and with significant help from my good buddies Elizabeth Arden and Max Factor. I appreciate compliments, but they bounce off me.

It's a fresh balmy night for late April and the nights are getting lighter. I look up at the sky which is streaked with lemon and pink as I step out into the busy city street, feeling optimistic about what the rest of the year will bring. I snigger anxiously to myself as I make my way to the wine bar to meet Oliver. Blind dates have always been for other people – the brave and the desperate. I guess I'm the latter.

Oliver and I briefly chatted online, but I'm still ridiculously nervous, and barely able to smile with the tension in my jaw. I'd thought about getting drunk beforehand and now, even as I arrive I'm still not convinced this is a good idea.

I walk into the softly lit wine bar and spot Oliver at a small table for two. At least he looks like his photograph, but my instant reaction is disappointment and I've not even spoken to him yet. I join him at the table and as we begin to get to know each other I discover Oliver is relaxed and chatty. There is plenty to talk about; but there is total lack of chemistry.

Two large glasses of Pinot Noir later, I've mellowed. While Oliver excuses himself, for what I think is a trip to the bathroom, I glance at my phone and at that exact point a text comes in from Giselle. The text reads – *Have you got panties on? How's it going?*

Simultaneously Oliver's face appears eagerly right in front of me. I'm startled and confused. Did he see the text?

"What the...?"

He comes in close and smothers my words with a kiss. I'm taken back but I go along with it, wondering what I'd done that gave him the green light. I'm a little excited, but hugely mortified. I self–consciously glance around to see if the bar staff have seen it. Either they haven't or they're too polite to meet my eyes.

"Mm, nice kisser," says Oliver.

He overdoes a seductive look and reminds me of Pepe le Pew. *I need to get out of here.* As he disappears to the bathroom, I quickly send Giselle a blank text. It's our pre–agreed code if I needed an excuse to end the date. Right on cue, as Oliver is coming back to the table, Giselle calls. I snatch up the phone and sympathize with Giselle's feigned distress – I have the excuse I wanted.

"I'm sorry. My friend is in trouble," I mouth to him, muttering my apologies then quickly leave. I'm giddy with adrenaline. Chalk one to me. There is only one first blind date. I take a cab to meet Giselle and Simon who are in our usual haunt. I walk in to a round of applause from the exuberant pair, drawing attention from others in the bar and I grin like a lunatic; becoming a public spectacle for the second time tonight. We laugh ourselves limp. It turns out that a surprise tongue sandwich on the first date seems to be customary. Giselle is the expert on dating etiquette – she's also single.

Afterwards I make my way home and the trivial triumph of going on the blind date only lasts until I turn the key in the door of the apartment. It's another night where I go to bed alone, and face the recurring nightmares which have been plaguing my sleep. There is only my job to look forward to, and I'm increasingly averse to that.

I worked hard to get through law school, so when I got offered the job at Sheldon & Napier, I jumped at the chance. For seven years, I've juggled a hectic social life with many late nights spent in the office. Now with promotion in sight, I'm stressed to hell, but bored to death. On the plus side being a lawyer is a lucrative career and as an independent singleton financial security is a huge driving force.

I'd always been ambitious and driven to fulfil my expectations of a successful life. Now I'm living the dream, but the ferociously high–powered and drama laden life in New York hasn't given me the high I'd expected. Happiness has proved elusive.

I turn out the lights and stand in the shadows of my bedroom, gazing out of the window at the bustling street in the city that never sleeps. I watch spirited teenagers hanging out on the street corner and a cosy couple walking slowly arm in arm before I climb into my empty bed.

Next morning at work I find myself staring out the window and searching for the blue sky which is obscured by the tall buildings – my mind won't stay on the job. I have the concentration span of a rocking horse, probably due to the lack of sleep. Again last night I had a bad dream; again I woke just before I died.

It's mid–morning and I'm already on my third water cooler break. I critique my reflection in the silver mirror of the executive bathroom. I draw back my thick hair into a ponytail, and adjust the chaffing waistband of my skirt. I look like a legal executive so what more is there to prove?

Today I feel like I've stepped outside myself and hardly recognise the impervious looking clone looking back at me.

Back at my desk thick files are multiplying. *Damn it.* I shuffle through the paper trying to find what I'm looking for. The court submission is imminent and I'm nowhere near ready. My stomach feels like I've swallowed a jellyfish. Recently the workload has snowballed and some joker speeded up time. This just isn't fun anymore.

I've recently been given a separate office, but much of this floor is divided up by white partitions, which blend into the austere monochrome and silver décor. Privacy isn't in abundance around here. Simon's camp, high pitched voice volleys back and forward, as he has a torrid exchange with Giselle. They make me laugh as she teases him that he only spikes his hair so high to make himself look taller. Because of his petite frame and cute boyish looks Simon looks much younger than he actually is.

"Ah! So where are you going to Miss North?" asks Simon as I approach.

"Well, I'm sure you'll know before I do."

"You're insinuating I'm nosey?"

"You said it, Agent Miller."

"You are lucky to have me looking out for you. Show some appreciation girl. Where would you be without me?"

Giselle's head pops up over the top of the partition. "Never mind him. He's just grumpy because his neighbors were partying and kept him up late last night."

"Oh, didums. Didn't they invite you?" I tease him.

"If you two lightweights hadn't called it a night so early I wouldn't have been in bed before midnight, with nothing better to do than sleep," Simon complains.

"I couldn't handle another cocktail. I need to detox. I'm going to book a colonic," says Giselle.

"Dear God, you're so anal, Miss Beau," says Simon, whose habit of calling people by their surname can get irritating.

"At least I'm not full of crap," Giselle retorts. "Tara. Are you on for meditation tonight?"

"Nope. I'm working late again. Maybe next week," I reply, knowing that probably won't happen either. I only tagged along out of curiosity anyway.

Giselle ducks back down behind the partition and out of sight. Since she joined Human Resources as a temp, the verbal exchanges between her and Simon have amused and irritated colleagues. It gets feisty at times, but their good natured banter eases the sombre mood in the office.

You can spot Giselle easily in a crowd: she's the one with the long, wavy auburn hair and wiry frame, attractive and authentic – two qualities which can be opposed to each other but in her exist side by side without conflict. She moved around Europe as a child, changing schools, picking up languages and making friends; it probably explains her confidence and adaptability.

Simon is moving files and shifting paper around his desk. "I push more shit around here than your average dung beetle," he snorts and rests his hands on his hips.

"I love your way with words, Simon."

"Can I have your autograph on these?"

I start signing the mountain of documents he's prepared while he mutters to himself, but I'm just not listening. I've got too much to do to get involved in high drama right now. I steady my shaky hand as I write; too much coffee on an empty stomach. My mind feels like a wheel spinning in mud, unable to grip anything solid. I jump when Simon's phone rings and I kill it with an angry look. Simon picks it up.

"Hi Patricia. Yes, she's here now. OK, I'll pass on your apologies," Simon responds.

I know what's coming. I've had the feeling all morning that this was coming.

"Patricia passes on her apologies. She can't make the lunch meeting with you and Tray Buchanan, but she says you're not to postpone it," cautions Simon, gesticulating with his eyebrows and tipping his forehead at me.

"Fine. Hold all my calls between now and lunch. I need to read up on their file."

Annoyed at being let down by Patricia at the last minute, I turn sharply to walk off, but my feet tangle and I tumble into the wall with a grunt. Simon's raucous laughter reverberates around the room as I head back to my office.

Patricia Napier has always dealt with the Buchanan family's business. Now she wants me to start taking it over. That's the reason for the lunch meeting today – to lay the foundations.

I don't know much about Tray Buchanan but I'm sure I can blag it. Most of what I do know is by reputation. Tray is the son of a wealthy family, and several generations of businessmen, but he's best known as a philanderer and playboy, and features regularly in the gossip magazines.

I speed read the files before the meeting to get clued up. The dull headache I've been fighting all morning threatens my focus. I pop a couple of Advil in my mouth and swallow hard. I need a clear head. *Oh God, don't let him be too good looking in real life.* I'm a sucker for packaging and easily distracted. After an hour of reading, I've summarized the most important details.

The Buchanans' companies are complexly structured, but regardless of the lack of transparency the international business appears to focus on land acquisition for and on behalf of multi–nationals, geographic research, global mining projects and commercial property development. I don't feel prepared for the meeting and I expect him to be challenging. I snatch up the phone on the first ring.

"I have Mr Tray Buchanan waiting in reception for you," says the receptionist.

I wipe away a smudge of eyeliner, hoist up my bra and tidy my hair, tucking back the lighter golden brown tendrils which broke free. I glance disappointingly in the mirror, sling on my grey wool jacket and head for the reception.

Stepping out of my office I tilt my chin, ready to meet the playboy millionaire. I round the corner to the reception and there is Tray sitting on the white leather sofa, staring at the pert bottom of a pretty young woman reaching for a magazine.

"Hi. You must be Tray Buchanan. I'm Tara North," I interrupt his blatant ogling, extending my hand out to him.

His eyes snap forward to look at me as he slowly and deliberately rises to greet me. He shakes my hand, holding it a second longer than is necessary.

"Unfortunately Patricia can't join us today. It'll be the two of us; I hope that's not a problem?"

"Ah. Shame. Not to worry," he replies.

Tray's mouth pulls back into a tight smile as he drops his eyes southwards in clear and obvious appraisal of my breasts.

"It will give us a chance to get acquainted," he smiles confidently, like someone who knows he's good looking.

Mildly irritated I give him a mental slap.

"I'm sure it'll be beneficial nonetheless," I reply, now aware that my breasts feel conspicuous, despite being hidden behind a neatly cut white shirt.

I notice Tray's manicured hand, the immaculate tailoring and well–practiced suave demeanour which exudes affluence. I wonder if despite his expensive education, his emotional intelligence is below par. His privileges and position in the family business are based on birthright rather than merit.

Loud muffled whispering distracts my attention from him. I glance sideways and see two familiar heads bobbing over the partitions. Wide eyed and open mouthed Giselle and Simon are spying on us. The corners of my mouth lift up. I stuff down the giggle and compose myself. We need to leave before they get more embarrassing.

"Shall we go?" I ask.

"After you," Tray gestures magnanimously. "I've reserved us a table at Mario's."

It's as though I should already know who Mario is. He gestures to the glass door and I lead the way to the elevator without waiting for his reply. The elevator opens and as we step out into the foyer several female heads do a double take on Tray. *What do they see in him?* He's handsome in a boring way: with short brown hair and blue eyes on an oval face which lacks angles and intrigue. Tray's driver is waiting outside the building ready to chauffeur us to Mario's. When we arrive the waiter shows us to our table, addressing Tray with familiarity and charm. He's clearly one of their regular clientele, who can call up and get a table in an instant.

During lunch it becomes apparent that Tray has no interest in talking business, and that's a great relief. I haven't remembered much from the file I read earlier. Tray's main interest and favorite topic of conversation is himself, yet there is a definite vulnerability and charm to the guy which I hadn't expected, although his conversation is purely output only.

The image of him being a cut-throat, power-hungry businessman is a complete illusion created by the media. He keeps glancing at his reflection in the window as he talks endlessly about his skiing trips to Aspen. He recalls his sailing adventures and regales me with vivid tales of his college days. He talks about his twin brother Vaughan, and how they had swapped girlfriends for a week as a prank. I didn't know he had a twin. Tray eventually gets around to asking about me.

"Are you single?" he asks.

"I thought we were here to discuss business? I was expecting to learn more about Buchanan enterprises."

"You come highly recommended. I'm sure you'll learn all you need to know in due course."

He lunges over and places his hand on top of mine. Here's another guy who is unable to read the subtleties of body language.

"Tara, I'd really like you to accompany me to a charity event tomorrow evening...if your boyfriend wouldn't mind? We won't call it a date if that makes you more comfortable, but I'd like to introduce you to my father, since you will be working on behalf of our worldwide interests. It's a great opportunity to network. What do you say?"

Before I know it I hear myself agreeing. It's happening again: the people pleasing! But it's a good career move, and it might be vaguely interesting to mingle with New York society. It wouldn't hurt to accompany him. This is Tray Buchanan, who I'd only seen before in magazines, a harmless socialite with an express ticket to have fun.

"Are you sure I'm not stepping on anyone's toes? I was under the impression you had a girlfriend."

"*Had* a girlfriend," he remarks casually. "Francesca. We broke up. She was paranoid I was seeing other women, acting crazy jealous all the time. So no, I'm a free agent now."

"Then yes. I'd like to come," I say, glad to have clarified the point.

Just as I'm pulling my hand free from under Tray's, a series of flashes go off and we're abruptly and intrusively photographed by a guy, who then bolts from the window of the restaurant.

"What the hell! Does that happen a lot?"

"Yeah, don't worry yourself," he says nonchalantly. "Coffee?"

I shake my head and frown in bewilderment, clueless to why someone would be interested in us, while Tray remains casual and unperturbed. He openly glances at his window reflection with a narrow pout, and a shoulder lift, checking which angle the photographer got. I don't know the potential ramifications of being snapped with the pouting, preppy bachelor, but one thing is for sure – it's out of my control. I toss the white linen napkin on the table, accepting this crazy world and sit back, amused by his vanity, and the fact he probably has more beauty products than I do.

He flashes his ultra white smile at me, and gives my throat a long suggestive look. He's playing me. I sit silently defiant.

"I'll get the check." Tray nods to the waiter, who has been lingering subtly in the shadows waiting for his cue. Although relieved to be going back to work, there is a twinge of trepidation about tomorrow night, and my future working relationship with one of Sheldon & Napier's biggest clients.

2

Running full tilt I glance over my shoulder but can't see the hunter – my heart is palpitating as I try to escape him. He raises his arm to take the shot and with a sudden jolt I awaken from yet another nightmare. The dreams are all different, but the theme is often the same: escalating threat and anxiety to the cusp of annihilation. The bitter twist is that I've started having visions in the quiet moments, seeing bizarre shapes and figures. A tall black haired figure is a regular visitor in these waking visions and I panic, although his presence feels benign, and try to think of something else.

I shower, guzzle my second cup of coffee and leave the reassurance of the small apartment, but at least the loneliness evaporates when I step out into the city street. As I arrive for work I have the usual sinking feeling.

"Morning Eric," I greet the security guard on door.

"Morning Tara," Eric gives me a sideways wink, and taps the side of his nose knowingly. I give him a quizzical smile as I make my way to the elevator. What does he know that I don't? He's such a joker. I walk past reception on the way to my office but before I have a chance to put my bag down, Simon blusters in. He flings the door wide open in haste, as his head and arms arrive a second before the rest of his body.

"Oh girl, you've really done it now, haven't you? Look at this!"

He flings down a newspaper on my desk, opening it at a photograph of Tray and I looking cosy in Mario's restaurant. I can think of better ways to start the day. The caption reads – *Mystery woman splits NYC hot couple.*

"Dear God. What new hell is this?" I mutter.

Simon gesticulates wildly at the article then folds his arms at me.

"It was bad timing. It was a business lunch and that is all," I protest, even though I shouldn't have to defend myself.

Simon adds a foot tap to his stance. "Did he make a pass?"

"It's purely business."

"You better explain that to Patricia before she sees this. She will not be pleased!"

"I don't need this. Plus there'll be negative press if Sheldon & Napier are associated with it. They'll make the link between me and the company."

The short column accuses me of being the reason for Tray's split from Francesca. I'm uncomfortable with it, but the gossip column's credibility is weak. I dismiss the trashy story for what it is: a dishonest attempt to generate drama and make money.

"Thanks for the heads up, Simon. I'll defuse this. He looks better there than he does in real life."

"If I had the chance I would! He's hot. Get in there. Loosen your chains girl. You've a hard heart," Simon jokes, yet his words sting because they resonate.

"He's a textbook catch but I'm just not feeling it. I'm keeping it professional and going with the flow. If something develops then so be it," I reply, sounding more sure than I feel.

"Patricia has just arrived in," Simon's eyes flash to the doorway. "I'm out of here before it hits the fan." He is gone in the blink of an eye.

Wasting no time and ready to take the bull by the horns I stride to Patricia's office, knock and enter clutching the newspaper.

"Ah, Tara. I was just about to call you. How was yesterday's meeting with the Buchanans?" asks Patricia, as she distractedly shuffles paper on her desk.

"That's why I'm here–"

"Sorry to drop you in it like that but I'm just too busy. You'll be handling all their business from now on," she continues.

"Not much business was discussed. Tray Buchanan has his own agenda."

"He tried it on?"

"You know?"

"I'd be surprised if he didn't. It's his reputation...and it's all true. I've been dealing with his father for thirty years and he's a hard headed, no–nonsense businessman. The apple has fallen a long way from that tree," says Patricia accusingly.

With a mixture of relief and irritation I place the newspaper article in front of her. Did she set me up yesterday by ducking out of the meeting? Was she testing me? Patricia glances down and puts on her glasses.

"Crap!" she snaps. "There's no truth in it, so I'm not bothered about that. But is something going on now?" she asks, eyeballing me directly.

"No. He has asked me to go to a charity dinner with him tonight and I've agreed, only because it's a chance to network."

"Yes it is. Just keep it professional, or at least be seen to be professional," she looks over the top of her glasses to makes sure I understand.

I leave Patricia's office and roll my eyes to the ceiling. A fleeting vision of a peaceful country landscape with a feeling of tranquillity flashes through my consciousness and lifts my spirits. I longingly wish to be there, or anywhere else but here. Somewhere beautiful I can escape the politics, complexities and stress of this current existence. I should've been a vet after all.

I used to dream of a second home in the country – maybe move there permanently one day. Right now I'm light years from idyllic lakeshore living. I put that dream on the backburner years ago to carve out my career. If I work hard for a few more years, I can save enough cash and move somewhere peaceful and have a better life. With that in mind, right now I'd like to find 'the one', my soul mate: chatty, interesting, intelligent, ruggedly good looking, funny, a professional guy with a similar outlook, someone I could join forces with for a more contented life. The excitement of city living has lost its lustre but I must keep going. Unless something unexpected happens I'm here in New York for the long haul.

Giselle looks up from her desk when I walk past and I give her the thumbs up on the way. She always says how thoughts are prophetic and create your reality. I don't have time for a situation analysis now. The cell phone is vibrating in my pocket; I pick it up, not recognising the number. I always screen my calls, but for some reason I feel compelled to take this call. I press answer, half expecting a sales call. There is silence on the other end.

"Can I help you? Hello?" I frown at the phone.

No one speaks, but there is some background noise which sounds like a radio or television, and another wind–like sound. It could be someone's breathing. The silence carries on until I end the call. I rationalise it; someone must have accidentally pressed my number by sitting on the phone.

Later, when I pick up my dry cleaning on the way home from work I wonder if the little black dress I had in mind is glamorous enough for the charity event. I certainly don't want to be under–dressed, so maybe I need to wear something more extravagant. I need to know the dress code for such an occasion?

When I get back to the apartment I fire up the laptop and search *charity events Tray Buchanan*. The search brings up images of charity dinners Tray has attended with a stunning blonde beside him: all bouncy hair, exposed cleavage and a vacant far–away stare. This must be Francesca, his glamorous ex–girlfriend. For a brief second I wonder if it's wise to go to a public event with Tray so soon after their split, but I'm not after him and it's his issue anyway.

With one glance at the pictures of the party–goers' I know I need to vamp it up in the glamor stakes. The little black dress is way too conservative. From the back of my wardrobe I pull out a long, black lace, fish–tailed, strapless dress which is still protected by its plastic cover. It has never been worn, but it's the right dress for this occasion.

I shower, blow–dry my hair and pull on the figure hugging dress, easing it over my hips. Now I remember why I haven't worn it before. I pull the zip up to the top, catching sight of my rear end in the mirror. I self–consciously try to smooth it flat. I turn quickly towards the mirror several times, but I notice the same pronounced curve each time. It will have to do.

With little attention to detail I finish off my make–up with smudged black eyeliner around my green eyes and apply red lipstick. Dropping my head backwards, I let my hair hang down my back and spray it with product to separate the layers. Tray will be here in ten minutes.

I toss the lipstick into a tiny black clutch bag and pour

myself a large glass of Merlot to take the edge off. It goes down easily, flooding my empty stomach, making my arms and legs temporarily numb. The buzzer to my apartment rings and I try to dash to answer it, but I'm abruptly restrained by the fishtail of the dress, which forces me to take tiny tottering steps to the door. *Damn formality.*

"Hello."

"Tara. It's Tray."

"OK, I'm just on my way down."

Damn. I feel heady and I haven't even left the apartment. Grabbing my clutch bag and cell phone, I notice I've missed a call from Giselle but I don't have time to return it now. I totter out into the hallway, frowning and feeling resentful that I'm trussed up so tightly.

"Wow, you look lovely," Tray slathers on the charm.

"Thanks."

The driver opens the door of the black limousine and I clumsily get inside, shuffling my bottom over to the far side as Tray slides in beside me.

"Glass of champagne?" Tray passes me a glass of Bollinger.

"I don't think I should, but I will." I take the glass and discover I've quite a thirst to quench. "It's been a hell of a day. Did you see the photo of us in that gossip column today?" I ask.

"Yep."

"Aren't you bothered?"

"Nope. Are you?"

"I don't care much for the spotlight."

"It'll be old news tomorrow when they have someone else to demonise."

"You've got a point there. That's not a world I want to

be part of." My guard is dropping, my senses altered by the alcohol. I notice, and ignore, the unwelcome wave of foreboding that comes over me. Tray leans forward to speak to the driver, giving him instructions. As we approach the hotel, my eye is caught by beautifully dressed women and men in tuxedos gathering around the entrance of a grand building. The traffic near the hotel is heavy and the driver pulls over on the opposite side of the road.

I'm captivated by the grandeur of this beautiful classical building. Two elegant Grecian style columns stand either side of the wide entrance, with its beautifully lit golden lanterns, against a backdrop of wispy variegated ivy. A sparkling three–tiered fountain reflects light across the half–moon driveway.

The car door opens. Tray gets out and beckons me to follow. I do my best to gracefully slide to the edge of the seat, keeping my knees and ankles together. Tray takes my arm and I'm grateful for his steadiness, though he seems preoccupied by my cleavage. He looks like he's willing my breasts to escape over the balcony of the black lace dress. He places his hand on my lower back as we walk to the crossing. I remind myself that I'm here on business, because right now it's slipping my mind. We wait side by side for the crossing to change and I step out just a split second before Tray.

With dim awareness I hear a car revving hard. Tray steps back and I realize it's screeching towards me. I feel his hand grab my shoulder, but it glances off. I'm too far away. I need to get out of the way of the speeding car. I attempt a long stride, but I'm restrained by the damn dress, which sends me into a dive. The hurtling car levels with me.

With brutal impact the metal tears into my flesh. The sickening blow throws me onto the car. My neck snaps backwards, before my head smashes into the windscreen with full force. A black hooded figure is driving. I only know it's human from the glint of the eyes.

Everything is out of control. In slow motion I freeze frame the images and capture every split second of what is happening. The onslaught of images suspends then vaporizes into darkness.

3

My spirit separates from my body very naturally and I float above the human form of myself. I hover above; watching the doctors and nurses working on my still form which is lying in the emergency room. I feel no pain. I'm not scared. But I know my body is in a whole lot of trouble. There is bright red blood oozing from the open gash on my head. I don't want to watch.

A brilliant light is shining above me, beyond the limitation of the ceiling. I'm swept into a shaft of multi colored light, and the hospital scene disappears. Moving at great speed, the colors around me blur to brilliant white. I'm completely at peace with what's going on. The Tara who is lying on the hospital bed would be freaking out at this, but I've no concern for what's happening to me.

Through the radiant light I step into the most stunning landscape I've ever seen. There's nothing quite this beautiful on earth. I'm in an exquisite terraced garden on the side of a mountain. Around me there are golden translucent arches coiled with greenery, white sparkling marble, and flowers so incredibly bright they actually shine. A smooth shallow pristine pool is hewn from the pure white marble and the water within twinkles invitingly. The golden sky has a fine layer of pearlescent shimmering pink clouds. There's amazing peace and elation here. Death is so effortless and easy to accept. I'm glad to be here.

Tiny golden flecks drift towards me then expand into faintly human forms; welcoming me without words. I step forward without my feet touching the ground and I magnetically drift towards a whirling mass of energy in what looks like a swimming pool. Someone, I don't know who, tells me I'm not to go there, but it's hypnotic. Suddenly there is a man beside me, or was he there the whole time because he feels familiar? I look into the kind, noble face of a Native American man with liquid brown eyes.

We speak only with thoughts. I tell him how beautiful it is, but the man tells me to go back. Although we're still talking, I can see other things too, as if on multi-screen. I feel like I'm being plugged into a power source, and I can see what looks like mathematical codes flashing through sequences. I ask why I have to go back. He replies that I have to return to walk between worlds – whatever that means, it sounds like a burden. All I want is to be here in paradise. I don't want to go back.

I want to know who the man is, but before I finish forming the thought he tells me his name is Lehman. The tugging is getting stronger. Lehman's strong gentle face begins to fade and as I watch he communicates that the bonds with nature are to be rebuilt. His presence, and that of the light, begins diminishing and I'm no longer in the garden. I hear a rhythm which is faint at first, though it's steadily increasing. I'm being pulled along on a current. The rhythm is my heartbeat. I'm falling back through the tunnel and all the time the rhythmic beat continues.

A sudden jolt brings me rudely into a bodily world of pain. I panic at the intensity of my senses. The pain sears through my body: splitting through my head, over-spilling and cascading around me. I acutely hear the metallic sounds of clattering instruments, loud terse voices seem harsh amongst beeps and hisses. The pain is torturous. I try to scream, but no sound comes out. They can't help me if they don't know.

I need to return to the blissful garden. I need to go back,

but how? I'm alive, but I've no gratitude for that. It's intolerable. I push at the boundaries of my body, looking to escape and I find it.

I'm flickering out of my body, repelled by the pain. I look down at myself twisting in the hospital bed and watch the nurse prepare an injection. I drift away; because I can. I pass into the waiting room where Giselle sits alone with her head in hands and I feel the love she is sending me. I can feel her fear, and my concern is for her. I place my arm around her shoulder, but it passes through. Again I try to reassure her, and again my arm drifts through, but Giselle's startled expression shows she is aware of me.

"Oh God, no!" Giselle quietly mutters and I know she feels me beside her, though she fears the worst has happened.

"I'm OK," I whisper unheard, but suddenly I'm moving back to my body. I glimpse the nurse who has injected me and she is watching my slowing eye movements. The arcing and twisting of my body stops. Numbness connects my veins and the morphine takes effect. I slip into darkness.

4

I have no idea how much time has passed, but I recognize Giselle's voice, and it must be her hand that is holding mine. I blink hard, focussing on Giselle's smiling face. Although my vision is blurry I can see I'm in a hospital room. Excitedly she calls the nurse and starts manically gabbling, hardly pausing for breath.

"You being chased by the devil?" I croak.

"Don't you ever do that to me again! I thought I'd lost you!" Giselle snaps but her face is soft.

My mind is blank as I struggle to take it all in. Giselle explains how I came to be in hospital, and how the police found my phone at the scene of the hit and run accident. They contacted Giselle because her number was the last call on my phone. Apparently, before he was taken to hospital suffering from shock, Tray hadn't been helpful to the police. He hadn't given them any of my personal details.

"Bloody idiot," remarks Giselle, who has no patience for ineptitude.

A young nurse breezes in, already on first name terms with Giselle. The doctor explains I've been kept sedated for two days because of the head injuries. The doctor's voice is low and serious when he tells me I'm lucky to be alive. They're keeping me under assessment for a few more days which is not good news – I want out of here.

Giselle had retrieved my phone from the police and contacted Aunt Rosa and my brother Anthony; my two closest relatives.

"Anthony was fresh out of sympathy," says Giselle, "but your Aunt Rosa is flying out as soon as she can. She's been phoning the hospital constantly." Giselle emphasizes the latter comment.

I'm relieved my aunt is coming. She has been such a small part of my life recently, but I miss her desperately. Aunt Rosa is a kind, motherly woman: generous to the point of being a doormat, who always overstretches herself and worries what people think. If there's trouble, Aunt Rosa would be the first to drop what she's doing to help out.

It saddens, but doesn't surprise me that Anthony wasn't bothered about me. I've been making excuses for my brother's cool, irritation with me – but I simply can't explain it. I wouldn't say we'd ever been close but we share a sibling bond, which now seemed stretched thin. I'd noticed he was on a short fuse around everyone, but I'd been inclined to take it personally. When I first noticed his annoyance I'd asked him what was wrong. He responded with a hard eyed, semi–smile and a questioning sneer to his tone that 'there's no problem'. It was the male equivalent to that common female refute 'I'm fine' which actually means 'work it out, stupid'. Anyway I couldn't work it out, but suspected his heavy drinking was playing hell with his blood sugar.

Giselle's summation of my sibling was that he's 'such a dumbass' and now in every conversation where I mention my brother she begins by saying 'he's such a dumbass', but he really isn't that bad, which I often point out. For someone who endeavors not to be judgemental, Giselle sometimes struggles with her Rottweiler alter ego, which jumps to loyal, but unnecessary, defence. Oddly though, today she referred to Anthony by name, and not by 'dumbass'.

I'm shaking off the bewilderment of being in hospital. Although I've no immediate recollection of the accident, I'm slowly regaining a faint memory of getting out of a black limo.

It's late afternoon when two solemn faced police officers come to take a statement. The doctor tries to stall them but the police get their way. Straight off the bat I tell them I can't help because I truly don't remember much about the accident.

"Miss North, we already have a suspect for your attempted murder. The car was fitted with a false number plate, but we've located it and found your blood on the vehicle's bodywork," says the policeman.

I think I'm going to throw up.

The policeman continues oblivious. "Miss North, do you know someone called Francesca Evans?"

I shake my empty head.

"Francesca Evans is an ex–girlfriend of Tray Buchanan, the man you were with at the time of the accident."

"Oh right, yes." Now something is making sense.

"We believe she was driving the car, though Mr Buchanan seems to be unable to confirm that." The officer's tone raises a suspicion about Tray's honesty.

"Why would...? Oh." I already know the answer.

The policewoman nods, seeming to read my mind and I presume the officer also knows about the press article too. My brain throbs when I think of the lead up to the accident.

"The thing is, we have been unable to apprehend Miss Evans. We can't locate her. What do you know about her? Did you two have an argument?" quizzes the policeman.

"No. Why do you think I know her? I've never even met her."

The policeman casts a look at his colleague.

"What did you two talk about on the phone on the day of the accident?" the policeman presses.

"I've never spoken to her," I answer getting exasperated.

"Your phone shows you took a call from her, in addition to several missed calls," the policeman contradicts me.

I raise my eyebrows and inhale deeply before I continue. "I vaguely remember a call where no–one spoke, but I guessed someone pressed the button accidentally."

"I see. We believe Francesca Evans is in hiding. No–one seems to have seen her since the accident. She may also be dangerous. If you remember anything that may help, call us," instructs the policeman.

"Do you think she'll come back to finish me off?" I'm ask, only half joking.

"There are cameras all over this building and the security guards have been given a photograph in case she tries to enter. Don't worry."

"Really!" My mouth is dry and I reach for the water jug.

"We'll have her in custody soon." They abruptly leave.

This can't be real. I close my eyes, trying to shut it all out. My mind keeps going over the events, trying to make sense of the drama I've found myself in. I want to escape in sleep, I remain awake. Bright daylight streams in through the window and I'm thankful for the warmth of the sun's rays on my face.

Lying here I have nothing better to do than think. *Someone wanted to kill me.* Now that's a bizarre and sinister thought. The near death experience, if that is what you call it, is also on my mind. I'd read about it, but I would never have imagined how incredibly lucid and real the experience is. I try to recapture the wonderful feeling of peaceful euphoria, but I can't, so I simply linger on the memory instead. For a brief while I died. Death doesn't frighten me – but going insane does.

I could ask the nurse about what happened, and omit the near death experience in case she thinks I'm having a post traumatic melt–down. I don't want to give them an excuse to keep me here longer than is necessary either.

A walking smile comes in carrying a bouquet of flowers, which is so enormous she has to peer around it. The middle aged nurse remarks that I must mean a lot to someone for them to send such an outrageous sized bouquet. She passes me the attached card and disappears to find a vase large enough to hold them. The card simply says – *Get well soon. Tray xx.*

No visit, no phone call, no use whatsoever, but he sends me flowers to sooth his conscience. I toss the card onto the cabinet but it misses and falls on the floor. The nurse comes back in with a large vase and arranges the bouquet in it. She picks up the card from the floor and gives me a perceptive look.

"Not from someone special then?" she shakes her head.

"Not at all."

"I'll move them away from you. They'll only get up your nose," and she kindly moves the flowers to the other side of the room.

"Were you on duty on the night I was brought in here?"

"I was. For a while we didn't think we'd get you back. You suffered serious blood loss. That leg injury was dangerously close to your femoral artery. You're very lucky to be alive."

I choke at the irony. *What's lucky about it?*

"Do you get used to it?"

The nurse gives me a sideways look, stops folding a towel and sits down beside me.

"What do you mean? Blood and sickness?" she asks.

"Death."

The nurse smiles. "You get to know the look and smell of death very well, but you know what honey, you detach from it. I've been a nurse for thirty–two years and I'm certain death isn't the end. To some degree it's whatever you expect it to be. I've watched dying patients reach out to something that I can't see. I remember hearing a patient ask someone they knew, if they could go with them, but there was no–one in the room; that I could see anyway. She died peacefully a few minutes later. A patient once told me he'd been visited by his dead brother and that he was coming back for him. He said his goodbyes to his family, smiled and died peacefully. He chose to go when he did."

The nurse is watching me intently.

I only manage a nod because I don't trust my voice not to break.

"Did you see something, honey?" the nurse asks too kindly, touching my arm.

Uh no. Not sympathy. I can feel tears brewing.

"I...died...but I had to come back. I just need to know I'm not crazy." I wipe away unbidden tears, feeling relieved, not judged.

In the early evening Giselle visits. I'm utterly exhausted by this time and blurt out about the near death experience. I can trust her not to think I'm completely insane. She's a walking encyclopaedia on all things metaphysical and some of it had rubbed off onto me. I'd been to a couple of workshops, which were interesting, but I was turned off by some of the guru worship and some of the leaders seemed to be on an ego trip. I don't like being told how to live, no matter where the dogma stems from.

"Well, I'm surprised they'd let you in at all," Giselle laughs. "We've got a lot of living to do yet. Near death experiences exist. They're well documented. I don't fancy putting it to the test myself just yet."

"When the doctor was working on me, you were in the waiting room. You felt me there didn't you?"

Giselle blinks sharply and stares at me. "I did feel you there. I thought it was because you had passed on."

She touches my arm and I can see her eyes moisten at the memory of it. So now I've told two people and neither have called for a straight jacket. Giselle doesn't stay too long and she hugs me tightly when she leaves.

I lie back and think about how Giselle and I are like two sides of the same coin, yet her unorthodox upbringing was completely unlike my conservative childhood. I grew up in the small town of Fort Jarvis, Washington. My mother was a housewife. My father was a lawyer and town councillor. We did everything by the rules. We never moved house, and my father would only drive Ford cars. He said they were reliable and cheap to fix. By the time I was a doubting teenager this sounded bizarre; if it's so reliable why worry about it breaking down? My father's favorite sayings were 'if and when' and 'worst case scenario', which prompted an undercurrent of fear; to be prepared for what was going to go wrong. At home anything unusual or abnormal to them was scorned and ridiculed.

My mother went with the consensus and always acquiesced with my father. She also referred to him as 'father' and for some reason it made me cringe when she did that. I remember the black cloud feeling I'd get from her. Now I recognise that my mother was depressed. She deferred all responsibility, and lost the opportunity to have any influence.

Their marriage worked because they stuck to their fixed ideas of their familial roles. They didn't look beyond their niche. To the exclusion of everything else, they rigidly adhered to routines and beliefs. They were active in the church, the golf club and charities. They were always 'helping the less fortunate' by dishing out pity, platitudes and mashed potato.

My father was fierce if he didn't get acknowledgement for his community efforts. The one year he didn't receive an accolade at the golf club dinner, he came home in a narcissistic rage, and took it out on us. I knew by his stiff carriage when he came in the door there was trouble brewing. He was a different man at home to the one most people saw. We swallowed it down. That's just the way it was.

Anthony and I were the targets of his verbal abuse and aggressive tirades. We handled it by putting on a different face to the outside world – following the example we had been set. We were pathetically grateful for our dad's attention, sickeningly so. Regardless if it was negative, it was at least a substitute for love. It was around that time my heart fuse had blown, and I disconnected.

I'd become a lawyer, like my father, and like him, real happiness has eluded me. Anthony has suppressed anger issues, which he channels into hunting animals and bullying his wife. As products of our upbringing, it crosses my mind that perhaps Anthony and I are both a couple of fruit cakes.

5

It's dark now, so sleep should come soon. Noise from the corridor and the squeaking of the door disturbs me. Another nurse enters and tweaks my pills. The medication eventually kicks in and I fall into a restless sleep. I awaken under the influence of a hollow, wretched feeling. A cuddle would be priceless right now. I feel vulnerable. In truth I've felt like this for a long time and avoided dealing with it. Everything I usually cram into my life is suspended indefinitely and I can't escape my feelings. The fallibility which has been threatening me pushes me anxiously to the edge. I can't justify this panic, but my fear is that I'm losing my mind. Then what? Asylum? Medication? More isolation? My troubled thoughts escalate.

I smack my fists down on the bed, twisting and trying to find comfort. There is none. The last time I was alone in hospital...*no, I'm not thinking about that*. Regardless of attempts to block them out, the images of being in this hospital one year ago this very week, come crowding in. I'd had an incomplete miscarriage. But I don't want to think about the pregnancy, or the miscarriage, and once again I push it out of my mind. Apart from Giselle I told no-one until it was all over.

Through my closed eyes I can see faces shifting and changing as though they're trying to communicate. Are there distant voices too? What the hell is happening? I'd seen similar things as a child. I'm frightened because there is no rest anywhere. My heart races and I'm sweating. I need to get this under control. I breathe slowly and eventually the panic subsides. I've no idea what time it is but daylight is beginning to break through. The squeaking door distracts me and someone comes into my room.

"Just checking to see if you're awake," smiles another new nurse. "I know it's early, but you have a visitor that's come a long way to see you. It's Rosa Cummings. Do you want to see her?" she asks.

"Aunt Rosa! Yes."

I push through the greyness and turn on the overhead light. As soon as she walks into the room I throw my arms around the rock of comfort that is my Aunt Rosa. Her natural homely scent is a mixture of freshly baked bread and newly ironed clothes. *How did she manage that after being up all night travelling*? I inhale her deeply before she pulls gently away, taking care not to touch the bandages on my head.

"I'm so glad you're here." I stretch my fingers out and wrap them around her hand.

"I would have been her sooner if I'd known, darling. How are you? Can I get you anything? Pillow? Water? Soup?"

"No, no, nothing. Just be here." I sound unusually and ridiculously needy. She places her other hand on top of mine.

"How long will you be in here?" asks Rosa.

"I don't know, but I want to be out as soon as I can. The doctors want me out of bed today and I'm having physio. I just want to get back to normal."

"Is that realistic? You'll need to recuperate and you can't do that when you're working."

"Well what else can I do?" I shrug.

"You could come and stay with me for a while. Some wounds may be on the inside," says Aunt Rosa sagely.

The thought of being nurtured and cared for in the peace and tranquillity of the country is very appealing. I've been an orphan long enough.

"I'd like that, but I've got to get back to work," I reply, thinking about the rent, the apartment and the credit card payments.

"I'm sure there's an answer. Leave it with me. How did this happen anyway?" asks Rosa, swerving topics. I can tell from the change in her usually gentle voice that she's looking for someone to blame. I explain to her about the accident, leaving out the important detail that Francesca Evans is not in custody.

We're interrupted by the physiotherapist who comes into the room. With belligerent perseverance it goes better than the doctor expected; I'm determined to get out of here and retreat to the mountainous countryside of Big Spruce for at least a little while.

Aunt Rosa orders a taxi to my office to meet with my boss for an update and to discuss sick leave. I smile at her, standing there in her casual floral print blouse and long canvas skirt. She looks soft and parochial and a sharp contrast to the austere, clinical, surroundings of the Sheldon & Napier office she is heading to. I thank her for what she is doing and she brushes it aside. It feels great to have her in my corner.

Later Giselle visits and recounts how the patronising Patricia Napier had her ass kicked by a humble country lady. Using, for leverage, the fact that I was on company business when the accident happened, crusading Aunt Rosa negotiated extended leave for me, on full pay, until I'm fit to return to work. Apparently Aunt Rosa shone when she left the office. Typically, she'd stood up for someone she cares about, in a way that she wouldn't have done for herself. Now her task for the day was over she'd gone to her hotel to get some sleep.

After days of physical therapy I'm mobile and eager to discharge myself. The scan shows that the brain swelling has gone, and now that the bandages have been removed I can see the shaved area around the scar, though my hair hides most of it. When I wash it for the first time the caked blood runs a revolting purplish brown. I wince and take care not to disturb the wound.

The cuts and bruises have healed well. I can now apply the Bio Oil that Giselle has given me to stop the scarring. It's part of the emergency lotion and potion pack she brought me. *God, I love that girl.* Because of a damaged ligament in my knee I've been given an embarrassing crutch, which I plan to discard. Giselle calls me from work to arrange my discharge from hospital.

"This is so meant to be. Everything has just come together. Simon's place gets flooded and becomes uninhabitable–"

Giselle is interrupted.

"And you see something good in that?" Simon is shouting in the background. We're now having a three way conversation on speakerphone.

"Yes. You get rinsed out and now you've Tara's apartment to move into for the time being. That's great timing," says Giselle.

"I'm glad it helps you out Tara, and I'm sorry I haven't been able to visit but I just can't stand hospitals. They freak me out enough without seeing you lying there all mangled. All that blood and gore. They'd need a bed for me," says Simon dramatically. I can't get a word in when their conversation turns into a double act.

"You're a total wimp, Simon," accuses Giselle.

"I had flashbacks for years after I had my tonsils out," he replies. "I got a gastric virus in hospital and vomited blood everywhere. It was like a scene from a horror movie."

"Well, you're coming with me to pick her up. No excuses," Giselle tells him.

Aunt Rosa has already returned to Big Spruce. She stuck it out in the city for four days, having spent all of her time with me or in her hotel. I collect my things together and I'm ready to leave this hospital once and for all. I've had no more communication from the police. There doesn't seem to be much urgency to find the car driver. *Maybe no news is good news*, I reflect as I sit on the bed waiting for my lift.

I can hear them before I see them. Simon's high pitched voice echoes down the corridor, drawing attention to himself before the nurses shush him. Giselle has him by the arm as they bump through the door frame together. Simon complains in a loud whisper that he's going to faint.

"Oh shut up and pull yourself together," scolds Giselle.

Simon is not listening. In one stride, he has his arms around me with a grip like a drowning man.

"I'm so sorry I've not been to see you, but you know what I'm like," apologizes Simon, making a fuss. I don't care because I'm ecstatic to be discharged, and I'm so glad to see my two best friends.

"Let's just get out of here," I pull away from him and move toward the door.

"Too right. I've got you!" says Simon taking my arm.

"What! Who has got who? Stop leaning on me."

We, the commotion, head out into the corridor while smirking nurses watch us, hiding their mouths and muttering into their coffee. We reach the entrance and I pass my crutch to the security guard.

"I won't be needing this," I say with a wink.

It's good to be in the outside world again and I'm relieved to see the back of the hospital. Next stop, Seattle: en route to Big Spruce for rest and relaxation.

6

I don't have much time to collect some belongings from my apartment before the flight leaves for Seattle. I toss my most comfortable clothes into a holdall: pull on a pair of loose jeans, a blue hooded sweatshirt and navy Converse sneakers. Comfort is what really matters to me right now. The freedom of being able to go wherever I like puts me back in control of my life again. As I lift my bags into the trunk of Giselle's car something makes me look back at the apartment building. It weirdly feels like the end of an era. I hand the keys over to Simon, knowing that the place is in good hands and that it'll be immaculate when I get back.

"Come on, let's get you to the airport," says Giselle, starting the engine and we set off to JFK. When we arrive Simon grabs a trolley and loads up my bags as we make our way to check–in.

"No second thoughts?" asks Giselle.

"None. I want to be there already. I want to escape before something stops me."

"Wrong answer. You're supposed to say you'll miss us."

"I will. But I'll be back before I know it."

There's a pull to stay in New York, and even though I'll only be gone a short while I only booked a one way ticket because I don't exactly know when I'll be back – it's hugely liberating – just like not having a diary to adhere to.

"You're not getting away from us that easily you know. We'll come and visit," threatens Simon.

"Oh good. What would I do without you two goons?" I roll my eyes at him.

After check–in, we hug and say our quick goodbyes, then I make my way to airport security and join the queue of passengers waiting to be scrutinized; the tedious procedure takes longer than usual. By the time I board the steps to the plane I need to grip tightly because dizziness and fatigue overpowers me now that the adrenaline has subsided. I finally wilt into my seat with sweet relief.

The six hour journey will give me plenty of precious time to let my mind idle and contemplate the past couple of weeks. I let go of the tension I've been carrying. *God, I'm so grateful to be doing my own thing again, free from doctors, nurses and a hospital bed.*

"Sorry," the passenger next to me nudges me from my thoughts. "I'm a nervous flyer," he apologizes. The man re–fastens his seat belt and starts fiddling with his watch. Moments later we take off, bound for Seattle. I remember the Rescue Remedy which Giselle gave me, so I fish it out of my bag and offer him some.

"It's good for stress," I explain.

He looks at me like I must be joking – well I guess it could be anything.

"I'm not trying to poison you. Look." I drop four drops from the dispenser onto my tongue. The man takes a few drops and raises his eyebrows.

"Tastes like brandy. Speaking of which..." he presses the call button for the cabin crew. The passenger introduces himself as Steven and we chat amiably for a while. Amazingly, he turns out to be from Big Spruce; the town where Aunt Rosa lives and where I spent much of my time as a child.

"No way. Small world," says Steven. He begins to tell me his life story and about how he recovered from chronic fatigue syndrome with the help of an acupuncturist in Big

Spruce. He opens his wallet and gives me the business card for his acupuncturist, even though I didn't ask for it.

I absently drop the card into my handbag, having no intention whatsoever of ever contacting the acupuncturist. I'm needle phobic so I'm not about to sacrifice myself as a human pin cushion for anyone, plus I'd had enough needles to last a lifetime at hospital.

Thoroughly exhausted I try to tail off the conversation with Steven. In my window reflection the dark circles under my eyes stand out like skeletal hollows, in marked contrast to my pale face. I wish Steven would stop talking. He doesn't take the hint. I exaggerate a yawn and look away from him to disengage from the conversation. Steven continues talking and leans even further forward into my space.

The flight attendant comes around the cabin and gives out blankets. I tuck it round me, pulling it over my shoulders, shielding myself from the onslaught of Steven's monologue. Finding space between his sentences I interject.

"I'm going to get some shut–eye." I smile, then recline my seat, and lean towards the window, away from him.

"Oh right. Good idea. I think I'll do that too," says Steven.

I close my eyes, but by the restless sighs coming from him and the distorted tinny sound of music, it sounds like he's now listening to his iPod. I let it wash over me and settle into a light sleep, only waking up when we start our descent to Seattle Tacoma airport. Steven has already latched onto a lady on his other side. I wish him well and edge down the aisle as far as I can, hoping to be one of the first off the plane.

I make my way through the terminal building, discovering that walking isn't all that easy. I hide the limp, trying not to not draw attention – they might offer me one of those embarrassing, buggy rides. I hoist the oversized handbag over one shoulder, and make my way to baggage reclaim feeling detached from the hordes of people in the airport. I just focus on what I have to do. I make my way outside and spot Aunt Rosa's green pickup truck at the arrivals collection point.

It makes me smile to hear the different accents, and the air smells so good: light and fragrant as though there had been a recent shower. It's feels great to be back and I welcome the familiarity – yet with it comes a heaviness I can't explain, but it reminds me of my previous life. The one I tried to leave behind.

My mood soars when I see Aunt Rosa. She throws her arms around me when I reach the pickup truck and I feel like I've come home. Inside the truck a large, black shape bumps against the windows. Hudson, her huge, burly, Newfoundland dog sticks his twitching muzzle out of the half opened window, licking and snorting as he tries to get out.

"Hudson! You crazy big bear. Who's gorgeous?" I wrap my arms around him and bury my face in his thick black fur. He whines and writhes, trying to jump on me from within the confines of the pickup.

"He's glad to see you," says Aunt Rosa. "We both are," and she beams a hearty, honest smile at me.

The journey from the airport will take at least three hours, more if the traffic is bad. We head north, away from Seattle on a beautiful journey I've always loved. The roads become quieter and I take in the beauty. The watery blue–grey inlets recede until they're only visible in the rear view mirror, replaced by an abundance of trees bordering our route to the country.

I love Aunt Rosa's upbeat chatter, but I'm happy to just listen and stare out the window. Always prepared for whatever is ahead, Aunt Rosa has brought a small wicker picnic basket, covered in a red and white gingham cloth. It's a lovely touch.

She pulls the truck over at pretty wooded, roadside picnic–spot to break–up the journey and to let Hudson relieve himself. For years she's been using the truck to carry gardening supplies for her work, and there's a fresh, earthy smell from the back of it where soil has recently been spilled. I unroll the cloth from the top of the picnic basket: the smell of fresh baked bread in my nostrils is divine – my stomach groans in response. We tuck into overstuffed cheese and pickle sandwiches, while I pat Hudson and he drools on my sneakers. He watches us intently, waiting for something to fall. His rear end twitches with anticipation.

"We've not forgotten you, Hudson," assures Aunt Rosa. She gives the amiable dog half of her homemade chocolate muffin – clearly begging pays off. He snaffles the muffin with one swallow and a gratuitous dribble.

Rosa was widowed many years ago and Hudson, with his protective, gentle nature, had been a canine replacement for a partner. She treats him like a human being and Hudson goes along with it because he considers himself human too. Rosa lavishes love on him, plus every home comfort she would offer any visitor; and the bonus is he's allowed to sleep on her bed. For the life of me I can't understand how she gets any sleep, with him spread–eagled on top of her handmade quilt.

We get back on the road and the sharp splitting pain in my skull reminds me to take the painkillers.

"You need to keep taking those regularly to prevent the pain before it starts," says Rosa, who is no stranger to medication for her arthritis.

"I only take them when I need to," I counter.

The painkillers kick in, and with a full stomach I feel drowsy. I lean my head against the window and muse over how much I adore my aunt. She is in my happiest and most cherished childhood memories. I remember vividly the family vacation to rural Kansas and how at dusk Aunt Rosa and I had caught fireflies as they flew out of the long grass. I remember how mesmerized and excited we were by the little bugs, and how we stayed up long after the others had gone to bed. She is the one safe haven amongst the harshness of life's reality. I don't know what I'd do without her. I fend off that thought. So why, if I love her so much, haven't I spent more time with her? I could even move back to the country permanently? I think it's too late for me. I've become citified, but I let my mind rest on the possibility. I hadn't felt like part of a family since the death of my parents, and before that family life had been pretty bleak anyway. New York had been an amazing blank canvas.

I always follow the proverbial dangling carrot, only pausing to change the carrot. My identity is based around my life in New York. The isolation suited me when I wanted to leave my past behind and carve out my own life. But now I'm questioning if I want something different. Maybe I could blend into the town but maybe I'd be swallowed up by it. I need a change, but I don't know if I can cut down my life for something untested; and besides would it be any better?

Aunt Rosa shrieks. Suddenly the braking of the vehicle

propels me from my sleep. Lurching forward, my adrenaline spikes, then I'm roughly restrained by the seat belt. A large elk is galloping across the road in front of us. Aunt Rosa swerves the car, nearly colliding with the hulking animal. The side panel of the pickup passes within inches of the elk's muscular hind legs. The elk carries on galloping, reaching the grass verge and disappearing into the trees.

"You OK?" I ask, noticing Rosa has her hand over her heaving chest.

"Yes. Sorry, that creature had a death wish. It jumped out from nowhere," she apologizes, and raises her eyes in gratitude to an unseen force. My heart is still racing and I steady my shaking hands.

"You're white as a sheet," says Rosa.

"I'm fine."

Actually the near miss brought me back to the accident and the moments before being hit by the car. I feel a surge of fear that I hadn't during the accident. I remember how it felt like time had paused. I look outside for something to focus my attention on.

"We're nearly there," Aunt Rosa nods her head towards the sign which says *Welcome to Big Spruce. Please drive carefully.* I have a childish impulse to drive faster.

Big Spruce is a peaceful, pretty place which was originally inhabited by Native Americans, until they were moved to the reservation on the outskirts of the town. The small town is made up of low rise buildings: mostly two–storey, and no more than three. At the heart of it is the pretty lemon and white Town Hall which proudly flies the American flag, and is set back from the street by a neatly manicured lawn.

The main shopping street is fed into by numerous quiet streets, where muted timber–framed houses nestle comfortably together. At the end of the adjacent streets lies a recreation area alongside the peaceful lakeshore. The small, sulphurous spring beside the lake attracts tourists. Big Spruce feels like it has been created from the forest, and hewn from rock, surrounded on all sides by coniferous forest, and protected on one side by a small mountain which always reminded me of a friendly, sleeping dragon.

I remember how I used to think the name lacked imagination because there are so many trees here – which 'Big Spruce' could they be referring to? As we drive into town we slow down behind a funeral car, which stops alongside the pavement. The coffin is about to be brought inside. A small crowd of mourners have gathered outside a tiny, white clapboard church. It's the oldest church in town, with a diminishing congregation now there's a much larger and newly built church which now attracts many more followers.

"Who's died?" I ask, pulling down the mirror. Shocked by how terrible I look, I flick it back up.

"It must be Blanche Whitelaw's funeral. I doubt there will be a big turnout for that one," says Aunt Rosa, surprising me with the derisory tone in her voice.

"You didn't like her much?" I ask, puzzled because she's such a community spirited sort, and as there are very few people she doesn't know it would be strange for her not to attend.

"Hateful woman! I didn't really know her. She messed about with the occult. At least she kept herself to herself. Pastor Shimlow told us to stay away from anyone working with the devil," Aunt Rosa stares, oddly passive, at the funeral gathering.

What the hell was that? For a split second I could've sworn Aunt Rosa morphed into someone else. Her mouth opened and someone else spoke, unzipping a ray of hatred. I feel slightly uneasy with this, like that sunny world of hers isn't the haven of hearts and flowers that I thought it was.

A stocky man, presumably a coffin bearer, stands alongside the funeral car. He lifts his head, and looks straight into the car at Rosa, his face blank. I look back and forward between the two. After a few seconds Aunt Rosa lifts her hand in acknowledgement. He simply nods back.

"Who's that?"

"Sheriff Whitelaw. Blanche Whitelaw's son," states Rosa, and offers no further information.

I have the unsettling feeling that I've walked on an anthill. There's more to this, but it isn't going to be unearthed today. I glance back at the kindly faced man, feeling some sort of connection, but I don't know why. I think I've met him before.

"Home at last," says Aunt Rosa, as she cheerily hops out of the pickup, letting Hudson out too. He bounds up the steps to the porch and beats his thick black tail against the door, scraping at it in a hurry get in.

Rosa grabs my bag before I get a chance to do it, then heads inside the house, talking away to herself, or the dog, because I'm not listening. I stretch out my legs and look up at the charming home, aptly named Evergreen. It's just as enchanting as I remember.

The double–fronted house is painted a warm, mellow,

cream with a complimentary sage–green veranda which wraps around it. The same old cane swing hangs in the same place it always has, amongst the wicker seats and old terracotta flower pots, filled with geraniums in pink and white. The house sits within a lovingly landscaped corner plot at the end of a quiet cul–de–sac, behind a short, flower–filled garden which is laid to lawn in the middle.

Aunt Rosa's love of her garden is apparent everywhere you look. I walk around the side of the house to the rear garden, which extends way back and leads to the forest beyond. The two sequoia trees stand proudly at the bottom of the garden. A simple wooden seat has been built around them and the vegetable patch is distinguished from the rest of the garden by some paving. I remember how I used to lie on the paving, picking peas off their stalks and eating them raw.

"Aren't you coming in?" Aunt Rosa calls from inside the house. I walk up the steps and open the back door, just as Hudson barrels through it. He jumps against me and lands his two giant front paws on my chest. I love the feel of his soft wavy head. I pet him, and push him aside to get through the door.

"I've put your bag in your room. You must be exhausted. I put a casserole on this morning, so it's there whenever you want it. I'll make us a drink. Come and sit down at the table."

I pull out a wooden chair which is topped with a red checked cushion and sit down at the age–smoothed cedar table. I feel so at home. Virtually nothing has changed in this house in twenty years. The richly patterned rugs have faded from the sun, and the wooden floors look worn, adding to its warm, rustic atmosphere. The paintwork around the doorframes has been scratched by dog claws, and fine sprays of mud have lightly stained the door where Hudson has rubbed himself.

My troubles are a million miles from here, as I sit in this cosy kitchen listening to Aunt Rosa endlessly chatting about the town's news, with Hudson softly snoring as he lies at my feet.

"Of course I don't gossip, I'm just telling you what I've heard," she says.

I grin. No reply is needed. I strain my ears to hear a low familiar sound.

"That's my cell phone ringing. Where's my bag?"

"Bottom of the stairs, honey," says Aunt Rosa.

By the time I get there, it's stopped ringing. The screen shows I've missed a call from Tray Buchanan. My heart lurches at the intrusion. Already there's trouble in paradise. I'm irritated by the reminder of that other world, and I throw the phone back in my handbag as if it's infected.

I plonk myself back down on the chair and I can feel Rosa's eyes on me.

"It wasn't important then? The call?" she asks.

"It was Tray Buchanan. The guy I was with at the accident," I reply.

"Then I'm not surprised you don't want to speak to him. Quite right too. Never mind. There'll be another bus along soon. I'll dish us up some of that nice casserole I've been keeping warm." She opens the oven door, and it smells so good. Hudson is suddenly awake and on his feet, waiting for his dinner. Rosa dishes up an enormous helping of herby chicken casserole and as I tuck in I can taste the love which went into making it. I've found my appetite again, but manage to leave the pattern on the plate.

"Seconds?" asks Aunt Rosa.

"Are you joking? I'm going to pop."

"I've made far too much." She starts ladling casserole into Hudson's bowl and he dusts the floor with his tail.

"I'm going up to unpack," I call, suddenly very thankful for the peace and solitude of my own personal space. It's been a very long day. I lie back on the bed, staring at the ceiling, not thinking about anything in particular, just idling. Then I remember I haven't let Giselle know I've arrived safely. I'm too tired to speak to anyone. Talking can take a lot of effort sometimes, so I quickly text her. Within seconds the phone rings; it's Giselle. I pick it up, hoping to keep the call short.

"So are you getting looked after?" Giselle asks.

"Yeah, and I'm loving it. I'll need two seats on the plane home if I keep eating like this. I feel like a kid again. It's lovely, but I may be ready to come home by the end of the week."

"Lap it up. Then you can get back here, guns blazing."

"Hmm. Right now I'm so tired I could fall flat on my face."

"OK, hint taken. I won't keep you, but I want your address. I've got some things to send you."

"What sort of things?"

"Just some books. I thought if you've nothing much to do they might be useful."

I'm relieved that it's not Patricia sending me work, though I've a smidge of guilt that someone else is having to cover for me; but not enough that I'm inclined to call. I remind myself that the Sheldon & Napier does not, in fact, own my soul.

I've just finished talking to Giselle when I hear the door bell, followed by the sound of voices. I step onto the landing to hear who it is. The voices, which seem to belong to a middle aged man and woman, reverberate upstairs and I can hear my name being mentioned. I level a guess that it's the notorious, tittle–tattling neighbors coming to find out the buzz. I'm not going downstairs and fuelling the gossips. The renegade niece returning from the city, smashed up by the ex–girlfriend of a playboy; it's a gossipmonger's dream. I don't know how much they already know, but they won't be learning anything from me.

I lie face down on the bed, kick off my sneakers and tell myself I'll call Tray back tomorrow. Maybe the police have found Francesca. It's still a puzzle to me, that with technology and prolific security cameras around the city, she still hasn't been found. But right now I don't care. My eyes are heavy and I blink too long.

7

I wake the next morning not recognizing the pink and green pattern of the duvet, until my mind synchronizes with the surroundings. I'm fully clothed and covered by the comforter. Rosa must have been in the room and covered me up during the night. I've slept well, but still feel lethargic and drowsy, probably because I've slept too long.

I lie for a while, listening to the comforting noises coming from downstairs. I can hear Hudson's happy barks as he gets breakfast. I drag myself out of bed and take a hot shower. As I let the water cascade over my face and head I imagine every trace of the past few difficult weeks washing away.

I fan my fingers through my hair, leaving it loose to dry naturally and notice how quickly the bruises have faded. I'm drawn to the tantalising smells coming from the kitchen. I throw on a bathrobe and pad downstairs, enjoying a wonderful sense of homecoming. I don't usually eat breakfast but it smells divine, and I'm ravenous.

"It's the fresh mountain air," says Aunt Rosa, dishing out smoked bacon, pancakes and maple syrup onto my plate.

"Not too much."

"Nonsense."

"Are you trying to fatten me up?"

"You're far too thin. There's more where that came from. Help yourself to coffee. I've got to take the dog for a walk if you'd like to come?"

"I need to get dressed and put some make–up on first," I reply, tucking heartily into the home–made pancakes.

"Make–up? What do you need that for? We're only going into the forest," she wrinkles her nose and forehead.

"I wouldn't even leave the house without mascara."

Aunt Rosa laughs and shakes her head, as she drains her coffee cup.

I devour my food in record time and push the plate aside.

"Thanks for breakfast," I shout, and disappear upstairs: re–appearing a few minutes later dressed in a fleece and jeans. I stuff my jeans inside a pair of long brown boots, and take the dog lead from the hook beside the back door. The act cues Hudson's ritual dance. He starts barking and circling around me.

We wander down through the garden: taking in the fresh morning air, ducking past the low branches and come out on the narrow worn path which leads into the forest. The soft springy pine needles underfoot make light crackling sounds when we step on them, before they spring softly back again.

We walk for a few minutes before Aunt Rosa stops and calls Hudson to come back. We're close to the lakeshore, and she doesn't want the water–loving dog to get wet. Unusually, he doesn't come back instantly. Aunt Rosa and I look at each other, saying nothing but listening hard. There is a sudden crash of branches close to us and the dog breaks through the undergrowth, barking anxiously he keeps on running, making me spin around. I quickly follow the dog along the path we've just walked. Aunt Rosa follows a few steps behind.

"What is that about? You'd think he was being chased."

"Crazy dog," breezes Aunt Rosa, not looking bothered.

As we approach the back door of the house I can hear a man's voice calling for Rosa, then Sheriff Whitelaw appears around the side of the house looking for her. Rosa is brushing twigs out of her hair.

"Barnaby, what are you doing here? Is this a social call?" asks Rosa.

"Not exactly," says Barnaby, smiling at me.

"This is my niece, Tara North. You remember my brother Frank? Well this is his daughter," says Rosa, introducing us.

Barnaby puts his hand out, and gives me one of those no–nonsense, death grip handshakes, that signify a strong, hearty individual.

"Sure I remember. I knew both your mom and dad. Good to see you again. I remember you and your brother Anthony way back when you were little."

"You do look familiar," I tell him honestly, kicking off my boots at the back door. People here are pretty friendly and go back a long way, so it's not unusual to clarify someone's heritage. I've forgotten how things work around here, and it feels odd but reassuring that a relative stranger knows my family and my background.

"Actually Rosa, I wanted to see you because we've had reports of a bear coming into the neighborhood. We think it's taken a few domestic pets and it seems to be making a habit of coming into town. I know you walk in the woods all the time with the dog, so maybe you should take a different route," warns Barnaby.

"The bear would be more frightened of me. We've had bears coming around here before. They do no harm," she dismisses his warning.

"Well, I'm just telling you how things are, but it's worth being careful," Barnaby replies.

"What? Hudson was frightened by something out there. Maybe it was a bear?" I ask, excited by feeling so close to nature.

"It's possible," says Barnaby in a measured tone.

"Oh don't be going frightening the girl. She only arrived from New York yesterday," Rosa chastises.

"We saw you yesterday at the funeral when I arrived in town," I pitch in, then realize that might not be the most diplomatic thing to say.

"Yeah, it was my mother's funeral. Sad day," says Barnaby quietly.

"I'm sorry for your loss," I tell him, thinking this would be a good time to be swallowed up whole cringing that I've made him uncomfortable. But I still find it odd that thoughtful, community–spirited Aunt Rosa hadn't gone to the funeral. If Barnaby Whitelaw and Rosa are old friends it would be courteous to pay your respects. I know for a fact she had been to the funerals of mere acquaintances. Something just doesn't sit right.

8

Apart from a walk down to the lake, I've spent most of the day happily lounging on the sofa, staring blankly at the television. I'm also procrastinating over returning Tray's phone call. I feel safe and content here being mothered; or could that be smothered I wonder, as I watch Aunt Rosa busily fussing around me. Giselle is right, I needed to recuperate, and feeling guilty for lying around is pointless. My cell phone rings and my mood takes a nose dive: it's Tray again.

I answer it, sighing unintentionally. "Hi Tray."

"Oh, hi. I thought it would go to voicemail again. How are you?"

"Living and breathing."

"Are you annoyed with me?" he asks tentatively. "I didn't come to the hospital because they said you weren't up to having visitors. I sent you some flowers. Didn't you get them?"

"What the hell happened, Tray? You saw who was driving that car, didn't you? You're withholding information, and given that Francesca can't be found, you could be more helpful."

"I'm sorry Tara, really I am, but I can't help."

"Can't or won't?"

"I'd like to make it up to you, if you'll let me. I feel awful about what happened."

"Oh sure, Tray, let's just brush it under the carpet shall we? I can forgive, but I won't forget," my voice rises unchecked; then I remember he's a client of Sheldon & Napier. "Look, I'm staying with family for a while, and it would really help me to know that whoever wanted me dead is put safely away. Do you know where she is Tray?"

"I'm sorry, but I'm sure the police know what they're doing. I'll call you again soon," Tray says amiably then rings off.

I'd tried to appeal to Tray's conscience, but perhaps he really doesn't know where Francesca is. Unfortunately Aunt Rosa has overheard part of the phone conversation and she pieces together what I hadn't told her about the hit and run.

"You were eaves dropping?" I quip.

"I couldn't help but overhear."

The lack of privacy is already niggling me. Aunt Rosa starts a verbal assassination of Francesca. It makes me feel worse instead of better.

"Why didn't you tell me in the first place that someone ran you down deliberately?" demands Aunt Rosa.

I open my mouth to speak but retract my words before they come out, and scrunch further into the big comfy sofa.

I opt for an early night and have the strangest lucid dream. I wake realizing the dream has become a physical image in front of me. Standing there is Lehman, the Native American I saw during the near death experience. There is static all around me and I try not to get anxious. I'm definitely awake now and the image is still real. I fight the urge to resist and focus on Lehman's message. His words feel like they're coming from a distance.

There can be no beginnings without endings. Look back to the past for answers. There will be opportunities and changes. To create a new life, cut down the old. Your ancestors welcome this. You have more power than you know. Meet trials with loving indifference.

Lehman's energy starts to dissolve until he disappears completely. I think about the cryptic message he communicated. Alone, with the silver blue moonlight streaming into my bedroom I feel strangely calm.

I'm not questioning my sanity like I did after the near death experience. I feel uplifted, peaceful and strong. I'm ready for something new and despite what Lehman said about endings coming first, I don't want to let go of my security. It makes no logical sense to alter my life for some mystic vision.

I stand at the bedroom window and gaze out across the trees. A pale blue oval light stands out, like a sentry against one of the trees. *What was that?* I squint to see better, but the light disappears completely. I remember years ago telling my mom about the hovering lights I saw moving around, especially in the forest. She said not to tell lies. After that I got wise and kept that sort of information to myself. Eventually I stopped noticing them, and then I stopped seeing them altogether. So why are these experiences happening now? Since the accident I've become sensitive again. I'm separated from the life I created in New York, albeit temporarily. That must be what Lehman was referring to. So now what?

A shiver runs through me and I have a sudden notion that my life is being deconstructed.

Over breakfast next morning Aunt Rosa announces that we're going to visit my brother Anthony and his wife Delphine.

"I know they would love to see you," Aunt Rosa breezes, though I'm not so sure.

"You go ahead. I think I'll just hang out here for the day," I reply, unable to think of a convincing excuse.

"Nonsense, it'll be good for you to get out and about."

"I really just want some peace and quiet."

"But I've already called Anthony and told him we're coming over."

"Ah. I guess we're going then."

I give up, wishing she'd asked me first. I've never felt welcome in Anthony's house.

"Delphine said they've been worried about you since the accident," says Aunt Rosa, and I know she believes this.

"Well if they were so worried, why didn't they call?"

I try not to stomp my feet like a petulant child as I walk out to the front porch, sigh and throw myself down on the swing, nearly landing on the floor. My mouth is dry. I gulp down my orange juice, mentally carrying on the argument with my aunt: annoyed that I feel so powerless and not even in charge of my own life. Jeez, I'll have to dig deep into my reserves before I see my brother and his brood.

The boys are all under the age of eleven, and are all lively, spirited kids, but with Anthony as a role model and Delphine's hands–off mothering approach, the boy's unruly behaviour is mostly ignored. It's not that Anthony and Delphine are oblivious to their boisterous antics – they can sit amongst it until it reaches fever pitch or a scuffle breaks out, then it erupts into yelling. The screaming glances off the boys with little, or no, effect – it's just another voice to join in the affray.

A squirrel scuttles across the garden and sprints up a tree to the top branches, where it tapers into the blue morning sky. It takes my attention away from my problems and I breathe deeply and relax.

We drive to my hometown of Fort Jarvis, which is a short drive from Big Spruce. Anthony has always lived here and is part of the fabric of the place. I inevitably begin to feel nostalgic. I partly revel in the familiarity of the town, but cloying memories of childhood dramas come flooding back.

As we pull into Anthony's yard the boys come careering outside, surround the car, and start having a shoot out. Several wrecks of old cars lie around the yard. Metal vehicle parts, tyres and old wooden pallets have been stacked together to make a den. The dirty, brown mongrel tied to a post barks savagely at us.

Delphine appears at the door dressed in a pretty fitted purple dress with matching purple sling back shoes. I've evidently underdressed. She hugs us and we follow her inside. Immediately I sense a strained atmosphere. Delphine's eyes dart around. She's nervous and distracted. I get the feeling we've walked in on an argument between her and my brother. We find Anthony setting up makeshift targets and taking shots from the veranda with his air rifle.

"Anthony, is that wise with the kids running around?" asks Aunt Rosa.

"My name is Tony," he replies slowly, ignoring the rest of what Aunt Rosa has said.

"I didn't know you were calling yourself Tony." I remark casually, greeting him with an arm extended for a hug, but I drop it when he ignores the gesture and re–focuses on the rifle. Anthony turns away from his targets and faces me, sweeping over me with a cool, wary look in his bloodshot blue eyes.

"You don't look too bad for someone who's been in an accident!"

"I'm made of strong stuff." I'm surprised he even mentioned it.

"Are you now? Must run in the family, huh?" Anthony contorts his face.

"The boys have really grown. I wouldn't have recognised them," I say, changing the subject.

"They sure have. Chip off the old block my eldest you know. Good eye for a shot. Do you want a go?" he asks, with an inscrutable expression but a hint of menace to his tone.

"Sure."

He puts the targets back up and runs his hand through his tufty black hair.

"Can you remember how? Don't suppose you've had much practice in the big city, or maybe you don't want to chip a fingernail," he sneers passing me the rifle. "Mind you, I'm sure you don't miss us now you've made it big."

"What's your problem?"

"Problem? What problem? There you go, our Tara, always looking for a problem. I've got three strong, healthy boys, the garages are doing well, I've got two now, plus a pretty woman looking after me. I've done well for myself, wouldn't you say?"

I aim, pull the trigger and miss the target.

"Oh dear, Sis!"

"Practice shot."

I take a deep breath, focus and try again. This time I hit several of the targets and knock them to the ground.

"I'm pleased for you Tony. I'm glad you're happy," I reply with utter sincerity.

"Happy? You're happy for me?! What would you know about it? It's always been easy for you. Princess, you couldn't wait to leave town."

"What are you talking about?"

"You left a trail of dust behind after mom and dad died."

"We had big decisions to make and we made our choices. You chose to stay here – I choose to go to college. I don't see what's wrong with that."

"There was nothing wrong with here, but it wasn't good enough for you."

"What happened to dad and mom was tragic but we dealt with it. We were nearly adults with our whole lives ahead of us. It's worked out alright...hasn't it?"

"Tara, you showed your true colors when you left." Anthony's voice is low and accusing.

I shake my head, looking at the ground. He isn't listening. He's living out the bitter resentment he's created from the problems formed in his mind – and I'm part of that creation too.

Anthony has always been such a tough nut. After our parents died he barely showed emotion. Neither of us did. Being familiar with denial, it was natural to detach from the quiet suffering. For my part, I'd seized the chance to bolt for the freedom I'd been missing. It was years later, when the novelty of freedom had faded, that grief surfaced and I mourned the loss of my parents. I'd used my career to escape. Anthony had used alcohol to the same extent.

"What are you two whispering about? Delphine has put on a delicious lunch. Come and get some!" calls Aunt Rosa cheerily.

I love my brother, despite his obvious antagonism with me. There's a scared little boy in there, and I'm stabbed by guilt for the part I played in the problem. Perhaps all those years ago he had needed me more than I knew? If that was true I'd certainly had no idea. I'd been caught up in my own pursuit of happiness. I'd been a flight risk, and the door had been open. But he was young and hadn't finished being mothered; I can see that now. I, as well as our parents, had abandoned him. The revelation of this new level of animosity is upsetting, but I can't rewrite the past.

Anthony follows me into the kitchen and grabs a beer from the fridge. Aunt Rosa tries to make conversation with him but he ignores her, disappearing outside again, amid apologies from Delphine.

"Hey, you little monsters! Leave me some," I shout, teasing the boys and pretending to chase them for a hug, while they grab handfuls of Delphine's precision cut sandwiches and run outside screaming.

I'm thinking I can't wait to get back to the peace and solitude of home when Aunt Rosa mentions we're stopping at the antique auction on the way back. My heart contracts with the lack of control I have over my movements. I can't imagine anything more tedious. It triggers a powerful resurgence of that old, familiar, claustrophobic feeling, the inexplicable need to escape and evade being sucked into something so suffocating it could kill me. I'm surprised by the strength of the urge to seek freedom. Oh to be back amongst the anonymous hustle and bustle of New York, drinking Satan's Circus cocktails and kicking back with my friends. In light of what I've said about Anthony, the irony of needing strong alcoholic stimulus to enjoy myself isn't lost on me.

On leaving I quickly hug Anthony's frigid frame, catching him in a loose embrace before he has a chance to spurn me. Aunt Rosa takes his chin and plants a kiss on his turned cheek, which he graciously receives. I look back in the mirror at the boys running around the yard, eagerly waving goodbye through the brown dust cast up from the wheels of Aunt Rosa's truck. I can't help but wonder to what extent history will repeat itself?

9

The auction is in the old town hall, and it's filled with second hand furniture, where prospective bidders sit on any available chairs or sofas, waiting for their auction number to come around. Dotted around are miscellaneous boxes of other people's junk. The room smells mouldy and I wonder what is living in the dusty, old Chinese rugs leaning against the walls. The auctioneer holds up the mounted head of a stag, and asks for bids.

Aunt Rosa waits pensively to bid for an antique cedar writing desk as her eyes move nervously around the room.

"What do you think I should bid?" she whispers with her hand in front of her mouth.

"What do you need it for? You have plenty of furniture."

"It would look great in your room. Do you like it?"

The auctioneer's voice echoes around the hall. "Lot number 204. The writing desk."

"That's it," whispers Aunt Rosa, her eyes glittering with excitement. She only jumps in after several bids have been already placed. She doesn't take her eyes off the auctioneer for a second. She makes the final bid. The gavel falls. Aunt Rosa reels back with delight then quickly straightens her face, trying not to look too pleased. At the end of the auction she goes to pay and collect the desk, curious to see what everyone else has bought.

"Pastor Shimlow," says Aunt Rosa, addressing a tall, thin, grey–haired man with a sunken, predatory face who is standing at the cash desk. "Good to see you. Have you found anything interesting?"

I watch them exchange formalities and I instinctively recoil from him. From Aunt Rosa's enthusiasm I get the impression he is someone she reveres, yet my skin crawls from this man's presence. Rosa proudly introduces me to Pastor Cain Shimlow. We shake hands and a quizzical looks passes through his small charcoal grey eyes. He limply lets my hand slip from his grasp. He has also seen something in me he doesn't like. Pastor Shimlow's thin insincere smile pinches his otherwise taut face into narrow lines.

"I do hope we'll be seeing you at church," says Pastor Shimlow, in a tone that couldn't be any more condescending.

"Actually, no I'm–"

"Oh, I'm sure you will. It's a good way to meet people," interrupts Rosa cheerily.

"I don't think so," I snap, bouncing with annoyance, struggling to contain my irritation at having been spoken for. Aunt Rosa blinks rapidly several times then closes her mouth.

"I'm sure everyone will take you under their wing," says Pastor Shimlow, snubbing my opinion and turning his attention fully to Aunt Rosa. He turns his shoulder and freezes me out.

"You'll excuse me," I say sarcastically, knowing I've already been dismissed. I stride off, heading for the door. *What is with people?* I'm a fully fledged adult, yet here I feel like a child again. And I get treated like it. I resent others forcing theirs on me. I'm beginning to ferment with frustration. I squeeze past a few people hovering in the doorway on my way outside.

"Tara. You look like you're in a hurry."

The voice comes from Barnaby Whitelaw who is sitting on a bench outside the town hall.

"Hi Barnaby. I just needed some air," I reply, and he watches me keenly.

"I know what you mean. I didn't want to go in yet. I just thought I'd come by and see what's been sold," says Barnaby, staring off into the distance. My initial annoyance at having more unwanted company is soothed by Barnaby's presence.

"You've been selling something?" I ask, sitting down on the wall next to him.

"Yep. My mom's stuff. The old place has already been sold. Still…it's time to move on I suppose," he says, turning his head to face me he raises a half–hearted smile.

"That's a big step."

"I don't have room for it all, though I don't think people nowadays want that old fashioned stuff anymore. If they've found out that stuff came from Blanche Whitelaw's none of it will have sold." Barnaby chuckles.

"What difference does that make?"

"My mother wasn't very popular with some of the locals."

"Why not?"

"She was psychic. A born healer. They were sceptical of her gifts. Then she learned how to use herbs and people were more accepting of that. They came from miles away to see her; but round here they'd condemn her, but visit in secret. They said she was a witch in cahoots with the Devil. People fear what they don't understand."

"I realize that."

"You've been away a long time. Maybe you see things differently now?" asks Barnaby.

I look down and nod.

Barnaby raises an eyebrow and I sense a listening ear.

"Anyway," I change the subject, "did you inherit your mother's gifts?"

"No. Anyway if I had I think I would keep it quiet! A

psychic Sheriff? I'm the butt of enough jokes already." Barnaby laughs at himself.

Several people walk past us carrying all sorts of bric-a-brac and furniture from the auction.

"I'd better go and find my aunt. She's bought a writing desk."

"Maybe she needs a hand," says Barnaby getting up and following me into the auction room. Pastor Shimlow walks tall and aloof towards us, carrying the mounted stag's head with such pride it's as if he had killed it himself.

"Sheriff Whitelaw," nods the Pastor.

"Cain," nods Barnaby, and the two men pass each other.

Aunt Rosa is wrestling with the writing desk, single-handedly trying to lift and drag it towards the door.

"Let me do that," offers Barnaby. He puts his thick arms around the writing desk, gripping it and lifting it with his big bear paws, though his paunch awkwardly gets in the way as he manoeuvres the desk through the doors. He loads the desk onto the truck and covers it with an old grey blanket.

"I'm glad it's going to a good home," says Barnaby non-chalantly, wiping his dusty hands on his trousers.

"What? It's your desk?" asks Aunt Rosa, looking surprised.

"It was my mother's desk. It's yours now."

"I didn't realize," Aunt Rosa glances around.

An ironic snigger escapes from me. I wonder if she'd have bought it had she known it belonged to Blanche Whitelaw. Pastor Shimlow might not approve.

10

"It's for you," calls Aunt Rosa, pushing the door open with her back, while holding a large brown package in one hand and a garden trowel in the other. I take the package and place it on the kitchen table, swigging back my coffee before I open it.

It's from Giselle. It must be the books she mentioned. Hudson comes to inspect the rustling noise by sticking his big wet nose in, searching for food. I open the package and find self–help and metaphysical books and even better, a large stash of quality organic chocolate. I smile. *The girl thinks of everything.*

The writing desk has a new home underneath my bedroom window, and looks made for the room. In theory you can look outside while you write. I put my laptop on it and log onto Skype so that I can thank Giselle for the books.

During the online chat with Giselle my cell phone rings. It's the police in New York. *What now?* I put my hand to my throat, feeling it constrict.

"Miss North, you'll be pleased to know that last night we arrested Francesca Evans for attempted murder," says the police officer.

"OK. Where was she?" I ask sounding more in control than I feel.

"We found her hiding at a house in the Hamptons. The house belongs to Tray Buchanan, although we didn't find him there.

"Tray didn't turn her in?"

"According to Tray she has been blackmailing him by self harming and making suicide threats. We're still investigating his involvement, but in the meantime Francesca Evans is undergoing psychiatric evaluation. Are you still there?"

I sit down on the bed because my legs are wobbling beneath me.

"Yes, I'm here. I'm just relieved. Thank you."

By the end of the call I've no animosity at Tray for hiding Francesca. A little part of me feels sorry for him that she emotionally and deliberately blackmailed him. I lie back on the bed and sigh with relief.

"What going on?" shouts Giselle's voice from the laptop.

"Christ! I forgot you were there," I turn my attention back to Skype. As the news sinks in I begin to unwind properly for the first time in weeks. I'm glad to have Giselle's virtual presence to talk it through. I disconnect from the Skype call feeling lighter. An unfamiliar feeling of relaxation unfurls in me. *Peace you've been a stranger.* I glance over at the mirror and catch sight of myself looking unkempt and colorless – I've let myself go. It's time to do something about it.

With a hair brush, eye makeup, lip gloss and foundation I set about a transformation. It's by no means perfect, but it's a definite improvement. I can be seen in public without scaring the neighbors. I pull my hair back into a high pony tail, because it's an unruly mess and in need of a cut.

I start to tidy my cosmetics away and try to open the desk drawer, but it jams. I wiggle it free and something drops down behind it. I pull the drawer completely out and stick my fingers into the space, grasping around for the obstruction. There is something hard and metallic. I wrap my fingers around it and pull it out.

It's a large ruby amulet on a gold chain. It's an unusual design. I've never seen anything quite like it before. The large round ruby is set in a gold surround, and has been overlaid with the moulded gold outline of a triangle, containing a circle which contains a square.

It's mesmerizingly simple. Am I imagining that it feels warm to touch? The sunlight passes through and it glows with such magnificent radiance; I'm transfixed. It must have been Blanche Whitelaw's, so I ought to give it back to Barnaby. The amulet is unlike anything I would normally wear, but there is no getting away from its beauty.

Against my better judgement I show the amulet to Aunt Rosa, who instantly decides it's a type of pagan ritual tool and shouldn't even be in her house. She calls Barnaby Whitelaw straight away and tells him she will return the pendant.

"He must know it's unlucky. He doesn't seem bothered about getting it back. It gives me the creeps. I don't want that in the house," declares Aunt Rosa vehemently.

I am in need of a haircut and some quality time by myself so I ask to borrow the pickup.

"Sure, take it. Try Barbara's salon and tell her I sent you. While you're at it you can give that monstrosity to Barnaby," says Aunt Rosa, meaning the amulet. "He's at home now, so if you're quick you can get there before he starts his shift."

I gleefully grab the keys to the pickup, take the amulet and leave. I push myself not to drive like a ninety year old. The accident is still fresh in my mind. I'm over–cautious and slow down if I see anyone on the pavement. I have a word with myself and press my right foot down harder.

Barnaby's house is within walking distance of the Sheriff's

office, so he's never far from work. It seems very fitting for such a down to earth, solid man to be utterly dedicated to his work; it's not in his job description to let people down. Then again he doesn't have any family depending on him either. He's a bachelor but I imagine he would've been a catch in his day. Even now, with his chocolate brown hair with flecks of grey, and warm friendly brown eyes, he has an affable charm. I'll bet Barnaby is sweetly unaware of his appeal.

The outside of the house is plain, with the sparse feel of a house without a woman in residence. I knock and after a few moments Barnaby throws the door open wide. His pants legs are rolled up to his knee, exposing bare legs and he's holding a large power drill.

"Oh. I wasn't expecting you so soon," says Barnaby looking mildly uncomfortable.

"Is this a bad time?"

"No. Come in, I was just doing my feet."

"With a drill?"

"No...well, yes." Barnaby looks amused. "I've a hell of a fungal nail problem. It's too thick to cut. So I use the drill," he explains, waving the power tool in the air.

"You're serious? Don't you know a good blacksmith?"

Barnaby throws his head back and laughs really hard at himself. It's so infectious I crease up in a fit of laughing too.

"I probably shouldn't have told you that," he says grinning.

"I'll tell no–one. They wouldn't believe me anyway."

"Rosa called. She said you found a necklace in that old desk. I'm surprised she didn't use it for firewood."

"It's got pride of place in my bedroom, and what a find, the necklace I mean. It must be one of a kind."

Barnaby pads back through to the lounge, unrolling his pant legs at the same time.

"Move those newspapers and grab yourself a seat," he says.

I shuffle the papers to another seat and sit down.

"Here it is," I draw out the necklace from my pocket, trying not to stare too wistfully at it.

"Ah, that. I remember that pendant. She loved that. Rarely took it off, so I can't imagine how it came to be in the desk drawer. All her other jewelry was kept in her jewelry box. She was careful with it."

"Perhaps she forgot where she put it?" I suggest.

"My mom was clear and sharp all her days. She knew she was going to pass away weeks before she died. She was getting her affairs in order. I just thought her age was beginning to catch up with her. I dismissed it. I should've known better. She was never ill. One night she just passed away in her sleep."

"I'm sorry."

"That's the way to go kiddo, just go to sleep. She organized everything down to the last detail. It wouldn't surprise me if she picked a day to die." Barnaby goes quiet, seeming to reminisce, then looks up decisively. "I have no use for jewelry. You keep it. Maybe she would've liked you to have it. There's no such thing as an accident – that's what she used to say."

"No really I wasn't meaning–"

"Keep it. I'm sure you'll have more use for it than me."

"Barnaby, it's probably really valuable. I don't know what to say...but thank you," I reply, not protesting too much in case he changes his mind. I gently place the amulet back in my pocket and a small thrill grows in my heart.

We sit chatting like old friends. He's really interesting and listening to stories of his adventures I feel uplifted that he has such strong friendships. He's entertaining and his infectious warmth of spirit is reflected in his story telling. He talks about how he loved hunting but he's losing his edge. It's difficult to imagine this amiable character as a force of law. He must morph into a Sheriff when he puts on his uniform.

At a lull in the conversation, I stand up, ready to leave, feeling a little awkward about the amulet. Barnaby comes to the door and waves me off. I'm not going to tell Aunt Rosa that the amulet is now mine, because I plan on keeping it; and if something goes wrong at home she'll blame it on the amulet bringing bad luck.

11

I find the hairdressing salon Aunt Rosa mentioned but it looks dated, so with a choice of two others I opt for the most modern looking salon, hoping I won't need an appointment; I'm in luck.

The hairdresser, who introduces herself as Jo, is chatty and inquisitive especially when she notices the scar on my head. I have to explain to the fascinated hairdresser how I got it. Sharing the tale of the hit and run incident seems to earn me some weird kudos, as though I've secured a place in the community. Gossip *really* is the local currency around here.

The wound on my head can be disguised by pulling hair over it. Now, with new well placed long layers, it covers the scarred area where hair is re–growing. Jo recommends the hot spring spa in town, telling me the spring water in the mineral pools have rejuvenating properties. I add a visit there to my 'to do' list.

It feels great to be getting out and doing something normal. I walk down to Emerald Lake and enjoy sitting by the lakeshore in the afternoon sun. I gaze out across the sparkling lake, soaking up the warmth of the sun's rays. Eventually I return to the truck and as I'm about to head for home the fuel light comes on. I'd better fill it up rather than leave it almost empty for Aunt Rosa.

I drive to the gas station on the outskirts of Big Spruce. I'm trying to remember when I last refuelled a car – with New York's abundant public transport I've no need for a car. As I walk into the gas station and approach the guy behind the counter, I have a sudden and acute loss of voice. I find myself face to face with a tall Native

American guy standing behind the cash desk. In complete awe of his presence my usual confidence falters. I glance shyly at the handsome, chiselled face, trying to memorize every detail that makes up this statuesque vision: his long, straight, black hair, prominent jaw, wide mouth, and keen hawk–like eyes. I steady my legs, committing every detail to memory while I rifle through the pockets of my jeans for my credit card.

Pull yourself together woman. I've met good looking guys and didn't bat an eyelid, but this guy has something indefinable: a powerful magnetic presence. I find and grasp my credit card and place it on the counter, not passing it to him to avoid him seeing my hands shaking.

His proud, flint–like face looks down at me, wide sensual lips evolving into a straight smile, as though he is amused by something. Picking up the card he looks at the name, before placing it in the machine and waiting for its response.

"So, how's Tara today?" he asks, keeping up the direct look which makes me squirm. The straight smile widens.

"Good thanks," I answer pathetically, forcing my voice to come out of my throat, but the rising color in my face is a dead giveaway. I can't think of anything to say. I sign and take it as swiftly as I can.

"Thanks," I manage to sound light–hearted, but the fierce heat radiating from my cheeks contradicts my voice and I think I'm going to die from embarrassment.

"See you soon," he answers, with that enigmatic smile that suggests he knows something I don't. I smile awkwardly over my shoulder as I walk towards the door. *Is he laughing at me?* As I return to the truck to put the gas in, I feel self conscious. *As if he would be watching me – get a grip girl!*

Not being familiar with the truck, I fiddle with the stiff fuel cap as I try to get it off. I glance up and see the guy's face turned in my direction and I give a small smile in acknowledgement when I finally release it and begin refuelling. As I replace the fuel cap I accidentally spill gas on the forecourt, splattering my shoes. I feel like an incompetent ass. *Damn, I'll have to go back in and tell him about the spillage. Maybe I won't? Oh, crap! I'll be quick.*

I wipe my hands on the paper roll beside the pump, take a deep breath and dash back across the forecourt into the shop: ready to confess. The guy is already watching me, smiling with a closed mouth.

"I've spilled some gas...I thought I should mention it... in case you need to put something on it," I say aiming for friendly, cool and confident, whilst fiddling with a strand of hair. He is grinning the widest white–toothed smile I've ever seen.

"Did you now Tara?" he walks towards me from behind the counter.

"Sorry. Does this mean I won't be allowed back?"

"That'd be a shame," his serious face flickers with humor, and something else.

My stomach flutters. A deep, delicious warmth spreads out from my chest and it's my turn to beam.

"I'll get someone to take care of it," he says, moving alongside me.

There is a pause for a few seconds. We stand connected by the space in between us – neither of us utters a word. The air sparks with friction, yet he looks poised and still: unaffected. Maybe I'm imagining that he can feel something too.

"Thanks...and sorry," I say apologetically, making towards the door.

"See you," he says, watching me walk away. I feel self-conscious and glance over my shoulder. I get caught looking back. *Crap!* I don't breathe out until I get back into the truck. I don't start the crazy grinning yet: I wait until I pull out onto the road for that. The radio is playing Sheryl Crow's "A Change Would Do You Good" and I let my voice rip, throw my head back, turn up the volume, and sing along. No–one can hear me as I accelerate on the open road.

I've been singing at the top of my voice to the loud music for a couple of minutes, when I check my rear view mirror and see flashing lights from another car. I hear the beeping horn when I turn the music down. *What's this about?* I'm not just about to pull over. The black jeep comes alongside me on the highway. The driver glances over. It's the guy from the gas station looking in at me. With a flick of the hand he gives a curt wave then drops back behind.

Shocked from my performance I slow down and pull over to the side of the road. My heart is flipping around wildly. *Oh God, How much has he seen and what does he want?!*

"You're embarrassing Tara," I mutter to myself, stopping the car, breathing out slowly. I'm bewildered as to why he wants my attention. The guy is already out of his vehicle and walking towards me when I open the car door and get out, totally bemused. He is coming towards me with something glittering in his hand, and as he gets nearer I recognise the ruby and gold amulet. My jaw drops open and my hand shoots to my mouth.

"You dropped this," he says.

"It must have fallen out of my pocket when I was looking for my card," I reply. "Thank you so much." The words don't equal my gratitude.

"That's quite a piece of jewelry you have there. What do you know about it?" he asks, passing me the amulet.

"Know about it? Nothing. I've just been given it." His implication is that the piece is more than mere decoration.

"I'm Shasta." He extends his hand.

"Tara." We shake hands and a powerful jolt shocks every part of my body.

"I know."

"Oh, yeah, right."

"So how do you come to have this amulet, but don't know what it is?"

"I found it."

"Or did it find you?"

"The owner died and her son gave it to me."

"Very generous."

"I know," I drop my eyes guiltily. I should never have allowed Barnaby to give it to me.

"That symbol, it's the Hermetic Seal of Light."

"Ah..." I close my mouth and lower my raised eyebrows, not wanting to appear clueless.

"It's sacred geometry," replies Shasta, as though that explains everything.

"Right...of course," I nod, then shake my head because I don't understand.

Shasta looks down at me and smiles, though offers no further insight.

"Take good care of it. You might want to learn how to use it," he turns and starts walking away.

"Use it? Don't you mean wear it?" I ask.

He grins broadly over his shoulder, oblivious to how casually sexy he looks and the tremble he's causing me.

"I'd love to stay and talk, but I've got to get back to the gas station. I'll be seeing you."

I stand rooted to the spot, watching as he turns the jeep and drives away with a brief nod. Stupefied, I turn and float back to the pickup truck. By the time I get back to Aunt Rosa's my head is whirling. I'm buzzing with questions and I've the strongest sensation that an unseen force is putting me in the right place at the right time – but to what end I don't know. Why didn't that guiding force steer me away from the hit and run incident? And yet that's how I've come to be here in Big Spruce.

I take the books Giselle sent me and nestle into a loom chair on the veranda. Hudson pads out and settles his heavy head on my knee as I begin speed reading the books. There's no mention of sacred geometry so I look it up online. The design on the amulet is, as Shasta said, the Hermetic Seal of Light but also known as Quintessence. Now this is what I'm looking for.

The Hermetic Seal of Light
Quintessence

Basically the symbol of Quintessence is made up of overlaid geometric shapes. They are elemental symbols of the triangle: representing fire, the circle: representing water, and the square: symbolising earth, blended together to represent 'all of creation'. They're also emblems of the material body, the soul and the spirit. It's believed that changes within all three are needed for spiritual and physical transformation. It's the essence of life in its most basic form. I want to know more.

The article describes how sacred geometry is found in natures shape and form: flowers, trees, shells, bee–hives, pine cones, crystals, trees, sun, moon, planets, and the shapes within our eyes. It mentions DNA of all life forms being created by geometric codes, and the geometry having the ability to subconsciously cause mood changes as we're attracted to pleasing shapes.

Symmetry reflects balance whereas irregular shapes are unstable and less appealing. The understanding is that geometry creates feelings of balance and regularity; because balance is what humans seek. Each state of mind is counter weighted to its opposite emotion but it's not that different, just a variation along a line of intensity. In the middle all things are balanced.

The Internet pages describe how the qualities and traits are coded into symbols, and that we're born with an intrinsic understanding of them. For a sceptic like me this is fascinating. When I was in Egypt a couple of years ago I had an awe inspiring visit to the pyramids. I felt uplifted for weeks afterward– now I have an idea why.

This article describes how the architects of holy monuments and buildings, prehistoric and modern day, used the principles of sacred geometry because they knew its deep affect on human perception.

But what's the significance of the sacred symbol on the

amulet, and why specifically the ruby? I do a Google search on the symbolism of rubies. It's said to shine in the absence of light, and in lore it's supposed to increase intuition. I remind myself this is just lore, with nothing to do with reality. It's interesting, fluffy and romantic but the idea that the amulet has some supernatural power is ridiculous. Right? I shake my head. *Jeez, I wonder if the trauma to my head has caused permanent damage?* I can't believe I'm even looking into this – for years I've teased Giselle about the hippy crap.

But where did this piece of jewelry come from? Did Blanche Whitelaw have it commissioned, or had it been given to her by someone else? I'm not going to find the answer to that question on the Internet, and I close the laptop down for the night. So many thoughts: none of them logical. What would Blanche tell me to do with the amulet? I clamber into bed exhausted.

I can't sleep. Tossing and turning – even the painkillers can't get rid of the pounding headache and the deep, heavy pain in my legs. I have a sudden, clear vision in my mind's eye of the Hermetic Seal of Light, lit from behind by a golden ray, shining through between the shapes like a silhouette.

I ask what to do with the symbol. I'm shown that I'm to visualise it on the palms of my hands, soles of my feet and between my eyebrows over the psychic third eye. Why? I question. In my mind's eye I see the words 'to secure and balance'. I visualize the outline of the Hermetic Seal, lit from behind by a golden light, and place it on my palms, soles and head. I instantly fall into a deep sleep.

12

Giselle roped me into one of her meditation groups a while back and I'd used guided meditations at home. However, today when I try it my mind is still coming up with worries: work, finances, promotion, spinsterhood.

To curb the negative chatter I close my eyes, trying to relax, but I notice a vague lingering depression pestering me from the sidelines – tears aren't far away. I've no idea why. My mind wanders back to work.

Sheldon & Napier could be coping so well without me that I'm at risk of losing my job. I've been putting off having a proper catch–up with Giselle, partly because she's prone to asking intense questions. I give her a call, hoping she'll be too busy to interrogate me about when I'm coming back to New York.

"We miss you," says Giselle loudly, trying to over–ride the sound of Simon's shrill voice in the background as he tries to butt in on the conversation.

"I miss you guys too."

Even before the words are out, I have a vision of myself back in the office, buried under paperwork and deadlines. I shudder at the thought and close down the idea instantly. I can't postpone it forever – I need more time.

"Has Patricia mentioned anything about me being off?" I brace myself for the reply.

"She's not mentioned you."

"I hope that's a good thing?"

"She's been in a worse mood than normal so we've been keeping our heads low. I think she's got a lot on," reassures Giselle.

I bring Giselle up to speed on my news, telling her about the amulet, and what I'd discovered about the symbols. I can hear her bouncing with enthusiasm – she loves anything arcane and mysterious. Eventually I get to the only point of interest on the romantic horizon; I describe meeting Shasta at the gas station and how he gave chase to return the necklace. I put my hand to my burning cheeks which are roaring red just from recounting the story.

"I can see why *you're* not eager to come back here. Maybe we should come and see you. Simon's desperate for a break. He's having a really rough time with Neil. I actually think they may split up for good this time," she whispers out of earshot of Simon. "Anyway I can't really talk now."

"OK. Give me a breather for a while longer, but I'll run it past Aunt Rosa. You know how she loves having visitors."

I feel better after the phone call, having organized and relinquished some of my thoughts. I lift Hudson's lead from the hook, but he doesn't come running so he must be outside. I walk to the front porch where Aunt Rosa is in the garden making up hanging baskets under the scrutiny of the next door neighbors, Pandora and Errol. So far I've managed to avoid the curtain twitchers from next door – but for no longer apparently.

Hudson is lying sprawled out on the grass. I try to

slip silently past...but no. Hearing the sound of his lead Hudson jumps up and comes lolloping towards me. Pandora and Errol's gaze follows him.

"This must be Tara. Your aunt has told us all about you. We have been dying to meet you," says Errol in a lecherous, smarmy tone. He quickly moves towards me with his hand outstretched ready to take mine. His slicked, comb–over hair slips across his face and he pushes it back up. I accept his cool, limp, hand and recoil at his touch the instant my space merges with his.

Errol asks me about the accident, but Pandora interrupts and pushes him aside. She grasps my arm and hijacks the conversation from her husband. Errol slides behind his short, wide, amply endowed wife and leers over her shoulder at me – I feel like a predator's breakfast.

"That's Errol and I'm Pandora," she gushes.

I've an extreme urge to ask about her box.

"Nice to meet you," I smile, hoping I can make a quick get–away.

"Now, when can you come over for supper? You really should come over and we can all get to know each other better. You MUST meet our son, Roger. He would love to meet you. He's an accountant, you know. He works very hard and he is about your age too, so I'm sure you'll have a lot in common. He's such a nice boy."

"Still lives at home though," Errol distances himself with a muttered disclaimer. Pandora ignores him.

A collusive glance passes between Pandora and Aunt Rosa – they've been plotting to fix me up with Roger. I'm repulsed. Nausea rises in my throat when I imagine a weak–willed mommy's boy who can't speak for himself.

"We'd love to come over, wouldn't we Tara?"

I'm being rail–roaded and don't have a plausible excuse: my social life is currently non–existent.

"Sure," I reply through gritted teeth. I'll find a way to get out of it.

"That's settled then. I'll arrange it. Errol, you help Rosa with the baskets. I'm sure Tara can help you unload them at the other end. That reminds me, when will you have my flower baskets ready? The Town in Bloom competition is coming up and I have just got to get a commendation again," Pandora's hands are on her hips as she leans forward into her words.

"They're nearly ready," Aunt Rosa appeases, but looks faintly harassed.

"I'm taking Hudson for a quick walk," I excuse myself and call Hudson to come with me.

I take a route through the forest, despite the warning from Barnaby Whitelaw about the bear. There is nowhere I feel safer than in the woods, and having a forty kilo dog for company helps too. I follow the path further than I've done for a while. I feel calmer the further I go into the forest. Hudson gets more excited and as the trees thin out, he begins a throaty whine knowing we are getting close to the water. He launches, outstretches his legs and splashes down in the water. I feel entirely relaxed as though everything I need is right here: beauty, love, laughter, and none of the drama. Nature is so magically healing.

In my lateral vision I see something light blue; it's strikingly out of place against the muted brown green and silver tones of the forest. I turn quickly to see who it is – but it isn't a person. It's an oval shaped light, and I can only catch a glimpse of it before it vanishes from my sight. It feels like I'm in company – really good company.

Feeling happy and relaxed I return home. I walk into the kitchen where my happiness is short lived.

"Tara, your phone has been ringing. It was Patricia Napier. It's there on the table."

Crap. That is the worst news ever!

I pick up the cell phone and go to the study, closing the door behind me. Patricia picks the phone up on the first ring. I don't get a chance to utter a word before she begins her directive.

"I know this is short notice but it's important. How are you by the way?"

"Ah...fine." Get to the point.

"Good. Things with the Buchanans have become a little...strained for various reasons, but all that publicity since your accident...well let's just say it didn't help."

"That's somewhat twisted out of shape, don't you think?"

Why the hell was she manipulating this one onto me?

"We need to do some damage limitation. They are valuable clients," she ignores my question. "Tray is due for a meeting in the Seattle office today. The Buchanans are doing some business in the Pacific Northwest. I want you to go along and show him some hospitality afterwards. Smooth things over for when you return. Restore any crumbling bridges."

"Patricia, Seattle is hours away, I–"

"I won't keep you then."

"What's this about anyway?"

"Land acquisition. Just sit in. You'll pick it up. Sorry I've got another call."

She rings off before I have a chance to ask anything else. Why the hell does she think she can just land this on me? Shaking with frustration I ring through to the

Seattle office to find out what time the meeting is. I've just over two hours to get there; impossible. Patricia has set an unreasonable task. I ransack my wardrobe and pull on black trousers and a plain black fitted t-shirt. Hardly the picture of professionalism but it'll have to do. Aunt Rosa tosses me the keys to the truck and I hit the road promising to be back as soon as I can.

My annoyance at having to go to the meeting is tempered by the knowledge that I'm securing my future career by going to meet Tray, but I feel like Patricia's pawn. I haven't seen him since the night of the accident. I can't comprehend how he managed to wrap up the whole messy business with the police and Francesca so quickly. Presumably it's a benefit of having money and friends in all the right places.

I hit every obstacle possible as I thrash the truck towards Seattle. I get stuck behind every slow moving vehicle, and hit every red traffic light and diversion possible. Even the GPS keeps cutting out.

I arrive at the Seattle office over an hour late; blustering through the glass doors of the reception, red faced and breathing heavily, just as Tray is exiting the meeting room, shaking hands with some men in grey suits. I only recognize one of the men. He is a lawyer at Sheldon & Napier, although I've only ever seen his picture before. I stride forward to introduce myself.

Tray spins around as though he's seen me through the back of his head. His blandly handsome face looks thinner than I remember. My hand is outstretched. He ignores it and puts an arm around my shoulder as though I'm a long lost sister in a sudden gesture which could be sincere.

"Tara."

He leaves his arm in place and glances proudly at the suits, staking a claim as he introduces me. I slip off the embrace as I shake hands with the men, who barely acknowledge my presence. They separate into muted conversations and drift off disinterested.

"You're Tara? I'm Robert Sargaison. I'm glad you could make it, but I have everything in hand. You didn't need to be here," my colleague points out. I explain my late arrival and ask to if he could copy me in on what was discussed. He agrees, but he seems reluctant – actually I don't see the point either; not until I'm back at work. I detect mild annoyance in his tone, which is understandable. I wouldn't appreciate someone invading my patch either. My brief for the meeting had been just to sit in and build bridges.

"I could do with a drink," says Tray checking his Breitling watch. "Tara I'm sure you could too. Robert will you join us?"

Tray walks forward, putting his arm leadingly behind Robert's back in a gesture which reminds me of President Bush with Tony Blair. Robert declines the offer. Tray suggests going to the bar in his hotel. I agree, not being familiar with other suitable options in the area, but obviously I'm acutely aware that with this arrangement his hotel suite is particularly accessible – I have *no* intention of getting snared into a scenario which would lead me to his room.

We perch at the bar in the amber light of the restaurant. Tray orders a couple of tequilas and eats handfuls of the nibbles laid out on the bar

"I asked for mineral water," I protest.

Nonetheless the tequila has a marked effect on

euthanizing some of the irritation I'm still feeling. Tray orders champagne and instructs the bar tender to bring it over to the table in the corner for us, which gives me the opportunity to ask him questions without being overheard.

"Did you know it was Francesca all along?" I blurt out, feeling sure he would now admit it.

He grimaces and throws back the glass of champagne as though it is water, then looks down at the table staring blankly at the flame of the candle in the center.

"Nothing? You're going to say nothing?"

"What do you want me to say?"

"I want to know what happened? I want an explanation."

He shakes his head.

"You won't want to hear this."

"Hear what?"

I wait for him to fill the silence as he refills his glass and swills the golden bubbles around distractedly.

"I don't believe it was Francesca," he whispers.

I wrinkle my nose in disgust.

"That's ridiculous. The police found her car with my blood on it. She's in custody."

He winces, pares back his lips and looks at me intently. "She's not."

"What do you mean?"

"She's been released into psychiatric care. She didn't do it, Tara. She isn't capable. She was framed."

A sick feeling is creeping slowly over me.

"By who? Why?"

"I've not made many friends, Tara. You're a smart girl. You know how the world works. You scratch my back...I didn't scratch theirs."

"Whose? What are you saying?"

He lowers his voice until it's barely audible, even with his lips near to my ear; his eyes are scanning the room.

"No matter how high up you get, how much power you have, there is always someone above you. The hidden power, the people no-one gets to see."

"Are you saying they were trying to kill you not me?"

He looks up and blinks subtly in confirmation.

"This is a joke, right?"

He remains tight lipped. I press further.

"Who?" I whisper. I'm wary that I could be being manipulated, lured into a fabricated tale, but Tray's demeanour is completely convincing. This conversation is making me edgy.

Tray looks out the window. "I'm not stupid. I know how things look. You think I'm a player. That's not who I am. I'm played too. I'm a puppet of my father's, but someone pulls his strings. It passes along the chain. There are obligations. Once you're in...you can't get out."

"Are you saying you're being blackmailed?"

"Drink up."

He downs another glass of champagne, grabbing the waiter's attention and pointing to the bottle before it is empty. It's an elaborate tale. One I hadn't seen coming. Francesca being free – that puts me on a knife edge.

"What are you involved in Tray?"

I'm surely being led a merry dance here.

"There's a hidden order to the world, controlled by a few."

He smirks and snorts derision.

"Still, it keeps me in a lifestyle I like. It's all just business. I buy and sell on behalf of clients. I'm actually just a glorified estate agent," he smiles casually.

"What wouldn't you do for money?"

"There you go again, thinking the worst of me."

"You're alluding to corruption, in which you're involved. It's a murky world you're describing. How else am I to think of it?"

He suddenly leans close to my face.

"Keep your head down, don't ask questions and don't step outside your remit. I mean it!" he quietly stresses and stares closely at me, as though trying to convey hidden meaning.

"I'll consider your advice," I reply flippantly, unsure whether to let him know that what he is saying is having an impact on me. He looks stressed: hunching his shoulders he fidgets and lines of tension have appeared on his brow.

With that I change the subject and suggest we order dinner. I'm lightheaded after the glass of champagne and in need of something to sustain me. Tray tells the waiter to send something out, that we'll have whatever the chef recommends. A lavish tray of the freshest and most delicious looking sushi arrives. It's a welcome meal which helps my head to clear after the champagne, although the prior conversation with Tray is sobering in itself. Dinner ends with a trio of pomegranate deserts and a couple of rounds of strong coffee.

When Tray drops the super smooth playboy act he's actually decent company. He prattles on about himself as usual, but some of his stories are actually quite funny. Some are 'you had to be there' moments. The two bottles of champagne are taking their toll; he's definitely a little worse for wear now, though not as much as you would expect. I'm glad I came because it's given me closure on the situation with him.

"Tray, I have to go. It's a bit of a drive back to Big Spruce."

As we're leaving the hotel restaurant I notice, for the first time, a couple of businessmen sitting at a table near the door. They both glance up and away quickly, but their swivelling eyes show they are taking a good look at us as we walk past them. I'm curious why they are interested in us. Perhaps they know Tray?

"Tara, I'll walk you to your car."

Remembering his warning about the hidden order I'm grateful he's escorting me back to Aunt Rosa's truck. Not that I particularly believe it, but I don't disbelieve it either – it's left me with an unsettling feeling. It's hardly surprising my imagination is fired up after the conversation. *I must get a grip.*

We walk through the quiet streets to the parking lot which, apart from a few vehicles, is deserted.

"I'm sorry about what happened to you," he catches me off guard with a hug. His body sways because of the alcohol. If I were taking bets I'd say if I stayed like that any longer he would make a full on move. Stepping back I put my arm on his shoulder, lengthening the distance.

"Good night, Tray. I'm glad we met up."

"Me too. I'm not the ogre you think I am."

Tray turns back towards the hotel. As I glimpse him in the rear view mirror I realize how glad I am to be able to close that chapter and move on. He's more insightful than I'd imagined. The city lights thin out as I head away from the populous into the darkness of the forests: towards Big Spruce, and the comfort and safety of home. Barrelling the truck down the highway I'm more relieved than ever to have a safe hiding place: somewhere pure and untouched, away from hidden menace.

13

Aunt Rosa has asked me to come to the garden center to help her unload the flower and hanging basket arrangements she has made for them. On the way through town we drive past a modern building, with a sign saying *Svetlana Wolfe Acupuncture*. The name sounds familiar; and I remember the conversation with the guy on the plane. Perhaps I'll give it a go.

Rosa sweeps into a wide white–fenced driveway of the garden centre and branches off to the left. This access is the trade entrance at the back of the store building, between workshops, greenhouses and pallets of compost. Several horses grazing in the adjacent field stop and raise their heads mid–munch to inspect the visitors.

A middle-aged lady wearing a checked shirt and jeans tucked into her boots gives us a robust wave and points to where she wants Rosa to park.

"That's Margy. She owns the place," Rosa clarifies.

We stop alongside an open–sided wooden building, where Aunt Rosa turns off the engine and climbs out of the pickup. The two women greet each other like they've known each other for years.

"I'll see if one of the guys can help unload," says Margy.

Well that saves us a job. Although Rosa mainly works freelance, she occasionally works part–time for the nursery, though she likes to take her work home with her. Gardening is her passion. She often says how lucky she is to be paid for something she doesn't class as work.

Hudson, who has been happily sitting in the back of the truck, begins to whine, but I leave him there when I get out. Rosa and her friend are deep in conversation and disappear into a greenhouse. I drop the tail–gate of the pickup when, suddenly, the passenger door of the truck is hurled open, banging against the wooden post. Hudson leaps out, barking. The door had closed on the seat belt, so it'd been ajar. Before I can get close enough to grab his collar he bolts at full speed; seizing his liberty he races off in the direction of the horse's field.

"Hudson! Come back here! Hudson!" I yell, but it has no effect.

Maybe I should just wait for him to come back, but he could scare the horses. He's such a gentle–mannered dog but he is wilful. I chase after to stop him causing havoc.

Hudson tries to squeeze between the low fence rails, but when he doesn't fit, he jumps it instead and vanishes around the corner of a stable adjacent to the workshops. Two roan horses in the distance lift their heads and prick up their ears in the direction of the dog.

"Damn dog," I mutter as I clamber over the fence in pursuit, hearing him barking playfully. I hurry, following the sound that is coming from the direction of the stables. I walk straight into a tall figure and raise my hands in reflex. Spellbound and stupid I stare up at Shasta's amused face.

"Sorry!" I exclaim. Paralyzed by surprise, I can't seem to move.

"Hi...again," he speaks slowly, staring down at me, not breaking eye contact – equally not moving.

The spell is only broken by the sound of barking dogs. I'm suddenly aware that my hands are resting on his broad chest. I step backward, without losing eye contact. I glance over at Hudson playing with a long–haired shaggy, Golden Retriever crossbreed.

"That's my dog," I say lamely. "I came looking for the

dog." I'm tongue–tied and stuck for something witty and intelligent to say.

"You weren't looking for me then?" asks Shasta, and a trace of a smile hovers on his mouth.

"Ha ha. No. Um...I didn't know anyone was here," I giggle nervously. What is wrong with me? It's like I've been possessed by a giddy love–struck teenager. *Get a grip girl. It's not your first rodeo*, as Simon would say. "Hudson took off. I guess he knew your dog was here."

"He recognizes my jeep. They're old friends."

"So what are you doing here?" I ask, looking around at the horse shelter, tools and the gas burner. "Are you having a BBQ?"

"I'm a farrier."

"Oh. I know someone who could do with your help," I remark, thinking of Barnaby's thickened hooves. Shasta raises one eyebrow – I smile and shake my head, dismissing my comment. "I thought you worked in the gas station?"

"No. My friend owns it. I just help him out occasionally."

"You get outdoors and you work with horses. Lucky you."

"It works for me. What do you do?"

"I'm a lawyer."

"Here? I've not seen you around before."

"No, I live in New York, but I'm taking time out," I look off into the distance because I don't want to elaborate.

"Why?" asks Shasta, not for a second removing his dark, probing eyes from me. I twitch from the intensity of his scrutiny. I look back up at him, feeling vulnerable to exposure. There is nowhere to hide.

"I had an accident and I wanted to get away for a while. My aunt lives here, so I've come to stay with her."

I've given him the facts hoping to switch his attention

to light conversation, but instead Shasta continues his questioning silence, but I catch his eyes flickering over my hands and neck.

"My aunt works for the garden center. She's the hanging basket lady."

Shasta just nods, still scrutinizing me. "Why did you want to get away?" he asks.

Damn. I don't really want to talk about me.

"That's what I'm here to find out," I say, surprising myself with the answer hoping that'll be enough to satisfy his curiosity. It isn't. He doesn't fill the silence that's stretching out between us. Instead he just continues to look at me, waiting for me to continue. I don't trust myself to open up without the flood–gates opening. They say it's easier to talk to strangers and what would he care? It doesn't really matter if I tear up, I quickly reason with myself.

"I hate my job. I've lost the point. My values have shifted now that I've achieved everything I've worked towards. I don't feel it matters, but it's my security – I'd hate to lose it," my throat constricts and my voice breaks.

"You have many things to be grateful for though?"

"Sure my friends are amazing. I'd be lost without them… more than I am now. They've been my adopted family for a long time." I didn't plan on telling him this much.

"What about your real family?"

"My parents died when I was seventeen."

"Sorry."

"Don't be. It was a long time ago."

"Be grateful for the things you value. You'll encourage more of them."

I narrow my eyes and look back up at him, feeling irritated that he clearly doesn't understand my predicament.

"Everything I've achieved has been down to me, through hard work and perseverance. I haven't had anything on a plate, not least support from a family, so I'm not sure I owe gratitude to anyone else," I hear myself and instantly regret such an indignant response.

"And yet your friends have been there, keeping you anchored and helping you flourish."

"Sure…but apart from them, it's just me – kind of always has been," I swallow down self pity, feeling tears stinging the back of my eyes. I'm never usually this emotional. I wonder if I'm having some kind of post traumatic melt–down.

"It makes you strong and self–reliant. If you're motivated to get what you want from others, you'll be disappointed when you don't get it – be what you seek. You're a constant beacon, sending out ripples of energy. Once the ripples hit substance and return to you, they bring back the same thing you sent."

"What are you, some sort of psychiatrist?" I ask, screwing up my nose.

Shasta laughs. "It's just the way of the universe, nature's principles if you like. Drop a stone in a pond and watch what happens; that's nature's laws in action. There is a season for everything. We aren't separate from each other anymore than we're separated from nature and animals. It's all the same life force that animates us all."

I don't feel like he's judging me, and my irritation subsides. He's sharing knowledge – for that I'm grateful. It also resonates. It's the power of attraction again, and I've heard it all before, but listening to the words spoken with wisdom feels different.

"The nature here is a big pull for me. I feel good outside,

especially around pine trees – I could become a tree hugger. I came here after I was in a hit and run. The most bizarre thing was I had a near death experience while I was in hospital." I find myself opening up easily.

"The Shaman's way. They move between worlds," says Shasta.

"What?"

"Some experiences force you to change your life. Sometimes you face death before you can go any further. It shows you another realm."

"I thought I was going crazy. During it I saw this Native American, Lehman he called himself. I've seen him since too, and then there are the lights in the forest." It's all coming out now.

"The lights are guardians and spirits. They're everywhere. It's the critical mind prevents them being seen more."

"Do you see the lights?"

"Since always."

I nod, wide–eyed, impressed and massively relieved that someone else perceives an alternate reality. I feel less alone – less of a freak.

"You're awakening. As your energy rises you'll have more insights and can use your gifts more."

"Not sure about that."

"Sometimes they're dormant from lack of use and fear of rejection. Didn't you ever have visions or just simply know things when you were a child?"

"I used to see people, as real as you or I, but I grew out of it – it just stopped. Sometimes I know when something has happened to someone. I still get that."

"Only what resonates for you is right. Not what others want you to believe."

I'm intrigued and inspired by this beautiful enigma standing beside me.

Hudson bounds up with a stick. The two dogs have been frolicking in the field, while we've been talking. He drops a stick at my feet, with a plea to throw it for him. I toss it automatically, lost in thought.

Shasta goes to the light–grey mare tethered to a post. I quietly watch him appreciating the graceful, effortless way he moves. His tall, lithe, frame looks weightless, seeming to glide across the ground. As his muscular tawny hand touches the mare's shoulder she turns her trusting head towards him, lovingly nuzzling his arm. He grips her firmly, running his hand down the length of her leg to the fetlock. I'm ridiculously jealous.

I approach the horse, gently stroking her dignified, velvety head. Shasta picks up the mare's foot and she shifts her weight, leaning heavily on Shasta's shoulder with implicit trust.

"No you don't girl," he tells her, pushing her as he moves his back away from the horse, making her stand up straight – yet the palpable bond between the horse and the human remains.

I murmur to her, quietly losing myself in the horse's exquisite brown eyes. Blending with her I feel a powerful connection with the horse and my eyes brim with tears. An unexplained and overwhelming love envelops me and I feel myself merge with the horse's spirit. The horse shares her gentle, yielding warmth and kindness. It's not the spirit of a subservient animal, but that of a purposeful, free–spirited being; willing to serve in return for man's leadership. I have a clear vision of bucking horses, galloping across plains together in high spirits – one hundred animals, one shared spirit answering an ancient primal call. It creates a yearning in my heart for the same freedom and euphoria – that sense of oneness.

I pull back from the horse, trailing my hand away from her neck; now aware of the tears streaming down my cheeks and falling on the dusty ground as a silent sob escapes, bringing me back to the present. I blink hard, tilting my head, letting the tears fall to clear my vision.

Shasta rises and stands beside me. He doesn't say a word. I can feel my heart beat to a different rhythm as though it's recalibrating. Without interrupting, Shasta quietly holds the space. His hands look taut with restraint, but he remains still and solid beside me.

I keep looking down. I don't want to explain. Raising my hand to the horse's soft muzzle I look into her eyes once more, conveying gratitude to the horse.

"Thank you," I mutter.

I turn to Shasta, whose intense eyes show no concern, only a kinship of mutual understanding. He looks down and nods. I quickly bring my sleeve up to my chin and try to subtly wipe my tear stained face.

"Sorry," I tell him though I don't feel embarrassed. Instead I'm strangely comfortable. "I felt her joy, her reason," is about all I can say.

"You felt her magic: her spirit. You let her touch your heart," says Shasta.

Tears well up again, but I keep them in check this time.

"I need to find my reason."

"Or accept it."

What did that mean? I'm puzzled and can't instantly grasp what he means. Was that a random comment or is there something I need to accept?

"I've got to go," I say, quickly distancing myself. I walk away from the stable, then stop and look over my shoulder at Shasta.

"Thank you," I whisper, my voice sounds husky and barely audible. I stand silently for a moment, time feeling like an awkward concept, pondering if there is anything else I need to say. He smiles at me knowingly and turns his attention back to the mare as I leave, feeling more at peace than I've done for a long time.

14

"Breathe in... and out," instructs Svetlana, as she turns the needle in my skin. I release the breath and grin with relief that I braved the fear of needles.

"See, it's not as bad as you thought it would be," she says triumphantly.

Svetlana Wolfe, I'm delighted to report, seems to know exactly what she's doing – it truly isn't painful, just a curious tingling sensation. What's really surprising is that I barely felt the needles, and hadn't been aware they were still in until she told me not to fidget so much.

"My hands are sweaty," I laugh, and wipe my palms on the tissue paper beneath me. "I enjoyed that! Is that wrong?"

The rapport with Svetlana was instant. The strident, petite, fifty–something Svetlana, with the confidence of the worldly wise, and a rasping, throaty voice which reminds me of an old Hollywood actress who is a forty–a–day smoker. When Svetlana took my case history I felt at ease, plus I went in with the opinion that whatever I tell her she would probably have heard before anyway.

She asked me about relationships and I told her I came out of a three year relationship last year. She paused long enough to suggest she wanted me to elaborate. I haven't spoken about it for so long and tried not to think of it at all. The shock, then delight, of the positive pregnancy test, the hideous continual nausea some joker called 'morning' sickness; but it would all have been worth it. Maybe if I hadn't been late for work I would have missed the mail man, then things would be different – but they weren't. I couldn't change what had passed. David, my ex, was a nice normal guy who ticked all the boxes; from an intellectual point of view anyway. Only now I can admit the chemistry had been weak – but I could have made it work; for my baby I could have done that.

It was the day before Valentine's Day, I had collected the mail and found one red envelope addressed to me. The thrill at the romantic notion David had posted the card became a waking nightmare the instant I opened it. It was a woman's distinctive bubbly handwriting and vindictive heart that had written the card. In two short sentences my world fell apart.

She hinted that David had been having an affair with her and she had also sent the same card to him to arrive on Valentine's Day, I presume to test that I would know of his guilt by his reaction. I dismissed it as best I could – there could be any number of reasons why a woman would send such a thing. Maybe he had rejected someone's advances I reasoned, but the cold, hard shell forming around my heart wasn't budging.

The next day was Saturday. We weren't at work. I asked David to check the mail when it arrived, and watched his reaction as he shuffled through the envelopes in his hand, and faltered when he read the handwriting on the red envelope. From his neck up he turned deep red, like a tourniquet had been tightened around him. As I lay on the sofa watching, praying he would open it and tell me it was a terrible practical joke, he slipped the red envelope in his back pocket and tossed the rest of the mail on the table.

"Nothing important, just junk mail. Anyway, I've arranged a game of squash with Barry." David had stumbled over his words, overcompensating with joviality and a plastic smile.

After a chaste kiss on my forehead he was gone. He had failed the test his lover had set up. The next day I found the scrunched up Valentine card in the bottom of his sports bag. I had to look. Inside the card his lover called him a total bastard and told him that she had also sent me the same card – that I already knew his secret. It was suddenly all too real for me.

It was then the gnawing pains got worse. They'd started overnight with cramping and aching at the top of my legs. I felt dizzy and sick, more so than normal. Something was wrong inside and I knew it. I lay down on the thick pile of the cream rug on the floor, tucking a pillow next to me I held on to my stomach, willing the baby to stay with me, promising I would make everything alright, that I would make his world a safe place to come into. I begged for it not to be happening – my prayer wasn't heard.

I got to ten weeks but the pregnancy didn't hold. I miscarried there on the lounge floor. I cried like I've never cried before; gut wrenchingly, unable to breathe between sobs. I lay there until the scarlet blood seeped through my clothes.

The hardest part had been coming to terms with the loss of that new beginning, that tiny new life which had been unfurling but never did. The inevitable breakup with David had been emotional and messy, but I never looked back or regretted our parting.

So I ended up explaining the whole sorry story to Svetlana who made no additional drama. I felt happier for the opportunity to tell someone other than Giselle who was so close to me and the situation. I hadn't been aware how much of that trauma I'd still been carrying.

Eventually she asked me if I was happy being single and I admitted after a year as a singleton I was more than ready to be part of a couple again.

She gave me a cursory look over, from head to toe.

"You won't have to wait long," she said in her warm Polish accent, as though she were party to such knowledge.

I told her that in New York there are five women to one man so it was like piranha feeding time. Behind her friendly, easy going demeanor I reckon Svetlana is a force in her own right. I hadn't realized she would be considering my emotions until she prompted me to talk about myself.

"Sit up slowly in case you get dizzy," instructs Svetlana, then she leaves the room to let me get dressed in private. I swing my feet round to the side of the treatment couch, and sit up too quickly because I'm trying to look at the acupuncture meridian charts hanging on the walls. I look around with greater acuity and clarity, feeling more present than I have done for months. Everything in the room seems vivid, almost surreal.

I pull on my shirt and jeans, which I have virtually lived in recently, then secure them with a black belt which is essential due to the weight loss since the accident.

"You OK?" asks Svetlana, sizing me up as she comes back into the room.

"Yep, a bit strange, but in a good way. It's like I'm looking out from my eyes, instead of watching from the back seat. I didn't even know I'd felt like that until now."

"Good. It'll take a little time for your treatment to settle in. Just for today, don't drink any alcohol and have plenty of water and rest," says Svetlana, sitting down at her desk to schedule my next appointment. "You have my number, ring me if you've any questions," she says as she shows me out to the reception.

Back out in the quiet street I squint in the late afternoon

sunshine, feeling light and springy, like a weight has been lifted from me. The bright blue sky lifts my spirits even further. Instead of heading for home, I take a detour to the coffee shop on my way to the lakeshore. I remember Svetlana's instructions, and no, she definitely didn't say not to drink coffee.

I catch myself daydreaming of having a partner to share the afternoon with. I have an inclination the universe has been giving me space for a relationship detox recently. It's probably better for me to be single right now, but it doesn't stop me thinking about Shasta non–stop. I've become completely and reluctantly infatuated by him.

My phone vibrates in my pocket, which reminds me to turn the volume on again. There is a text from Simon which reads:

Hey Northy. How would you like a visitor? You free for a chat later? xx

I text him back while I'm walking along, taking tentative steps as I turn the corner onto the main street.

Check out flights. I'll call you later xx

I press send, open the door to the busy coffee shop and drop the phone into my bag, becoming engrossed in reading the menu board behind the counter.

"A large latte to go, please."

"I'll get that," says a deep voice next to me.

I stop breathing and my heart flips around like a landed fish when I see Shasta beside me. I look to my side and realize he was there all along.

"Thanks," is all I manage to say, pretty certain my voice isn't noticeably quivering. Shasta turns slightly towards me, dropping the money into the barista's hand.

"Do you want to join me?" he asks.

"Em, sure. But I was going to head over to the lake."
"Oh, right."
"But you could join me? We might as well enjoy the sunshine." I get such a thrill from using the word 'we' that I may be about to faint.

"Great," says Shasta casually. "Make them both to go," he calls to the barista.

I put my lips together and blow out slowly, aiming to calm my erratic breathing as my heart hammers out of my chest. I spot my reflection in the mirror opposite and roll my eyes to myself, giving away my internal conversation. Then I notice I'm being watched by Shasta and do a double take. I smile lamely at him in the mirror. *Damn.* I always act so foolish around him.

I steal several quick glances at him, taking care not to get caught in the mirror this time. He must be at least 6ft 3in in height. His slim hips and narrow waist taper into his lean back. Straight broad shoulders and taut muscles are faintly traceable through his white t–shirt. I repress the purring noise in my throat. I take in the smooth shapely tone of his tawny arms and the deep brown of his wide sinewy hands. *Jeez.* What was I saying about staying single? All I can think about right now is what it'd be like if he kissed me.

Together we walk out of the coffee shop. It's crazy how amazing I feel just being with him. He radiates great confidence and authority – I feel shielded in his company. The electricity fizzes and sparks between us: the invisible force joining us together. I'd swear I am taller, as if a coil is pulling me upwards. I didn't know it was possible to feel this connected to someone.

Does he feel it too? We don't speak. Three inches of

dazzling space separates us, and right at this moment I feel luminous.

"I know a great spot. Let's take my car," says Shasta.

I step up into the jeep, and as I pull the door closed I notice Pandora Walsh coming out of a store with an armful of groceries, rapidly talking to a friend. She notices me. Crikey, in this small town there is no getting away from anyone. She stares over with her mouth open then fervently resumes chattering with her friend and keeping her eyes on me. With the bags in her arms Pandora can't wave, and thankfully she is out of earshot. She contorts her face with exaggerated gestures, which I presume are an attempt to engage me. I deliberately misunderstand, and give her a cheery greeting then slam the car door shut.

"Drive!" I laugh, and grab the hot drinks off Shasta.

"Who's that?"

"Our neighbor, Pandora. That'll give her something to talk about for a while," I tell him, feeling rebellious and pleased with myself.

We drive a short distance to a quiet grassy area beside the lake, which is well away from the public lakeside. I can just see the water twinkling through the foliage of the trees, and I follow Shasta through them to a small rocky cove, sheltered on one side by a large boulder.

A large pale tree trunk that has been worn smooth by the elements lies uprooted, jutting out from the shore into the water. Small ripples lap around it, covering the sand and light grey pebbles, glistening below. It is breathtakingly beautiful: rustic and magical – it's one of 'those' places. A gentle shore–bound wind touches my skin: creating goose–bumps and heightening my senses.

"You're cold," remarks Shasta, and vanishes back into the

trees. He re–appears with his jacket and drapes it over my shoulders. The heady mix of his tangy scent and his close proximity completely intoxicates me.

We clamber onto the fallen tree, using the old branch stumps as a foothold. Shasta is alongside and we shift further along, using the tree as if it is a jetty – we sit above the surrounding water.

I drink deeply from the paper cup, feeling the warm liquid sooth my restless insides. I have the urge to fill the silence, yet there seems no reason for speech and Shasta doesn't seem to waste words. I'm utterly present in this moment. Are we both under the same spell? I'm actually on the brink of daring to believe that, but self–doubt nags that perhaps I'm the only one having these incredible feelings. Maybe my misguided romantic notions and wishful thinking are causing me to mistake his friendship for something more.

This guy is powerful and deep, exuding the robust confidence of a warrior, which borders on arrogance. The shadow beneath his high, flat cheekbones nestles beside the chiselled jaw line. I need to rein myself in. This guy is out of my league, and just because I've had a few chance meetings with him and a free coffee doesn't mean he's interested in me. I can't keep up the silence any longer.

"Do you know...you have the advantage on me? You already know a lot about me and I know nothing about you," I say, hoping to get more of a measure of him. I turn my face towards him and get caught in the intense, deep brown eyes.

"Yes you do," he says obscurely.

"Huh?" *Crap*. I'm going to fall off this log.

"What do you want to know?" he asks. Is it my

imagination or is there another separate conversation going on between us? This one is the tip of the iceberg.

"Did you grow up here?"

"I've mostly lived around here. I grew up on the reservation on the outskirts of town."

"Did you ever want to live somewhere else for a while?"

"I've done my share of travelling. I trained horses professionally until I didn't want to travel anymore. I wanted to settle back here. For generations my family lived on this land and took care of it. Now it's up to me to carry it on. I've travelled and lived in places where the energies are so fractured. If I'd continued to live there I'd have become like that. What I need is right here. The answers are around us when we are quiet enough to hear it," says Shasta looking out across the lake and gesturing with his hand. "I needed a simpler life."

"I can understand that," I echo his sentiment as I look across the rippling lake.

"Now I work as much as I need to and my clients are grateful. My other job, the one I don't get paid for – I enjoy it the more."

I give him a quizzical look.

"Earth healing. It's like nature's acupuncture."

"How funny! I've just had acupuncture, but I don't see how that relates?" It's bizarre to be having this conversation right after my visit to Svetlana's.

"The principles are similar. The earth's geopathic energy has meridians in the form of grids and ley–lines. Sometimes these get out of balance. It's important to keep the portals open."

"Why?"

"Light codes arrive through these portals. They bring

in new energies. There's another way to live which we're being prepared for, but we haven't the full picture yet. The portals need to be cleared and strengthened to help the process along."

"I just get a feeling from a place. I know where I feel good, and I know where I don't. Like here..."

"That's it. This is a power spot. I come here to re-energize. Places which are out of sync lower the energies in that area. It's instinctive. Huge changes are happening in the earth right now, and it's more important than ever that the grids are open and clear."

"So, are you saying you use giant needles and stick them in the ground or something?"

"Some people use rods or magnets, after they've dowsed, but I use my intuition and sometimes symbols to work out what's needed."

My ears prick up particularly at the mention of symbols.

"How do you do that?"

"Marking the symbol on the ground but sometimes also using visualisation. It works better when you get your mind into the theta brain wave."

I raise my eyebrows, not understanding.

"Like in meditation, or we sometimes use drumming," he explains and I'm marginally wiser.

"Do you use the Hermetic Seal, like on my amulet?"

"No, there are other symbols traditionally used – but maybe we could use it," it seems like the thought has only just occurred to him. I linger on the 'we' reference. He skims over me with a glance.

Overhead an eagle is coming in low as it flies over the water, swooping down to land on an isolated tree which is growing from a small, earthy island in the centre of the lake. From a distance it isn't obvious that the island is a separate entity, it blends into the background scenery. But now in the changing light a fine mist drifts across the surface of the lake, showing contrasting muted colors between the island and the backdrop.

"You know the animals bring messages?" asks Shasta, watching the eagle land. "They're metaphors for life."

I smile back at him and we sit silently, melding into the shifting mood in the cove. I wish I knew what he is thinking.

Shasta draws his right leg up and over, to straddle the tree. He lifts my hand and moves me round to face him, keeping intensely deep eye contact, as I drape my legs over either side of the log. Now we are both completely facing each other.

"This is what I'm thinking," says Shasta.

I can barely breathe as his eyes flicker between my eyes and mouth. He slowly closes in, pulling both my hands towards him. The air sparks with anticipation. I want to feel his mouth touch mine and I lean towards him. My lips part and his mouth softly traces them. I'm lost in the moment, melting into him. He lifts my face with both hands, stroking his hand along my cheek to the back of my neck, where he holds me still and I'm locked together with him.

We kiss so deeply and passionately that I'm aware of nothing else. I place one of my hands on his warm chest and the other around his neck, drawing my fingers through his thick satiny hair. We move closer into each other, pressing hard, trying to get under the other's skin. It's impossibly and unbearably not enough.

When we break apart our breathing is erratic. I look into

his face as his hand gently tugs my hair and my chin tilts up towards his mouth. He firmly slides his mouth over mine, his lips and tongue probing. We linger and hug tightly. I don't want to part from him.

We lean our foreheads together our noses touching as we study each other's faces. I capture every detail of Shasta's, touching his mouth and chin with my finger, storing the memory. I touch the scar above his left eyebrow but nothing can mar this noble face.

"Turn around," he breaks the spell and I turn to face the lake, with my back to him, moulding into his chest. He wraps his arms around my shoulders, kissing me from my hair to my shoulders. We gaze out across the water, tightly bound to each other, absorbing the beauty all around us. I wish this time were endless.

There is a cool nip in the air now and we eventually begin to make our way back. I jump from the log, but he catches me as I launch, and holds me close, sliding his hands around my bottom as he lowers me to the ground, keeping me there while we kiss again. He brings his hand up and cups my breast through my shirt. He tugs the shirt open and pulls down the lace of my bra, exposing my nipple to a puff of cool air. He quickly lowers his head to kiss my breast. I laugh and scold him, but feel my insides clench excitedly.

"Next time," he breathes, touching my neck.

Oh, such sweet promise...

Driving back towards Big Spruce my phone springs to life and a series of texts and missed calls appear. We've been out of range of a signal and I'm in demand. Abruptly I'm back to reality as I scan the texts from Aunt Rosa.

Don't forget supper with next door tonight xx
Followed by:
Supper is 8:00. Are you on your way?xx
And finally:
Where are you?

I have completely and conveniently forgotten dinner with the Walshs next door. All too soon we are back at Aunt Rosa's.

"Sorry, I've got to run." I turn to Shasta, still hardly daring to believe he is here, with me, like this. We share a lingering kiss before I jump out of the jeep and he watches me walk up the path before driving away. I'm flushed and warm through but prepared for a chilly reception from Aunt Rosa.

15

I bolt through the door of Aunt Rosa's house, running seriously late. She is a stickler for time-keeping because she doesn't want to keep people waiting.

"Sorry! I lost track of time."

"Where have you been? You look like you've been dragged through a hedge backwards."

"Sorry, I'll just freshen myself up, it won't take a minute!" I bound upstairs in an exuberant mood, not willing to answer questions.

"Honestly Tara, I've been calling and texting you. You know how proper the Walshs are. We're already late. How long are you going to be?" calls Aunt Rosa, her irritation is unmistakable as she clatters noisily around in the kitchen.

I rake a brush through my hair and throw on a skirt and top. Rubbing the smudged make-up from below my eyes, I quickly apply a lick of mascara, before running downstairs while still applying lipstick and putting on shoes simultaneously.

"Ready?" asks Aunt Rosa, watching me as she paces the room.

"I'm ready. We aren't too late after all." I try to pacify this rare display of anger from my aunt.

"What do you mean not too late! We were supposed to have been there forty-five minutes ago. My ears are burning! I'm sure they're saying all sorts of things behind my back. What must they think? It was so good of them to invite us Tara, and you don't even have the courtesy to turn up on time."

I've really lit her fuse. I've never seen her so irate. But I do know that she fears disapproval so much and perhaps

I should've known better. I hadn't intended to be late. I wouldn't have done that. So I march next door behind my fermenting aunt, feeling anything but sociable.

The door opens before we can knock, and the stench of cologne wafts out, or is it air freshener? Either way I try not to inhale the overpowering synthetic floral scent which is suffocating my nostrils. The house is, as I expected, immaculate; nothing less than a show home. Although the elaborate bright décor of pink, blue and lilac, with matching wallpaper and curtains isn't to my taste, it's probably expensive.

A bust of an unknown solemn gentlemen stands at the foot of the stairs and I resist the sudden urge to drape my coat over his head. Errol and Pandora fuss around us like yapping poodles, while my aunt apologizes profusely for our late arrival.

"Sorry. It wasn't Aunt Rosa's fault it was mine," I say, passing a bottle of red wine to Errol, who gives it a curious look. Pandora thanks my aunt for the home–made brownies and flowers and passes them to her underling, Errol; issuing an order to take them to the kitchen. I sigh under my breath, grateful that it is a small gathering. I can bear it. I'm secretly in a state of sweet mania, chuckling to myself and remembering Shasta, and our amazing time together. My mind is far from here, occupied by its reverie. A dark–haired guy is reservedly walking into the hallway looking uncomfortable as he shifts his glasses further up his nose. He gives me a shy, innocuous smile as he approaches. This must be their son, Roger.

"Shall I take your coat?" he asks.

"Thanks, you must be–" I start to say, extending my hand, but I'm brashly interrupted by Pandora.

"Darling you must meet Roger," Pandora directs, tilting her head to the side with a phony grin which she converts into her best 'isn't it wonderful' face.

Roger looks acutely embarrassed as we shake hands. I have instant sympathy for this ordinary guy and we already have in common the humiliation of being roped into this hideous dinner date scenario. Romance is not on the menu for us. Roger is conventionally dressed in trousers and a shirt, looking all set for a day at the office.

"Oh isn't it great that you two kids can finally meet," says Pandora.

What the hell! Kids? Scotty, beam me out of here.

"Now Roger, Tara here is a lawyer, so as you're both professionals I'm sure you'll have lots in common," Pandora declares, then turns back to Aunt Rosa, continuing an incessant commentary. Roger gives me a wry embarrassed look.

"That wasn't at all awkward, was it?" I whisper to him. It breaks the ice and I hear a low noise in his throat as he grins.

"Sorry," he colludes back. "Not my doing unfortunately."

"Now come in and meet everyone Tara," instructs Pandora, bustling past me so that she can stand centre stage, inside the doorway of the lounge.

"Everyone? I thought this was it. Isn't it?" My heart sinks. In the lounge, perched on the edge of an ornate green sofa, is Cain Shimlow with a pleasant–faced lady whom I presume to be his wife. On the matching sofa opposite, an elderly grey–haired couple sit nursing tea in china cups and saucers.

Everyone stands to greet us and seems very welcoming, especially Cain Shimlow. He gives me such an inflated welcome it makes me suspicious that it's for the other's benefit. Introductions are made and the friendly elderly couple, known as Sam and Violet, move along and encouragingly pat the sofa for me to join them. We barely get to sit down before Pandora and Errol announce that supper is ready.

"I apologize if the food has dried out while we have all been waiting for our guests to arrive," booms Pandora. I cringe for Aunt Rosa at the blatant dig.

The fancy dining room contains a long mahogany table, displaying an array of silverware. The matching sideboard is cluttered with silver candelabras, trinkets, photograph frames and stale pot-pourri. I thankfully spot my bottle of red wine sitting on a silver place mat.

Pandora directs us to our seats and I'm relieved to be seated next to Roger. Not for a reason the older generation would approve of, but because it keeps me at a good distance from Pandora and Errol.

"Dinner is served," announces Pandora with such flourish that you would think she is announcing a luxury banquet. In fact it's a meagre helping of pork and vegetables being dished up.

Errol, somewhat reluctantly, pours me half a glass of wine. I suggest he leaves the bottle on the table, to save him having to get up again. The others apart from Roger, all seem to be teetotal.

"Cheers," I say to Roger and we genially clink glasses and gulp down the mellow red wine. It goes down so smoothly. Just what I need to round off the sharp edges, and in a far corner of my mind I remember Svetlana the acupuncturist advising me to abstain from alcohol tonight. *Oops.*

The conversation revolves around local politics, gossip and church events. None of this includes me – nor does Roger have anything to say on these matters. Aunt Rosa is still chilly, although I think she has softened somewhat while she has been watching my interaction with Roger, which is becoming more animated due to the wine he's topping up our glasses with.

Pandora and Errol seem caught up in discussing their plans for the town fair. Seemingly it's even boring Cain Shimlow, who has tried changing the subject several times.

"So I've got some raffle prize donations from several stores," says Pandora. "Speaking of which, I was picking some up today when I saw Tara climbing into a car with some long haired native type. Didn't you hear me call you, Tara? I could have done with some help to carry them." blurts Pandora.

"No I didn't. I guess I was too far away," I feel defiant, but sure she isn't about to drop it at that.

"I expect you were too busy. Isn't he one of those Indians from over at the reservation? You should be careful what company you keep. They're a bad lot you know. We're all better off when they keep themselves to themselves and stay out of town."

"Well we're getting to know each other better and he's a great guy. I believe we shouldn't judge by our own prejudices, don't you?"

"My dear, you are new to Big Spruce, so you've much to learn. Those reprobates are responsible for all of the crime around here, with their drug habits, drinking binges, brawling and thieving. I'm sure you wouldn't condone it, would you?" asks Pandora provocatively, and she looks to the others for support.

Cain Shimlow has put down his knife and fork, presiding over the conversation.

"Pandora is right, of course. They've caused a great deal of trouble around here. We have done our best to bring them into the fold and teach them what is right, but they're beyond help. They're stuck in their pagan ways. It's just not acceptable to bring that sort of thing into civilized society. We'll pray for them," decrees Shimlow.

I'm utterly mortified and outraged that someone would have the audacity to own such bigoted opinions.

"Why would they trust us? Interesting you think our ways are better? I'm not sure the thousands of Native American women who had enforced sterilization–"

"It didn't happen," he interrupts.

"–*without consent*, would agree or have any confidence in what the dominant social group constitutes a better way of life," I drive my point home.

"I've read those ludicrous articles by disgruntled Indians too. It didn't happen," he snarls but wraps it in a measured tone.

"There is evidence of a policy of forced tubal ligation of Indian women to prevent them breeding. A young woman being admitted to hospital to have her appendix removed and coming out with her tubes tied is a travesty."

"I don't know where you get your facts from. They are wholly inaccurate."

"Do you agree with such a policy? Hypothetically speaking of course, because it apparently didn't exist – I'm just curious?"

All eyes turn to Cain Shimlow, awaiting his response. The atmosphere is thick with tension.

"I support stringent family planning," his grey eyes glitter.

"You would have recommended better access to contraception?"

Cain Shimlow is glaring across the table at me. I expect his eyes to glow red at any second. I raise my eyebrows at him. Pandora jumps in, uncomfortable with the subject.

"I'm sure your Aunt Rosa would not want you keeping bad company. Did you know about this?" Pandora asks, turning square on my poor aunt, who up until now has been sitting in silence with an unreadable expression.

"It's not up to Rosa, or anyone else, what company I keep," I interject.

A surge of white–hot rage wells up inside me. There is a social boundary and I've firmly stepped over it. Aunt Rosa closes her mouth and looks away from me. I need to be careful not to embarrass her further.

"We're looking out for you, Tara. You've been too independent for too long. You must learn to lean on others. You can do that now. There is no need for it here. You can depend on us. We want you to come into our fold," says Pastor Shimlow with sycophantic sweetness, which stirs the others into a chorus of approval.

"Thanks for your concern, but I really do believe that taking the moral high ground is in nobody's best interest, and making sweeping, toxic misjudgements only divides society. We could be looking at what we all have in common."

"Any more news on that bear that's been into the neighborhood?" asks Roger, deftly coming to the rescue and changing the subject. I appreciate the intervention.

"It's become too familiar now. It'll have to be shot,"

states Cain Shimlow emphatically, joining the conversation swerve. Sam and Violet look relieved at this diversion and jump on board, eagerly sharing anecdotes about their experiences of bear raids. Not to be outdone, Errol and Pandora pitch in.

I look at Roger with a smile of gratitude then finish my meal in silence, noting that Aunt Rosa is now avoiding my eyes, looking away when I meet her gaze. I sigh that I've embarrassed her again, despite being restrained in my comments.

I'm utterly exhausted, so I excuse myself when it is feasibly acceptable to do so. Aunt Rosa also takes her leave, and we swap air kisses with our hosts on the way out.

"Is that why you were late: because you were with some guy?" asks Aunt Rosa. I had expected an inquisition once we were alone.

"I'm sorry I was late. I completely forgot about dinner, but I *will* keep whatever company I choose."

"I was so mortified tonight I can't even tell you."

"Well I'm so sorry that you were uncomfortable, but it's not right to judge a whole culture like that. It's pure racism!"

"Tara, they didn't mean it like that, they are just upholding principles. Can't you see that? Sometimes you just have to toe the line. Sometimes you just have to do the right thing?" says Aunt Rosa, her voice loses strength and hostility ebbs away.

I'm puzzled. Why does it feel like she is talking about something else?

"I have principles. I also have a right not to have others force their opinions on me or try to take my power away.

It's a big world out there and I don't believe any one group of people can say they are always right."

She stops and turns to me, and it's as though a curtain has fallen away, and she really does understand.

"I know you have principles...and...I'm proud of you," she quickly turns her face away, but I've already seen her tears forming. I reach out from behind and hug her around her shoulders to reassure her that we are OK. She stands still, barely accepting my embrace. She puts her hands over mine. Something is wrong and I'm pretty sure it isn't about tonight's little foray.

16

When I awaken my first thought is of Shasta. I try to shake the foreboding feeling that I need to change course or this could lead to the sickening agony of heartbreak when I return to New York.

My second thought is that this is the first day I haven't woken up with a screeching headache. However that in no way means I'm ready to return to work; it's so liberating to not have to keep to a schedule. The prospect of adhering to a diary full of appointments and deadlines is grim. I'm dreading returning to the executive world of conflict, regulation and directive, but on the flip–side I'll be happy that I can keep paying the rent and the bills.

In contrast my life here has been a gentle routine. Concerns about work dominate my peripheral thoughts. I turn on the laptop to check my emails. I expect the worst when I see the email from Patricia Napier.

The email consists of two short paragraphs: polite and to the point, respectfully enquiring into my well–being and asking when I'm returning to work. There was no mention of my meeting with Tray. Either she had forgotten or it didn't matter all that much.

I draft a carefully worded response without committing to a time–frame. I offer to carry out work from home in the meantime, even though I know she won't take me up on it.

I'm just about to close the laptop when another email appears in my inbox. This one is from Simon. I'd forgotten to call him yesterday, with all the excitement. It's one sentence long.

Seems you've forgotten me so I'm coming to stalk you.

I can imagine the mock petulance. I click on the attachment which shows his flight arrival details; he's already booked it and I haven't even cleared it with Aunt Rosa. I pull on some clothes and go downstairs straight away to ask her. She loves having visitors and having someone to fuss over, but it would be a bad show if I didn't ask first.

"Aunt Rosa? Hudson? Where is everyone?" I call out but there's only silence. Downstairs is deserted, so I look out of the window and see Aunt Rosa in the front garden. I walk out on to the front porch and stop dead. My heart constricts as I watch Aunt Rosa slump to her knees on the grass, bending in half at her abdomen. She tries to stifle an agonised cry. Hudson is anxiously at her side.

"Oh dear God!" I hear myself shout while I run to her.

I'm vaguely aware that a car is pulling up. A second voice calls out and someone else appears but I'm not paying attention to them.

"What is it?" I toss away the trowel lying beside her, taking hold of her shoulders I pull her towards me. I do a double take; confused, because on the other side is Delphine, my sister–in–law, whose gaunt face is tear stained.

What the hell is going on?

Aunt Rosa's eyes close.

She silently fights the pain.

"What's wrong? Shall I call an ambulance?"

"No. I'm OK," says Rosa, forcing herself to sit upright and open her eyes.

"You're not! What can I do?"

"It'll pass. It's probably just my IBS. I just need to sit down for a while," says Aunt Rosa bravely, but she is ashen and her sky blue eyes have lost their focus.

We get her onto her feet and help her indoors. I'm shocked at her sudden vulnerability. I've never seen her so fragile; she's always so active and robust. I've never even known her to be ill, not that she would let anyone know if she was. I had seen her taking pain–killers recently but she said it was for her arthritis.

Aunt Rosa sits down at the kitchen table and drinks a glass of water. She seems to recover quickly and makes light of the episode. That leaves me to deal with part two of the drama: the appearance of Delphine in distress. I sense trouble with this one.

I leave Aunt Rosa sitting at the kitchen table and take Delphine to the side, so that we can talk privately. She's holding back tears. I quietly ask her what's wrong and her chin crumples. Delphine begins to sob. I don't want anything to upset my aunt, so we move further out of earshot.

"Anthony has lost it this time," says Delphine, and she begins to shake uncontrollably.

"Did he do this?" I ask, pointing at the residue of dried blood on her swollen lip. Delphine looks horrified and quickly tries to pull her sleeves down, which only draws my attention to the finger–shaped black and purple bruises on her forearms.

"He doesn't know what he's doing Tara. He never does when he's drunk. It's getting out of control. I can take his bullying, but now he's started on the kids."

"What's he done?" I ask, although I'm not sure I want to know.

"Last night, I finally got Brad to do some homework, but then Anthony came home, all riled up over something. He started goading Brad: criticizing his work, calling him a sissy and asking if he thought he was smart or something. Brad just kept quiet and took it, but that's when Anthony started getting physical with him. I tried to stop him... but I made it worse. Anthony turned on me. Brad started screaming and hitting Anthony, trying to defend me," Delphine breaks down into wracking great sobs.

"No child should have to endure that," I reply, but I was the last person Anthony would listen to.

"I'm afraid to look him in the eye in case it antagonises him. He's so angry at everyone and everything. Nothing is ever his fault. I love him Tara, but I can't live like this!" wails Delphine.

"Protect yourself and the kids. If he isn't going to leave, then you do it. Even if you manage to work things out, you need to be somewhere safe where you can do that."

"But the kids need their dad."

"Is this the example you want him to set for them?"

"It's better than having no father at all."

"Is it?"

"I couldn't bring them up on my own. I've never even lived on my own. I need Anthony to help me."

"How does he help you, Delphine? Seriously, I know he's my brother, but what is he doing for you guys that you couldn't do yourself? Is there more misery living with him than there would be without him? You don't have to accept it – you definitely don't deserve it."

"Don't I? I'm failing at my marriage. If I can change..."

I shake my head. "No. It doesn't have to be like this. Right now you're already a single parent with four kids, one of which is your husband – you're already coping with that."

"It's not abuse. He just lost his temper. It's the drink, not him," defends Delphine.

"It's still him, Delphine," I soften my words.

"I'm not like you, Tara. I'm not strong," she snaps.

"Delphine, I'm going to call Barnaby Whitelaw and ask him to stop by your place to have a word with Anthony," says Aunt Rosa, who is standing a few yards away with a determined look on her face. I don't know how much of the conversation she has heard but it's clearly too much.

"No! Don't do that!" Delphine sounds panic stricken.

"He needs another man to have a word with him." Rosa is emphatic.

"I'll just act like nothing has happened and smooth things over. That's the best way. Please don't tell him I told you, or that I was even here," begs Delphine.

"That boy has such a chip on his shoulder. I just don't know where he gets it from. He's had every privilege, and been grateful for none of it. I don't approve of what he's doing, but you are a family and you should be together. You two can work this out," says Aunt Rosa. I roll my eyes. How different opinions can be within one generation. Before Delphine leaves I hug her and remind her she has our support regardless.

Now that Delphine's drama has been defused, I take Aunt Rosa to the doctors for a check–up, just to be on the safe side. Despite her resistance she concedes and I bundle her into the pickup. I stay in during the consultation to make sure she does actually explain fully what happened, and doesn't get fobbed off.

When the doctor questions her, it transpires Aunt Rosa has had pain and bloating for months – if not longer. An appointment for an ultrasound scan is arranged with the reassurance that it was likely just an intestinal spasm.

"I told you so. It would take a bullet to bring me down," chirps Rosa and she is back on good form. There don't appear to be any chinks in her armor.

Despite this morning's commotion Shasta has been on my mind constantly and nagging doubts are pressing. I wonder if he's having second thoughts about me now he has had a bit of time to cool off. Why am I even concerned? I know I should resist him now or regret it later – but that would suggest I had some control over myself. The truth is even the memory of his scent and touch makes me crazy.

On the drive home I remember to ask Aunt Rosa about Simon coming to stay, and she merely asks why Giselle isn't coming too. Does she think Simon and Giselle are a couple? I dismiss the notion – no–one could mistake my gay best friend for a straight guy!

As we arrive home the phone rings. I have a mini–death when Shasta's name appears on the screen. The jolt of adrenaline goes through my legs and I answer it before my nerves really kick in. Even though we were close the previous day, speaking on the telephone can be more awkward. You can't read body language or just enjoy the silence. A smile or a look says more than mere words. Without formalities, he jumps straight in.

"You've been on my mind."

"You've been on mine too," and with that I'm grinning like a half–wit. *Willpower, where did you go?* Shasta offers to cook dinner for me at his place and suggests he picks me up this evening. I can hardly contain myself. After the previous night's dispute over the company I keep, it may not be wise for the next door neighbors to see Shasta here. Not that I care – but perhaps for Aunt Rosa's sake it's better to let the dust settle? No. I have to be honest. I agree for Shasta to collect me.

I'm torn between not wanting to upset Aunt Rosa, who may still be feeling physically delicate, despite the façade, and wanting to be open about my relationship with Shasta. I decide to give her the heads up, so she has a few hours to get used to the idea. I mention it casually in passing and don't make a big deal about it.

For someone whose home is open to the world, his wife and their pets, Aunt Rosa eyes me very suspiciously. I assure her Shasta is a decent guy and that she'll like him; I've my fingers crossed that both assertions prove to be true.

I wish she would at least give Shasta a chance before she passes judgement but I'm concerned that her mind is already made up. She's anxious of what people think of her association, and the potential judgements of her. I don't understand how this loving, kind and generous woman can be so fastidious in her opinion of what is right.

"I don't want to cause any trouble round here," were Rosa's final words on the matter.

The crucial moment will be when Aunt Rosa actually sees Shasta: long hair, aloof and proud. If he turned up with a neat short haircut, in a shirt and trousers she would approve. It irks me, but I figure I won't be able to change anything. I will just have to be open and honest if this relationship is going anywhere other than off a cliff; which is likely what some people round here would predict.

17

Carelessly sexy or girl next door? Deciding what to wear is a chore. I try a casual printed dress, hoping for an effortless sexy look – Little Bo Peep without the sheep looks back at me in the mirror. I change into a pair of black jeans, long boots and v–neck covered by a brown leather jacket. I don't want to look like I've tried too hard. I really want to wear the amulet, and as Aunt Rosa surely won't see it under the collar of my jacket I put it on.

I pace my room talking to Hudson, who is lying stretched out on my bed, raising alternate eyebrows as he watches me getting dressed. I intend to stay here until Shasta turns up because I can just nip downstairs and disappear quickly when I see the car. But due to fiddling about with my make–up, I don't see his car arrive.

The doorbell rings, my heart shifts into full throttle and my breathing falters. I take a long slow breath to compensate, and quickly make for the door, but Hudson gets in front of me, nearly tripping me up in his excitement to greet the visitor. I get to the foot of the stairs just after Aunt Rosa has opened the door. *Damn, I don't want an uncomfortable scene.*

I hold back a little and watch. Shasta introduces himself and extends his hand as Hudson barrels through to deliver his own welcome. Aunt Rosa shakes Shasta's hand and stands back, inviting him in. I know she doesn't want him on the doorstep any longer than he has to be; in case the Walshs spot him.

"I'm ready," I call and act like I've just breezed into the room, hoping to quickly breeze out again.

"I've seen you before, haven't I?" asks Aunt Rosa,

scrutinizing Shasta intently and placing her finger to her lips while she tries to remember where she knows him from.

"You've probably seen me around. I pop up everywhere."

"Oh, that's it. The stables at garden centre. That's where I've seen you," Aunt Rosa instantly seems more relaxed.

I guess his association with her friend Margy gives him credibility, and they chat briefly about people they have in common. I'm impressed with how it's going so far, still, better quit while I'm ahead; I wait for a pause.

"Shall we go?" I ask, checking that the collar of my jacket is still in place.

As soon as the front door closes behind us, Shasta leans in for a chaste kiss. I'm sure there is someone at the side window of the Walshs' house, but I don't look in. As we drive off I can see Errol outside, apparently watering the plants, but he's missing them completely and watering the path instead while he watches us. He gives a nasty smirk when I wave over.

Shasta's place is out of the way and I would never have found it myself. He's building a new house on the lake, beside the small rustic fishing lodge which once belonged to his grandfather and which has now been entrusted to him.

"The cabin is pretty basic," he warns, "but its home until the house is finished."

"It doesn't matter to me." It really doesn't, for I'm already lost in romantic notions of a lakeside hideaway. It's dusk and the dimming light is playing tricks with the shadows in the trees. We turn off the main highway to a quiet unmade road which is densely surrounded by trees. Shasta narrows his eyes and gives me a grin; oblivious to how sexy it is.

"Scared?"

"Should I be? Keep your eyes on the road," I laugh. Instead he teases me by taking both his hands off the steering wheel.

When we arrive and get out of the car I can't see much of anything while my eyes adjust to the darkness. I faintly make out the lodge on one side and the shape of a house on the other. I feel Shasta reach for my hand and a deep warm shiver runs through me. Thinking he's leading me to the cabin I step forward, and bump into him. He swiftly and gently pushes me back against the car with an urgent kiss. Warm waves of desire convulse through me as the surging heat from our bodies radiates into the night.

I want to make the moment last and escape time so that I can stay here with him like this. He takes my hand and this time leads me through the darkness. In the cloudless sky a bright crescent moon hangs in the deep indigo backdrop amid the lucid, diamond brilliance of the world above us.

A welcoming mellow light shines from the small window panes of the lodge he calls home, but Shasta leads me beyond, until I see the moonlight on the water and we stand at the edge of the lake. I'm mesmerized by the magical atmosphere and we just stand there silently; the frisson of expectation between us is palpable. Shasta leads the way to the cosy wooden lodge.

It is a museum of old fishing rods and tackle from generations back, and it's decorated with an array of hand-painted native artwork. The focal point of the room is a stone fireplace which is stacked with logs; beside it are two chairs and a sofa. Two bookcases are stuffed to capacity next to a cluttered table which is strewn with maps, plans and pictures. It feels lived-in: cosy and safe.

From the kitchen, a tantalising aroma reminds me that I haven't eaten; though my appetite has vanished. Excitement churns in its place. Shasta grapples with dishes while removing dinner from the oven. I stroke the long wavy golden hair of his friendly dog who has come to greet me.

"That's Scout," he calls over, and the dog trots over to him on hearing her name. I stroll around, looking at the books in the case, then hover over the pile of paper and drawings on his desk.

"Are these your house plans?" I ask, admitting my nosiness.

"Yes."

"Mind if I look?"

"Go ahead."

I pick up the blueprint, noticing the lovely triangular peaked roof above the glass-walled lounge, the upstairs balcony and vaulted ceilings.

"Wow, that's a beautiful house. Lots of wood."

"And it's nearly all from dead standing trees," he replies, as he clears the small round table beside the window, and lights a single white candle in the hurricane lamp and places it in the middle. He dishes up two plates of risotto and sits down opposite. I want him so much I wonder if it's even healthy.

"It's delicious," I tell him; because it is.

Then I toy with the risotto.

"Not hungry?" asks Shasta.

I place my hand over my heart and look him in the eye.

"I can't eat right now."

He smiles back.

"Me neither. It'll keep for later."

"Tell me about the maps on your desk," I ask just as we incline instinctively towards each other, our faces close together.

"You want to talk about that now?" he asks.

I've spoiled the moment. I'd like to know more, but all I can think about is him seducing me.

"You don't?"

"It's going to sound intense and lull you to sleep. They're maps I use for the geopathic balancing. The earth channels are connected to the portals. The portals dilated to let more light codes in, so anything which helps clear debris, and open the channels benefits the portals too. The vortexes which empty stagnant energy can get blocked. I help shift that."

"Sounds like putting out the trash..." I start backtracking, because that didn't sound very tactful. "But on a bigger scale...and a lot more exciting."

"You put it so well."

"Foot in mouth disease has been a problem of mine."

"Anyway, I want to know more about you. Let's go and sit by the lake."

Shasta grabs a blue wool blanket. He wraps it around me and we sit together on a wooden bench adjacent to the jetty at the water's edge. It's chilly, but I've an internal furnace which is raging. We both seem more relaxed out here, and it's as though we have all the time in the world as we get to know each other better.

The conversation eventually gets around to our romantic histories and I tell him about my recent tragic attempts to find a partner through online dating. In contrast Shasta has been contentedly single for a while; he had a couple of long term girlfriends and no shortage of partners when he was younger. His arm rests around my shoulder and I snuggle further into him, wanting to delve into his body and loose myself in him.

I've no idea what time it is, or how long we've been sitting talking under the stars beside the moonlit lake. My arm is around Shasta's waist and I can feel the warmth of his taut muscles. I'm aware of his every breath on my ear and neck. He places a lingering kiss on my neck and I drop my head to the side and close my eyes, savoring the feeling.

He pulls my face around and with cool lips he kisses me hard, urgently sliding his tongue into my mouth. A deep jolt of excitement shoots up through me and a small groan escapes my lips. He stands up and pulls me to him, placing my arms around his neck. I soften in his arms and give in to the sensation as he presses me harder into his body I drop my hand to just under his backside and feel his muscles flexing. I grasp under his shirt to his warm, ripped chest; desperate for more. I will him to undress me while I let my tongue trace along his neck. His hand reaches inside my shirt and I gasp.

He stops, and I'm bewildered when he steps back from me. He reaches into his pocket and pulls out his phone, which is vibrating but silent. He glances at the screen and snatches the phone to his ear. He steps away from me. No–one calls at this time of night with good news – unless it's a booty call? I watch him pace back and forward. I can't hear what is being said but his tone is short and abrupt. I remember my blind date with Oliver in New York, and the fake distressed phone call from Giselle. He wouldn't... would he?

"Is everything OK?" I ask when he rings off.

"I'm sorry. I have to go. It's important."

"You're kidding?"

"No. I'll drop you home on the way."

He takes hold of my shoulders and moves his face to mine until our noses are touching, but he is distracted and distant. On the way where? I shiver with frustration. I'm irritated and confused. Was it a booty call? Is he letting me down because there is someone else? He takes my hand and marches to the jeep. He fires up the engine and guns the jeep down the uneven track road, staring intensely and unblinkingly ahead.

"What is going on?" I demand, wondering if I actually want to know the answer.

"An ongoing problem, nothing to do with you," he replies, his face inscrutable. He offers no further explanation. He breaks the speed limit, and the dashboard clock reads 2:30 a.m. when we arrive at Aunt Rosa's. I glance at him looking for a clue as to what is going on. He smiles, but his mouth remains tightly closed. His hand shoots behind my head and he kisses me hard, then pulls away.

"I'll call you later," he says, as I close the door of the jeep and nod back at him, with a final hopeful smile. He quickly drives off as I quietly approach the house.

A curtain moves in a bedroom next door and a white face peers out as I tip-toe inside, feeling disappointed and rejected. What could have been so important? If there is a perfectly reasonable explanation for his behaviour, I would really like to hear it.

18

"I must have slept like the dead last night; I didn't even hear you come home. What time did you get in?" Aunt Rosa asks.

"After midnight." I withhold just how long after midnight it was.

"So how did it go?"

"Good..." I hesitate because I'm not sure I want to share what I don't yet understand.

"He seems alright." Aunt Rosa flashes a smile.

"Alright?" I exaggerate my surprise because this is quite an acknowledgement.

"Anyway, how are you feeling?" I ask, noting her yellowy pallor.

"Never better," she bats away my words. "So, are you seeing Shasta again?" She is unable to contain the curiosity that is spewing out of her.

"Yes...probably."

"That reminds me, I'm helping with preparations for the Summer Fair. There's so much to do. Any chance you could lend a hand?" asks Aunt Rosa.

"Sure I'll help out."

I wonder if she's as invincible as she thinks.

Now that I've been roped into community life, I find myself carrying folding chairs from a small church outbuilding to the main hall on the recreation field. I want to get the jobs done as quickly as possible. My heart lurches when I spot a familiar black vehicle parked in the road, and I look around to see where the driver might be. With one chair tucked under each arm, I peer hopefully around the street, when someone jumps out and pulls me back behind the wall. It's Shasta.

I drop the chair which clatters to the ground and giggles echoes around the building. I'm unquestioningly glad to see him. A man's grey head pops out of the door to see what the noise is, just as I vanish from sight. Shasta has caught me off guard, and is holding me by the waist and peering down at me. Whatever was happening last night, his mood has infinitely improved now.

"I'm training a colt at the riding stables. What are you up to later?"

"Seeing you?" I suggest, hopefully.

"Good. I'll give you a call later. The sooner I go the sooner I'll be back," says Shasta, smiling over his shoulder as he quickly walks across the grass to the converted 4x4 which contains his equipment

"Ah! I wondered what that noise was," says Cain Shimlow, who has appeared noiselessly around the corner of the building.

"It's just me," I tell him without eye contact while I watch Shasta who looks back and grins broadly. Cain Shimlow's face contorts as he bares back his thin lips over stained teeth as though he might bite.

"What was he doing here?" Cain asks.

"He was here to see me."

"Well, if something goes missing we'll know where to look."

"You haven't got anything he would want!"

I stride off to find Aunt Rosa, leaving Cain muttering to himself. The persistent chattering of several women's voices can be heard coming from the kitchen adjoining the hall. Clammy and thirsty from exertion I roll up my sleeves and go into the kitchen for some water, thinking my aunt is probably in there. Eerily, the incessant chattering stops when I walk in. It's like a scene from a bad movie. I look around and smile. Rosa isn't there. My eyes fall on Pandora Walsh standing in the middle of the women with a distasteful look on her face.

"Don't stop on my account," I say turning on the tap.

"You look tired Tara. Not much sleep last night? I didn't get much either, because you woke the neighborhood at 3 a.m.!" declares Pandora, pouting huffily with her hands on her hips.

"You know what they say: too much bed and not enough sleep." I smile provocatively at the group.

Someone quietly sniggers and Pandora glares fiercely at her.

"Are you staying in town much longer? We can't tolerate much more of your inconsiderate behaviour. And your poor aunt...you don't think of her. That bad company you're keeping is rubbing off on you. We'll pray for you!" she raises her voice venomously.

"Don't bother you condescending old bitch. You're hell's own gatekeeper!"

"Tara!" Aunt Rosa enters.

I roll my eyes at her and walk out, leaving the storm of disapproval raging behind. Rosa comes after me as I stalk out into the fine drizzling rain.

"You can't speak to people like that," she chides.

"She had no right to speak to me like that! Why are you taking her side?"

"Did you really come in at 3 a.m.?"

"I am an adult. It's no–one's business."

"It reflects on me."

"Why do you care so much? Why do you place more value on what people think than you do on happiness?"

"There have to be guidelines. It's the way it has always been."

"But why does it have to be?"

"Standards, Tara. We have to have standards."

"You're already the kindest person I know, so why do you have to prove your worth to everyone? You don't have to be anyone's conscience. Why don't you do something for yourself for once?"

She goes silent, her eyes widen and seems flummoxed.

"Why do you question everything? I don't understand it. I wasn't brought up like that. I can't just change who I am."

"I'm sorry. That was unfair of me." My irritation dissolves the instant I see her vulnerability.

"Why do you want so much, Tara? Why are you always battling something?"

"Am I?" I certainly hadn't considered that one.

"You're always looking to change things."

"I guess I am. A lot of things need to change. I don't like people trying to control me, or you! What do you want? Really and truly, if you could have anything what would it be?"

Aunt Rosa looks dumbfounded by the question and gazes at me blankly.

"I don't know. I already have everything I want."

"Have you?" I smile. It's me that needs to learn something from her.

"That's the difference with your generation. You want everything. You want to change things, and do it better than we ever did. Foundations and traditions hold us together. They're there for a reason."

"But is judging and criticizing part of that foundation?"

"You have such a fire in your belly. Where did all that spirit come from?" she asks disarmingly, with thinly veiled respect. We smile at each other.

"Come on, lunch is on me," I suggest, wanting to make amends.

"But we have plenty of food at home."

"And it'll still be there later. Come on."

I'm staggered the argument is over so quickly. My relationship with her feels like it's matured: with a renewed respect. I'm no longer the subservient child. I regret my harsh words to Pandora, only because I wish I could have made a cool, articulate rebuke instead of lashing like that.

Some might say I'm lovesick, because after missing dinner last night I couldn't stomach breakfast this morning either, but now I'm absolutely ravenous. Rosa is on friendly terms with Maria, the owner of the café, and she introduces me. Looking at the mammoth portions of lasagne it seems that we've been given preferential treatment.

We sit at a table by the window and can see the world come and go. Barnaby and another officer, who Aunt Rose calls Patrick, come in for a take-out lunch but join us instead. Patrick and Barnaby bounce off each other and are good, easy company to listen to. I feel very comfortable around them. Perhaps it's because Barnaby is a Sheriff. It's interesting how much more macho and authoritarian he is around another man. The three friends, share casual warmth and banter. I catch Patrick quietly watching Rosa when she isn't looking and I wonder what he's thinking.

Aunt Rosa is pretty and well liked, and I don't understand why she hasn't had a relationship since her husband Charlie committed suicide all those years ago. It'd been a shock; there had been no suggestion anything was troubling him. She never talked about it. Either it was too painful, or maybe she had simply moved on. Apart from an unobtrusive wedding photo in the lounge there is no trace of Charlie and Rosa's lives together.

I push the rest of my lunch to the side, then sit back and enjoy listening to Barnaby and Patrick regaling us with tales of their exploits. Patrick's laugh is so infectious.

I glance up and see Shasta's jeep enter Main Street. It quickly takes a left into a quiet adjoining street before parking up. My hands shake from the sudden burst of adrenaline at the sight of the lustrous, blonde hair of the passenger sitting next to him. My view is obscured by the reflections on the windscreen, but there is a woman with him, and it looks like he doesn't want to be seen. I can't breathe in case my heart cracks open and smashes on the floor – maybe I was premature in thinking it, we never said we were exclusive.

"I've got to go," I abruptly stand up to leave.

"Where are you going? Don't you want a ride home?" asks Aunt Rosa.

"I'll make my own way. I have to see Shasta."

I step unsteadily out onto the street. He has disappeared from view. The fine drizzling rain is misting my eyes and I blink away the moisture filling my eyelashes.

I have to confront him. I can't let it go. If the relationship is doomed I would rather know now. By the time I reach the end of the street my heart is hammering so hard that's all I can hear. I have no idea what I'm going to say. Now I can see his car parked up, and he is still inside – with her. As I approach the car he still hasn't seen me. I can't stand it – I'm about to see them together. He glances in the mirror. His head spins round and he jumps out of the jeep.

My mouth quivers and tightens as I dare myself to look in the window.

"I can't believe you..." my voice cuts off when the blonde passenger suddenly jumps to the driver's side with her tongue hanging out in delight.

Shasta's shaggy gold dog greets me affectionately. I'm ashamed and embarrassed.

"I'm sorry. I feel like a total idiot."

"What did you think?" his voice inflects laughter when he realises my misunderstanding. He stands close, clearly amused at my expense. I don't know what to say.

"Did you think Scout was a woman?" he acknowledges his dog and puts his arm around me. "You were jealous?" he is openly enjoying my shame. I put my arms around his neck and hug him passionately.

"Well after last night...I didn't know what to think!"

"Last night?" he looks puzzled. "There was another problem on the Reservation; someone was prowling around my parent's house. That's where I went."

"You didn't say much...so I thought the worst."

He slips his arms around my waist and I reach up as his lips press down on my mouth. Warm tingling pulses through me in waves; I'm completely overwhelmed.

"Wasn't this where we left off?" he asks.

I smile at him, nose to nose once more. He presses me against the car door and we kiss fervently but break off when a passerby makes a clucking noise at us.

"I want you," he whispers into my ear, before kissing it; provocatively caressing it with his tongue. My insides tighten and tingle in response. I tilt my chin towards him as a sigh escapes my lips.

"Shall we go to mine?" he runs his thumb along my chin and lifts his head away, gazing down at me but keeping his body connected to mine. With a quickening heart rate I nod subtly and he opens the door for me.

As we drive along I'm unable to stop gazing at him from the corner of my eye: the taut skin over the angular jaw and the sensuous mouth – he catches me looking and makes me giggle like a teenager and I flush even more. The thrilling images of what might happen sear through my imagination, quickening my breath. My neck flushes hot as my eyes dart to him. He is already tuned in. He responds with a sideways look, his eyes moving seductively from my mouth to my neck and presses his hand high on my thigh.

Eventually we arrive at the secluded lodge, though the sexual tension of the journey made it seem endless. Nothing is said but we both know what we want.

It's raining harder now. Shasta runs round, opens my door and grabs my hand. Together we run to get out of the rain. He suddenly stops on the porch before entering. He looks at me earnestly and I see his chest rise as he takes a deep breath. Something is wrong.

"What is it?"

"I've got something to tell you."

His eyes are so intense and serious. *Oh, God. What is it?* I'm thinking the worst.

"What?"

"I love you."

He catches my chin when it drops and he grins at me. I don't know how to respond. He answers my thoughts.

"You don't need to say anything. I just want you to know that." Our faces touch and my hand strokes his cheek as his finger brushes over my lips.

I've no reason to question his integrity. He doesn't need to tell me he loves me to lure me into bed – I want him regardless, and I've loved him since I set eyes on him. He picks me up in his strong bronze arms, kissing me constantly. I hold his face as he carries me towards the bedroom, pulling off my wet clothes. When I'm down to my t-shirt and underwear he places me on the edge of the bed. The hot tingle of anticipation is searing through me, the cold wet clothes gives me goose bumps. I pull at his damp shirt and jeans; he removes them as he takes control.

Passionately we grasp each other; hard and face to face. My breasts respond to his delicate touch. He swiftly smoothes his hand down my stomach stopping at the thin silky barrier of my panties. I arch my hips towards his hand.

"I can't get enough of you," he murmurs with stilted breath, right before he deftly pulls off the rest of my clothes and slides his mouth over my breast, circling until finally touching my nipple with his tongue. A spasm goes through me and I groan as he bites gently. My head rolls backwards.

"I want all of you." He breathes heavily, nuzzling my neck then looks intensely into my eyes making sure I understand. The desire is as strong as the urge to breathe – I can't wait any longer. He reads me entirely and draws himself towards me; lifting my hair off my shoulder he places his hand behind my head and brings his face to mine. With our noses touching the beating space between us is tantalizing as we lock eyes – conveying more love in those priceless moments than may ever be felt in several lifetimes.

I try to pull myself up but he holds me there; building up to an unbreakable bond that is about to be created. Our lips touch and our mouths open with the hunger to devour each other. I can already feel his erection pressing against my thigh. The passion I feel for this man, in this moment, is something so intoxicating it makes me want him more than I have ever wanted anything.

The wind rises furiously outside, thrashing against the wooden lodge. He thrusts gently at first then dives deep into me. He groans, and pulls my legs tightly around him. Possessing him, I greedily clasp him close to me. I lose myself in the waves of sensation ebbing and flowing through me. He winds a hand into my hair and tugs my mouth up to his. The wind rises outside. It whips into a fury, thrashing the wooden lodge, relentlessly matching our ferocity.

A flood of sensations and a feeling of completeness is overwhelming. I let go and begin to convulse and shudder. We're still entwined and watching each other's eyes. His breathing comes in short rasps as he reaches a tumultuous peak.

Lying here, side by side and face to face, I've never felt closer to anyone. The wind has diminished to a gentle rippling breeze. We gaze at each other, transfixed like animals.

The sheet falls from Shasta when he rises from the bed, and I admire every inch of him: the smooth chest, long lithe muscular legs and the round firm curve of his buttocks. Every inch of him is beautiful and he's uninhibited by his nakedness.

He lights the fire in the lounge and lays the damp clothes out to dry. Wearing his t–shirt I stand in front of the roaring fire, quietly sated in the afterglow. I stand as close to the flames as I dare – mesmerized and distant in my tranquil world.

"What are you thinking?" asks Shasta, drawing me close to him as we sink together onto the sofa, pulling me tightly to his chest. I drape my legs across him.

"Nothing. I'm thinking of nothing – I like it," I reply and kiss the line of his jaw, enjoying the peace of my idle mind, content to be cradled in his arms. I feel like I've come home.

19

Shasta and I spend as much time together as we can over the next couple of days. A highpoint was watching him work when he went to break in a young colt on a nearby ranch. He did it with such strength and sensitivity I felt like an intruder. Aunt Rosa is letting me get on with it in my own way. I'm dividing my time between his place and hers.

Today's plan is to go hiking when Shasta finishes work. He wants to show me some isolated known beauty spots. I'm wondering, well hoping, that it's code for al fresco sex.

"I've made sandwiches for you to take," Aunt Rosa calls from the front porch. I open the well wrapped lunch she has prepared and left on the kitchen table. It's a lot more than just sandwiches. I tuck the lunch into the small rucksack I'm taking on the hike.

Hearing voices outside I look out of the window and there is Shasta and Aunt Rosa chatting on the porch. I breathe out slowly between my teeth, taking in his statuesque profile: the jet black hair and wide sensual mouth – my heart hammers with excitement. He's early – that's no bad thing. It's a great relief that Shasta and my aunt seem to be getting along so well. All credit to her, she really has made an effort with him.

Shasta drives well out of town to a quiet hillside not far from the Reservation. He parks up the jeep in a lay-by and we set off on foot. We could easily have taken the jeep along the track Shasta is following. Two parallel ruts in the grass are visible so it would be accessible for the 4x4 – but that would spoil the fun of hiking according to Shasta. What I call a hike is merely a short walk to Shasta. Scout runs up ahead.

"So where are we going?"

"It's a mystery tour," he grins and takes my hand, dwarfing it in his broad palm.

"Don't keep me in the dark. Where are we going?"

"Nagual Creek. It's a power node."

"Somewhere you've done healing?"

"No, I want to show you the waterfall upriver."

On the way we talk about the earthwork, which this time last year would have gone right over my head. He explains how light codes travel through portals of focused energy and how it interchanges with the universe – they are gateways for energy to come in and balance the earth's energy. "Even dormant portals are activating now too. Am I boring you?" he asks.

"Not at all." He could be reciting the alphabet backwards and I'd be happy to listen. I watch enchanted by how his lips move over his perfect white teeth when he speaks.

"The more high vibration light that gets in the better the transformation and the more we evolve," says Shasta. "When that happens darker energies transform."

"Jeez. No offence, but you sound like Giselle. I can't wait for you to meet her by the way. She's always talking about the light versus the dark. She's stopped watching the news because she says the media propagates fear."

I remember Tray's warning about a controlling but hidden world order and the hairs on my arms stand on end as an epic chill passes by.

"She's got a point. Eventually there'll be more peace and freedom but there's a force trying to stop it. Everyone has a light quota. The higher it is, the better you feel and it makes it easier to see through the bullshit we've been fed as truth."

"So, if the portals are all up and running, what's going to happen?"

"Secrets will come out. There'll be a chance to live differently with higher consciousness."

"I guess a lot of people have a lot to lose," I mutter, breathing heavily. Shasta puts his hand on my back and gently pushes me ahead of him. We've been walking uphill for some time and stop by the river for a long drink of water. A couple of hikers are sitting on the riverbank drinking coffee from flasks. Scout goes to the water's edge and starts worrying stones as she tries to pick them up with her teeth. Shasta picks up the stone for her and throws it in the shallow water. Scout dives in to retrieve it, ducking her head underwater, and comes up snorting water out of her nostrils.

"She'll never get that out," I tell Shasta.

"That's what you think," he smiles that wide grin with the full lips. *Devastatingly sexy.*

Scout keeps ducking, snorting and barking then suddenly she pulls her head out of the water with a stone in her mouth. She looks like she's smiling because her lips are drawn back.

"I'm starving."

"Come on we're nearly there."

When we arrive at the waterfall the long walk becomes worthwhile. It's astonishingly breathtaking. The emerald green canopy of ferns either side of the dazzling cascade of water looks vibrant and lit from within. The white and silver curtain of water spilling over the ridge churns gently, before flowing into the crystal clear river. The soothing splashing of the waterfall is inviting but I'll bet it's absolutely freezing. The air smells so fresh: dewy and clear. I breathe deeply and sit down on a boulder beside the pool of water. A fine rainbow spray is drifting overhead as we tuck into the picnic Rosa prepared.

"How did you get so wise?"

"Am I?" he throws back and laughs. His long black hair catches around his mouth, like an arrow pointing to his tantalizing lips.

"Back in NY there are masses of groups and courses for self–development. Did you ever get involved in that?" I ask, devouring a home–grown tomato from the food pack.

"No. But I read a lot and avoid dogma; even in New Age culture there's some. I sometimes think it's just one step away from religion. We don't need another guru."

"How did you learn so much?" I ask.

"My grandfather was my mentor. He taught me to trust my instincts. I made so many mistakes and he would just say something cryptic, then sit back and watch while I got on with it. But it was a good way to learn," he says, shoving a mammoth cheese sandwich in his mouth.

"So are the portals all the same?"

Shasta shakes his head. "No, some are larger than others. There are sub portals too, which are smaller energy vortexes."

He reaches for a chunk of banana bread from the picnic.

"Jeez, your aunt can cook!"

"Oh my God. This is so good," I mumble through the banana bread. "So, how does that tie in with your culture?"

"My culture believes in respecting our next of kin, plants, trees, animals, and the earth; because we're the same, all crafted from energy. I believe old ancestral beliefs are coded into our DNA too. That's why patterns run in families and cultures that are locked in conflict. It'll shift with the higher energy," says Shasta, putting his hand on me and closing his eyes.

"Aren't you tired of talking?" Shasta lies back and looks up to the waterfall

"No, this is interesting."

"Do you fancy a swim?"

"No!" He can't be serious. That water must be icy. "Tell me more."

"I can tell you that what you believe today may not be what you believe tomorrow. Truth is evolutionary – as is value."

"Talk about shifting the goal posts."

"That's progress."

"One more question: I read about the Law of Attraction but I couldn't manifest myself a partner. Where was I was going wrong?"

"Oh, hello!" he points to himself with amusement.

"Didn't you like your own company?"

"Yes, but…"

"Did you find you talked too much?"

I laugh, and choke on the cake. "It's you that's doing all the talking."

"You keep asking questions. Anyway, there's your answer. You had a deeper belief that you wanted more time to yourself. It was counteracting the thoughts."

"I used to visualize or pray – even though I'm not into religion."

"Thinking is in the same thing. Prayers, thoughts, meditation, they're all ways to connect with the higher power – only the language is different. Imagine a hologram of your thoughts and beliefs, hovering outside the earth in an ethereal realm. It's an extension of you. It emits light, moves through levels of consciousness until it manifests," Shasta looks at me and raises an eyebrow, expecting another question.

I smile and shrug.

"Do you think that water's cold?" I ask.

"You said you weren't going to ask any more questions!" He springs up, grabs me by the wrists and drags me towards the waterfall pool. Laughing and shrieking, I plant my feet on the ground, trying to pull in the opposite direction, but it's pointless. He easily overpowers me. I end up shin deep in the freezing water. He looks down and pulls my face towards him; kissing me so deeply I forget about the cold.

Shasta pulls off his t–shirt and jeans: revealing a perfect swimmer's body – with long defined muscles skimmed with caramel skin. He dives in, swimming to the turbulent water plunging down from the edge of the ravine. I'm lucky he didn't dunk me completely. He calls me to join him, but he has no chance. Scout has plunged into the water and is swimming in circles. I perch myself on a waterside boulder, content to admire the view.

The sound of a vehicle breaks the stillness. Who would have brought a vehicle this far up along the track? Shasta's head turns towards the noise and he wades out of the water, dripping wet. A dark grey Land Rover comes into sight, pushing through the foliage as it makes its way downhill along the track, several metres from us.

Puzzled, I look at Shasta, as though he has the answer for the manmade intrusion all the way out here in the wilderness. When the Land Rover gets nearer I can make out four figures inside. The man in the passenger seat stares out, raising a finger to his narrow eye and points at me in a gesture that suggests he's watching – the next second the features of Cain Shimlow's face come into focus. I can't believe my eyes. He stares at Shasta with such utter contempt I can hardly comprehend it. All breath leaves my body as my insides twist angrily in response to the ominous signal.

It must be the lack of oxygen to my brain creating the illusion of Tray Buchanan, wearing darks shades, in the seat behind Cain Shimlow. The vehicle pushes on downhill; leaving us staring in its wake.

"What the hell was he doing here?"

"Developers? He wasn't sightseeing, that's for sure. The reservation territory was only thought to be valuable to us. Now apparently it's valuable to them," Shasta looks rattled.

"Do they want to buy it?"

"Rob it more like. They think the tribal council will take an uncompetitive offer. It's sacred land. It's not for sale whatever the price."

Shasta dries off using his t–shirt and we start to head back along the track. I don't tell him who I *think* I saw in the back of that Land Rover. I couldn't be sure it was Tray. Even if it was him, I don't want to be considered a link in a chain that leads to something underhand.

Shasta drops me back at Aunt Rosa's and heads off to meet with a friend on the reservation. As I close the front door behind me I can hear voices and laughter coming from the lounge.

"Tara, come in. Guess who I've got here? A friend of

yours has come to visit," says Aunt Rosa, her voice lilting with laughter.

The back of the visitor's armchair is facing me. I can't see who it is until he sticks his head around the wing of the chair.

What the hell is this?

"Surprise," grins Tray, flashing his fluorescent white teeth.

"Jesus Christ!"

"Not quite."

"What the hell are you doing here?"

"I was in the area."

"How did you find out where I lived?"

"That's not much of a welcome, is it?" he winks and smiles at Aunt Rosa, who is completely beguiled by his charisma. She chuckles with him.

"What do you want, Tray?"

"This girl is all charm," he nods to Aunt Rosa.

"I take it this is business? There's no other reason for you to be here."

"Relax. It's just your company I'm after."

It was him in the back of the car at Nagual Creek. There's no way this is just a social visit – I need to find out why he's here.

"Tara, I haven't prepared anything for dinner. Why don't you and Tray go out for a bite to eat?"

Here we go again. If it's not one person coercing me to dine with Tray it's another – and I can plainly see Aunt Rosa's motivation. Here is this nice, charming man with prospects and a silver tongue. In her eyes he's ideal husband material; once I've gotten over my dalliance with Shasta.

"OK, fine," I flick my hand in the air.

"Great. Rosa it was lovely to meet you," he takes her hand and kisses it gently. He's such a walking cliché, how can she not see it? I do get that he is pretty plausible though and there can't be many who are immune to his smooth patter, but he leaves me cold.

"Don't be a stranger now. Next time you're in town don't be wasting your money staying in that fancy hotel. There's plenty of room here."

My mouth falls open and I turn to look at her in disbelief that she's offering to have him under her roof. I don't know whether to laugh or cry. She has no clue that Tray is one of New York's elite and that 'fancy hotel' is a hostel compared to what he's used to.

I drive us to a local bar – it's time to keep it real and show him how we do it in the country. It's rustic and informal, with more spit than sawdust on the floor so some say it's a redneck joint; but it's a wholesome rustic place with decent food, country music and bags of atmosphere.

Tray doesn't bat an eyelid and chats away as usual. We settle in a cosy nook with a jug of beer and during some anecdote about something or other I interrupt him mid sentence.

"Why are you here Tray? Really, what's this all about?"

He deflates instantly and looks down at the table, pausing before he quietly looks at me with soft blue eyes. It's completely disconcerting and throws me, if only for a second.

"OK, please drop the wildcat routine for a second and hear what I have to say."

"I'm listening."

"There are two things."

"Which are?" I ask, gentler than before.

"I have feelings for you Tara," he pauses and waits for a response.

I raise my eyebrows, pretty sure these feelings don't originate from anywhere north of his belt buckle – if in fact they do exist.

"I saw you today with that guy. It brought it home to me. I didn't like it. Is there a chance you might feel something for me?" He looks sincere but I'm not convinced. I turn my head to the side, and subtly shake it – I'm not so callous that I'd shoot him down completely.

"I'm flattered Tray, but no. We work together," I dodge with the perfect excuse. He looks confused and stares at me as though he is expecting me to say something else.

"You are the only woman that's ever turned me down." He looks blank.

"That's why you're interested."

He smirks. "I've always liked a challenge."

"What's the other thing?"

He pauses and leans across the table, shuffling closer.

"I need your help," his voice is lower than before.

Now we're getting to the truth. I knew there was an ulterior motive. Tray just doesn't rack up in the middle of nowhere without a damn good reason.

"Did you follow me here?"

"No, it's just coincidence."

"Coincidence that we end up in the same town, thousands of miles from New York?"

"Incredible isn't it? I don't believe in fate. In my world it's just a chess game. One move justifies another – but I was suspicious."

"Not possible."

He smiles through tight lips, staring at me with such intensity and meaning.

"Your naivety is so refreshing." He looks away and finishes his beer.

"Why do you want my help?"

"It's not a legal thing, more of a sales role. Think of it as closing a deal."

"It's out of my remit Tray. Isn't that what you advised me to do? Stick to the remit and don't ask questions?"

"Usually. Not this time."

"Because?"

"My clients want to buy reservation land. However at the minute nothing gives and–"

"And you thought I could be manipulated to push the deal?" Anger explodes and I inadvertently thump my glass on the table. "You thought you could use my links with Shasta to put pressure on them?"

"Well we work for the same team. Sort of. I'm a client of Sheldon & Napier and I know for a fact your company needs our business," he offers up that little nugget as though it can be blown away in an instant.

"Are you threatening me? You'll quit with us if I don't help you?"

"I'm just suggesting you could use your influence: gain their trust, use your feminine wiles. Whatever it takes – it's a lucrative deal. More than you can imagine. I will obviously make it worth your while."

"Don't test my loyalties Tray. You'll be sorely disappointed."

"This has come out of the blue so don't make a decision. It's for your benefit too."

"What is your client after?"

He shrugs as though he doesn't know. It's a lie.

"That land has many valuable commodities perhaps. I know a lot of people would be happy to see the Indians moved on." It's a casual throwaway comment but it says so much.

"You disgust me, Tray."

"What did I say? I just said a lot of people may feel like that. Not me. That's all."

"This meeting is over."

"Oh, come on now don't be a bad sport. The night is young."

"Goodnight Tray."

"We can talk later. Sleep well," he smiles, unruffled, as though all is well.

I take my bag and stand to leave when he takes my hand as though to kiss it. He pauses and looks me in the eye.

"By the way, does your Indian lover know you're out with me?" he tilts his head and leers with innuendo.

I snatch my hand from him and don't look back as I head to the door; outraged at Tray's suggestions, and angry at myself for having walked into a precarious situation. I shove open the door and step out into the darkness of the dimly parking lot, my head reeling. My feet make a crunching sound on the gravel on the way to the car. The connotations of Tray's proposal are immense.

A fast shuffling sound in the gravel alerts me to something else, a split second before I see a dark shadow looming towards me. I turn in the direction of the footsteps and wheel around to face the shape. I don't get to see who it is before it's upon me. A hand grabs my throat and forces me up against the door of the car, knocking the air out of me and constricting my breath. The man's face bears down on me. The sharp, acid smell of halitosis is rank. Nausea rises.

"You need to decide whose side you are on. Get your boyfriend and his clan to sign the land over. You're already involved – whether you like it or not," the voice is disguised and thick with threat, but there is no mistaking the tone and tension of Cain Shimlow's terse threatening whisper. Reflected light from inside the bar glitters in his eyes – his beak nose is the only part of his face I can see.

I try to push him off but I can't move. I draw my knee up, aiming for his groin but the bony thigh pressing against me keeps me from reaching. He tightens his grip on my throat. I can't speak or scream.

"I'm sure you wouldn't want a loved one to meet with an accident. Would you? There have been a lot of them recently. Tragic really. You'll do it if you know what's good for you."

He releases his grip and I sink to the ground, gasping for breath as he vanishes back into the shadows. Fumbling for the car key I get to my feet, coughing off the feel of the tight fingers on my throat. I climb in the truck and lock the car door in case he returns.

I throw it into drive and race out of the parking lot. If anyone were in my way they wouldn't have been for much longer. I calm my breathing and get some perspective on what has just happened.

I feel alone and afraid, unable to tell anyone what has happened. Aunt Rosa would never believe that Cain Shimlow would threaten me. Shasta would uncover my link with Tray and I could lose him. Worst of all, if Tray is connected to some deviant powerful network, he knows where Aunt Rosa lives.

By the time I get home and put some distance between the incident and myself I feel safer. I'll keep it to myself, after all nothing actually happened. I determinedly try to shake off the threats as being cowardly attempts at control by spineless men flexing their influence. I can walk between the lines and tomorrow is a new day. But I've got a new uncomfortable awareness that life as I know it is changing. It's as though I've just woken in the night and found toys do come to life when we sleep.

20

As Giselle predicted, Simon has finally broken up with his boyfriend Neil. I can't wait to see him and give him some TLC, I just don't relish the interruption to my time with Shasta. I remember my tendency to lose myself in a relationship – I'm determined to keep hold of myself this time. Another co–dependent relationship is a no–no. It strikes me that marriage is the ultimate co–dependent relationship.

I've borrowed the truck and I'm driving to Seattle–Tacoma Airport to pick up Simon. The drive gives me time to recalibrate and reflect. I still haven't crossed the line with the old 'I love you' to Shasta. Although I have never felt these feelings for anyone I'm reluctant to commit; I've been wrong before. Shasta hasn't said it to me since that afternoon in the lodge. I'm going back to New York sometime soon and my reticence protects us both. Once you say 'I love you', it makes it true.

"Tara, honey!" shouts Simon from across the road, unaware he is attracting attention from all around him. He's struggling theatrically with his oversized matching luggage on the trolley. I adore Simon's directness and flamboyancy although on the flip side, sensitivity and diplomacy aren't his strong points.

We've been driving for about half an hour when he asks if we have much further to go. He looks nervously around as the landscape changes to countryside.

"Be afraid, city boy!"

It's great to see him, and the drive gives us a chance to catch up. Simon tells me all about his dramatic break–up with Neil, which isn't a surprise as their relationship has been a tempestuous on–off saga for years – but nevertheless he's hurting. Surprisingly I even enjoy hearing all about work and I'm relieved that nothing seems to have changed in my absence.

"She wants you back you know. I don't think her patience will hold out much longer," he says referring to Patricia.

"And just when things were looking up," I groan, but I intend milking my absence for a bit longer. Physically I'm fine, but I dread returning to the frenetic hustle and bustle of my New York life. My wounds have healed amazingly well and the constant anxiety I used to feel has now subsided.

"These roads are very quiet, aren't they?" says Simon rhetorically. "Do you have breakdown cover? You wouldn't want to get lost out here."

"Relax. Nothing is going to happen."

"You won't be saying that if we stop for gas and some serial killer stows away in the back and we're never seen again."

I look at him and roll my eyes.

"If you start asking 'are we there yet?' I'll make you walk."

We arrive in Big Spruce and Aunt Rosa gives Simon a warm welcome. She sits him down at the cedar table in the kitchen, where she plies him with hearty homemade food, and lots of it.

"You can eat more than that," she says and starts dishing out second helpings before he has finished the first. He takes a few more mouthfuls and leaves the rest, pushing the plate away.

"So what's the plan while I'm here?" asks Simon, ready to arrange his social schedule

"The plan is for you to get off the merry–go–round and

go with the flow. Life moves slower here. You might even get to like it."

"The annual town fair is on Saturday. I'm sure you'll love that. Everyone will be going," enthuses Aunt Rosa.

The disappointment flashes across Simon's face.

"I'll show you around later. We could take Hudson and do some walking. It'll blow the city fumes out of your hair. Maybe we can try the hot spring spa?"

"Hmmm. I'll look forward to that," he says sarcastically. "Is that all there is to do around here?"

I give him a look that suggests he pull his horns in before Aunt Rosa takes offence on behalf of the town.

"Why didn't you bring your girlfriend with you? Giselle is such a lovely girl," asks Aunt Rosa.

Simon chokes on his coffee, and puts his hand over his mouth, dribbling between his fingers.

"Giselle? My girlfriend? Oh no, not my type. For a start she's female!" says Simon. "Wow, you thought we were a couple. Hell no. She's my straight best friend."

I glance from Simon to Rosa. I can't tell from her expression if she thinks he's joking, or if she is shocked. Her raised eyebrows and weak smile give nothing away. It's time to wrap up this little get together.

"Come on. I'll show you around" I tug Simon by the arm.

During the next couple of days we visit the spa, take in the local sights, have dinner in a couple of lovely little restaurants and meet up with Shasta in the evenings. Not much seems to impress Simon. Apart from Shasta, that is. He's in awe of him and blatantly tells me he has the hots for him. He makes inappropriate references and tells

Shasta about his Village People fantasy. I love Simon and his wonderful lurid irreverence, which sticks out round here like an elephant in a pink tutu.

Saturday arrives and the town buzzes with activity as the Big Spruce Annual Fair gets underway. The recreation ground behind the Town Hall is now packed with stall holders, who unload trestle tables and lay them out with all sorts of goods, ready to be sold. Yesterday a couple of marquees were erected. They now house the beer tent and the hot food stalls, which are surrounded by tables and chairs indoors and picnic benches outdoors.

The fudge, cotton candy and popcorn stands waft a sweet, warm, smell in the air. Several cake stalls, hand–made jewelry stalls and an organic cosmetics counter intermingle with the children's games area. The maggot racing stall is already thronged with small children, picking maggots which have been coated in pink and blue flour. The fastest maggot wins by tumbling down the race track channelled into a board.

Aunt Rosa has her usual stall of potted plants, flower arrangements and assorted home–made craft pieces, with a few pots of jam adding to the variety. Simon and I help her set up, then as per her request, we leave her to arrange the stall as her various friends pitch in.

I get behind the table and start serving the customers. Simon has taken on the role of entertainer and is comically impersonating a market trader, flirting with everyone; which my aunt finds hilarious.

"You pretty lump of goodness, you." I overhear him flattering an elderly woman who is thrilled at his attention.

"Are you pregnant?" I hear Simon effeminately asking a

slim attractive woman in her thirties. She gasps at him in horror, and looks down at her abdomen.

"No. I'm not pregnant!" the woman replies.

"The day isn't over yet!" Simon nods and gives her a wink. The woman and her friend fold into giggles.

I haven't seen Pandora Walsh since the day of our confrontation, so I take a deep breath as she approaches the stall, with Roger following behind. If the opportunity arises I'll apologise to her.

"Hello," I say to her and smile with as much cheer as I can manage, but she blanks me; completely ignoring my existence.

"Didn't you hear her? She said hello!" says Simon, affecting an air of innocent impudence.

I cringe, not wanting a fuss.

"Oh. Hello Tara. How kind of you to help your aunt." Her contempt is thinly veiled.

"It's been a team effort. We've been up since dawn setting things up. Haven't we Tara?" Aunt Rosa surprises me with the speed of her defence. I ignore Pandora's attempt to antagonise me. She wants drama but she won't get it from me.

"Great day for it, don't you think?" I smile benignly at Pandora, who gives me a stiff nod in return. She pokes decisively at the plants and elbows another customer to get the pick of the bunch. I let Aunt Rosa serve her.

"Hi, Roger, can I interest you in some petunias?" I grin, looking over his mother's shoulder and give him a wink.

"Whatever the opposite of green fingers is, that's me," replies Roger.

Pandora sandblasts Rosa's ear about something or other.

"Isn't he gorgeous! He's just my type," Simon says in a

loud stage whisper. Roger flushes dark red and looks away through the crowd, pretending to have noticed something interesting.

"You are disgusting! That is my son you are disrespecting. Keep your filthy mouth to yourself," Pandora scolds Simon, then flounces off with her arms folded and her nose in the air.

Simon's mouth is hanging open as he turns to look at me and breaks into hysterical laughter. I put my hands to my eyes.

"Oh dear God. The world isn't big enough for you, Simon," I whisper, looking at the ground, thinking of poor Aunt Rosa's discomfort. I glance at her bemused face. She clearly didn't hear what Simon said and looks confused.

"What did I miss?" asks Aunt Rosa innocently, glancing at Simon and I.

"Nothing, just Pandora having a bad day," I reassure her. "I'll go and get us some lunch."

I push Simon's back. "Come on. Let's get you out of here before you incite a riot."

Simon and I wander between the stalls, looking at what is on offer for lunch. I didn't pay much attention to the charity and wildlife themed stalls – well, that was until I found Shasta standing in front of a small open tent with literature for the Native American Reservation & Wildlife Foundation. My stride automatically lengthens as I walk towards him, then I halt abruptly. He seems to be in an argument with someone.

A belligerent, suited businessman steps closer to Shasta in a face–off. It's obvious from the intense body language the stranger wants something which Shasta isn't giving. The businessman is trying to bully him, which is admirable because Shasta is a good few inches taller than the man, and much slimmer. I smile inwardly, proud of the way Shasta is holding his space: aloof, detached and dismissive of the stranger's rising angst. The stranger's fists keep clenching. It looks about to get physical. I'm riled, ready to interrupt. Who is this guy? From nowhere Cain Shimlow streaks past. The sight of him sends a jolt of adrenaline to my arms and legs as I remember the stench of his breath and the warning that came with it. Cain speaks into the businessman's ear. The businessman steps backwards, glowers and pulls out a business card which he flicks onto the table behind Shasta. He struts quickly away with Cain.

"What was that about?" I ask Shasta.

"Just someone who can't have what he wants" says Shasta nonchalantly.

"What does he want?"

"He's a representative of an otherwise faceless corporation that is after Indian land – and I guess an associate of Shimlow's. He says it's not worth anything they just want to bank it. They must have an ulterior motive. They've friends in high places. They've been trying for years but my people won't give up the land. It's a sacred site. At least the sequoia trees in the forest around the cabin are government protected."

It falls into place. The businessman must be connected to Tray. Jeez, what would Shasta say if he knew Tray is my client, and connected me with the acquisition of the Native land? If he finds out I'm a link he will think the worst. But I have no intention of acquiescing to Trays instructions, nor Shimlow's threat.

"They can't force you. Legally that land was granted to the Indians in the old treaties. Isn't it held in trust by the government on behalf of the Native Americans?"

"And we can always trust the government to keep their word, can't we?" he grimaces.

"Err, right."

"They've had teams of lawyers on it for years. Now we have intimidation, threats and vandalism. Nothing is ever done. Apparently there is not enough evidence – it's just our word against theirs; and we know whose word gets more credit don't we?"

It's on the tip of my tongue to spill the beans, to tell Shasta about my connection to Tray, but my job and my relationship with him are on the line. I can't tell him part of the story and withhold Shimlow's threat either – that would open a whole can of worms with Aunt Rosa once that came out.

There is a sudden commotion of raised voices behind me.

"Tara! Come quickly!" shouts Barnaby Whitelaw.

"What!"

"Your aunt has collapsed!"

Without thinking I turn and race off after Barnaby, but my train of thought derails trying to understand what is going on. Aunt Rosa was fine when we left her a few minutes ago. As I run I remember, with horror, Shimlow's threat to my loved ones. It's impossible. It was surely just an empty threat to provoke me? A cluster of people move to let me through and I get my first glimpse of Aunt Rosa lying still and helpless on the grass.

21

I don't believe or understand this nightmare. Aunt Rosa is lying in the ambulance, white and motionless. I wish it was me instead of her. I grasp her hands and don't utter a word, letting her focus her strength on fighting whatever this is. I pray silently.

"What's wrong with her?" I ask the paramedic.

"We're just giving her oxygen. We need to get her checked out at the hospital," says the paramedic.

I nod.

"The things you do for attention," I whisper to her, quickly wiping away one stray tear. Her eyes flicker open, widen and look around at the unfamiliar surroundings.

"Rosa, you're in an ambulance. You've been unconscious. We're just taking you to hospital," the paramedic reassures her.

He removes the oxygen mask and lets her breathe normally. She brings her hands up to her stomach, grimacing in pain. When we arrive at the hospital they take her away while I wait silently for what seems like forever. When they eventually let me see her she is sitting up in a hospital bed, with a drip attached to her arm. I hug her tightly, remembering that it wasn't so long ago our roles were reversed; now we've come full circle. She looks nervous, although I know she's trying hard to pretend everything is fine.

"Is everything OK?" I ask, knowing it isn't.

"The doctors and nurses are so nice, aren't they?"

"Never mind that," my voice fractures.

"They're just running some tests."

Aunt Rosa's chest heaves, but she is silent.

"Do they know what's wrong?"

"The doctor is coming around to see me."

"When will that be?"

"I don't know. The nurses look like they are rushed off their feet, so whenever they get a chance. There are some very sick people in here you know." She obviously doesn't categorise herself with them.

We try and make light of the situation and ignore the possibilities, at least for now. I have missed calls from Barnaby and Shasta, so I step out into the hall to call them back, all the while listening to the nurses at the desk with my other ear.

Two nurses and a very young looking doctor congregate at the desk, quietly discussing results on a chart. The doctor starts to walk toward Aunt Rosa's room. I cut the phone call short, and dash in after him. The doctor stands, fumbling with the chart.

"I'm sorry, Mrs. Cummings. The ultrasound shows you have a large mass in your pelvic cavity. We'll need to run some more tests, we'll be keeping you here in the meantime," says the doctor.

Aunt Rosa nods stoically and accepts the doctor's words, but she is translucent with shock.

"What does that mean?" I press the doctor, because it doesn't look like Aunt Rosa is present enough to ask anything.

"At this stage we don't know enough to give a diagnosis," the doctor hedges.

"When will you know?"

"We'll run some tests and take it from there," he replies.

"So when you say there is a mass, do you mean cancer?" asks Aunt Rosa, looking the doctor directly in the eye.

"Let's not jump the gun, it could be benign. I'll organize tests straight away, and put a rush on them."

The doctor puts his hand on Aunt Rosa's shoulder then leaves the room. *This is not happening.*

"Are you OK?" I ask, shocked; trying to think of something positive to say.

She smiles and nods and I put my arm around her, but she doesn't look like she wants reassurance. She looks off into the distance and doesn't make eye contact.

"At least he's getting the tests pushed along quickly so you shouldn't have to wait too long," I try to lift the stony atmosphere which has fallen on the room.

"And it means, I've not put on as much weight around my belly as I thought," she attempts a joke, and I smile with her. "Let's not make a fuss until we know. Right?"

"Right."

"It's been a long day. Would you go and check on Hudson for me?" asks Rosa.

"Sure. I'll come back in the morning and bring some of your things."

I get the feeling she wants to be on her own for a while.

Shasta collects me from the hospital, although I'm not much company because I don't feel like talking; I'm just grateful for his reassuring presence. When we get back to the house I hug Shasta tightly, and we say goodnight. I'd love for him to stay over but that's pushing Aunt Rosa's goodwill to the limit, although she is unlikely to find out.

Simon is still up and watching television, with Hudson lounging on the sofa beside him. I tell him as much as I know about Aunt Rosa's condition, then head straight to bed for some solitude.

In the morning I gather together some things for Aunt Rosa and apologize to Simon for not spending much time with him. He seems happy to amuse himself, which is unusual. I want to be at the hospital just in case the results of the tests come in. When I arrive at the hospital there is a nurse with Aunt Rosa, chatting away about everything and anything. I hug Aunt Rosa and notice she has a slight yellow pallor to her skin, but other than that she looks better than she did when she came into hospital – that must be a good sign. The arrival of the doctor feels like judgement day. He pulls up a seat – that looks like a bad sign.

I take a deep breath and shakily exhale. I will him to get on with it.

"So you're here to give me good news?" Aunt Rosa raises her eyebrows, tempting him to the point.

"I'm sorry, Rosa, it's not good news," he says, then starts to reel off medical jargon, but Aunt Rosa cuts him off.

"In simple terms doctor, are you saying I have cancer?"

Please don't answer that! Please don't answer that! I'm silently begging. It's such a direct question, and can only have two possible answers

"Yes, Rosa. You have ovarian cancer."

Damn the man! How dare he be so brutal! He's casually served a termination notice on her life. *Damn him!* A crushing weight falls around me.

"But you can treat it though, can't you?" I ask, scrutinizing Aunt Rosa's face, looking for something which tells me the doctor is wrong. She looks the same as she always has – this can't be right. Maybe they've got the results mixed up. She leans her head back on the pillow and looks off into the middle distance.

"We do have treatment options. We will decide on the

best way to proceed, but surgery, chemo and radiotherapy are all possibilities.

"So she could make a full recovery?" I'm desperate to find an exit from this hell.

"There have been advancements in treatment, and we've still more tests to run, but it's possible," says the doctor sounding evasive.

"You're going to be alright. You'll see," I'm begging, not reassuring. I want to fling myself on my beloved aunt, to hold her tight, to stop her going anywhere, because no-one can take her away if I hold on tight enough. Instead I hear myself being strong and resilient. I tell Aunt Rosa all sorts of implausible reasons why she will get better. I won't buckle. Not yet.

"I didn't see it coming. Cancer is for other people, not for me," says Aunt Rosa.

"That's the spirit."

"I've got too much to do yet."

"And you'll get to do it. If anyone can overcome this it's you. You're a tough old bird."

"Less of the old," she replies, but the vacant expression doesn't leave her face. It's as though a soul fragment has already drifted off.

"I don't fear it, you know," she says.

"Fear what?" I don't want to hear this.

"Dying."

I knew it.

"Please stop talking like that. It sounds like you're about to slip out before the show's over."

"After this...life goes on, Tara. Believe that or not."

"I do believe that, but I also believe in life before death, and there's plenty of life in you yet."

She just smiles placidly. I sit with her in the hospital room until dark and she falls quietly asleep, snoring gently. Sitting watching her trance–like in the dark, I send out gratitude for her life, for she is irreplaceable to me. A tiny, brilliant–blue orb of light is hovering around Aunt Rosa's head. It starts to vibrate, jiggling faster and faster until it disappears from my vision. I know I can leave her tonight in safe hands.

I leave the hospital and return home feeling hollow. They will remove the mass, and life will go back to normal very soon – it smacks of denial and I know it. I walk into the stillness of the house, drop into the nearest chair, and lower my chin on my hands. Hudson meanders over from his bed, dragging Rosa's old cardigan. He nudges my hands away so that he can lick my face. Even he seems subdued. I wrap my arms around him, burying my face in his thick rug–like coat. We share a need for comfort. He sits stock still against me; a beacon of love in a storm.

The absence of just one person can make a house feel so lonely and dim. It reminds me of being in a room after the fire has gone out. The wonderful feeling of belonging I've had for the past few weeks feels like it's fading now. I ponder the prospect of being more alone than I was before, of returning to New York without the distant reassurance of my anchor. The idea of leaving Shasta behind creases me even further. I lie wide awake for hours and snatch some sleep just before dawn.

Later Simon comes into my bedroom. He's shocked to hear about Aunt Rosa's diagnosis. We sit hugging and his eyes are glassy. I can't cry. I can't plug into any emotion properly. He sensitively retreats and takes Hudson out. It's so unlike Simon to be by himself for any length of time. I smile at the thought of him taking Hudson out. He has no experience, nor a particular affection for animals, but there is an obvious bond developing between him and the dog.

I spend the rest of the day hanging out at home with Simon; we put the world to rights and eat every morsel of chocolate we can find, but Shasta is constantly in my thoughts.

Shasta calls round after work and finds me in my lounge wear, not exactly dressed to kill. I thought he would call beforehand. He asks me about Aunt Rosa and lets me talk while he quietly listens. I've know about metaphysics, mostly through Giselle, and how people can manifest illnesses based on their trapped emotions. But it doesn't explain to me why Aunt Rosa has ovarian cancer. I don't understand how this correlates with her past experiences. I hope that Aunt Rosa does believe she will get well. I don't want her to succumb to the disease just because she accepts a bleak prognosis.

"She can fight it. She can beat this," I tell Shasta.

"She'd be fighting with herself Tara. The disease is a part of her that is suffering a hurt. Maybe something that she repressed," says Shasta.

"So what then? What are you suggesting? Do you think she should just accept it: roll over and die?"

"Accept it, yes; because denying it is avoiding the real problem. Tara, there has to be willingness to change,"

"Well isn't that the ultimate disclaimer!"

I'm riled by his unorthodox complacency for someone's life and I want to vent my anger somewhere.

"Why are you shutting me out Tara?"

"This isn't about you, Shasta."

"I'm trying to talk to you but you won't let me in. You seem to find it hard to believe, but I'm here for you."

He wouldn't be thinking that if he knew I'm working for Buchanan Enterprises. I'm racked by guilt at my association. My sympathies lie with the Native Americans – not that it counts for much when my salary is paid by Sheldon & Napier. This could blow my relationship with Shasta out of the water completely.

"Sorry. I guess I'm not used to being around a good guy."

Shasta puts his arm around my shoulders and draws me protectively into him, but I don't feel worthy of it.

"I'll do what I can to help, but I think you know that."

The guilt is welling up like a dam in my throat. I gulp it down and move away from him, looking out the window, staring at nothing in particular. How can I not tell him? He deserves to know the truth.

"I do know that."

"There's something else isn't there?"

I glance up at him, not meeting his eyes.

"Someone else then?" he asks quietly, but his dark eyes lock into mine and don't let go. He's noticing every miniscule movement.

"No, I don't want you to think that." The words fly out of my mouth so quickly, trying to extinguish any truth that it looks suspicious.

His eyes narrow at me, excluding everything else. He is already on his guard and there is no point in me withholding anything from him any longer. It's his mind to make up.

"You're not going to like this, but I didn't know myself until recently."

"What?" his voice snaps before I've even begun to explain.

"My company have a client who is trying to acquire the

Indian land. I work for that client. It was him I was with the night of my accident."

Shasta's face is stony. Only by a flicker in his eyes do I know he has understood me.

"The client is new to me so I had no idea what they were involved in until...well I saw him at Nagual Creek."

"You didn't tell me?"

"I couldn't be sure."

"Was it just business with you two?"

I hesitate a split second before answering, but Shasta notices and lifts his head back with a deep breath.

"It was on my part. I've met him a couple of times since too. He turned up here out of the blue looking for me. I went out with him solely to find out why he was here."

"He was at this house?" the tone of his voice is escalating.

I nod.

Shasta is motionless but his eyes are burning coals and the flare of his nostrils shows his anger. In a rush to explain my words tumble out all at once. I tell him the whole story: about being called to an urgent meeting with Tray in Seattle, him turning up at Aunt Rosa's and finally the discussion at the bar and his intention to remove Buchanan's business from Sheldon & Napier if I didn't use my connection with Shasta and push the deal forward and help to secure the Native American land.

"Why the hell didn't you tell me sooner?" his voice is low but unmistakeably angry.

"I didn't want to wreck what we have. Also..."

I'm frightened what trouble it'll cause if I tell him about Cain Shimlow, but the dam has burst.

"There's more?" he visibly winces.

I explain about the threat from Cain Shimlow the night

I left Tray in the bar, how he threatened to hurt people if I didn't play ball, but that I had no intention of doing what Tray asked. I even told him how Tray alluded to a higher, sinister network of control.

Shasta strides angrily to the door. He stops and places his hand on the frame. He looks to the floor while raising his other hand to his eyes. I can't see his face but I know he's ready to blow. He raises his fist. For a moment he looks like he's going to punch the door, but his hand slows with restraint before it comes to rest. He spins round to face me; chin jutting out and eyes blazing ready to take the war path.

"You should have told me," his voice is low and controlled but brimming with anger.

"You can't lay a finger on them Shasta, you'll play right into their hands. They'll see you behind bars."

"It has to stop, Tara! Too many people are going to get hurt, "he raises his voice.

Simon walks in unnoticed at first. He looks warily between Shasta and I.

"Is everything OK here?" he asks.

His question goes unanswered.

"I'm sorry, but I thought it best not to tell you!" I implore.

Shasta steps forward to me and wraps both his arms tightly around me.

"Don't keep secrets from me. Ever."

"He said my loved ones would get hurt. You're one of them. I thought I was protecting you."

"Me? Christ, Tara. I can look after myself," he snorts ironically. "It's up to me to protect you. I can't do that if I don't know what's going on."

"OK. No more secrets," I look up at him.

"I love you. I wish you understood how much," says Shasta with his nose to mine.

"And I love you," I reply feeling like the heat raging between us could melt me to a puddle on the floor.

"Jesus. Barf–o–Rama," Simon mutters, busying himself; and we remember he is there.

We break apart and grin at each other, suddenly back from that little spell, aware that Simon is looking on.

"Do you think they would actually hurt people?" asks Simon anxiously, wanting to be brought up to speed on events.

Shasta looks at us with a dry semi smile.

"Two months ago I found the body of my friend at the foot of a cliff near Nagual Creek. His death was recorded as a suicide. I don't believe that for a second. Mount Nagual is sacred and some of my people think it shouldn't be climbed. He was so superstitious. I know he wouldn't have gone up there.

"You think he was murdered?"

"I think it was made to look like a suicide."

"Will you two stop with the creepy crap! I'm just getting comfortable in the woods on my own," Simon pipes up and diverts the conversation.

I'm relieved Shasta has accepted my explanation of things and it reinforces our relationship with a trust, the like of which I've never had before. Our connection deepens because of it. I just don't know what the repercussions will be now the information is out, and whether Shasta will take an action which could have serious consequences all round.

"Are you staying over here tonight?" Simon asks Shasta boldly. "I'd feel much more relaxed if you were in the house. "You could sleep in front of the door in case we get an intruder."

"Simon, grow a pair. I'll protect you from the hooded claw," I tease him deflecting the slight awkwardness.

"I'd like to," Shasta turns to me for an answer.

"If Aunt Rosa were here she would have a fit. But she's not. For Simon's sake I think you should stay," I reply, imagining Shasta's arms wrapped around me and feeling safe in the warmth of his chest.

Shasta grins. "OK. Just for Simon's sake." He gives me that casual sideways seductive look that makes me ripple with pleasure.

"Oh, God. What was I thinking? I'm gonna need ear plugs," moans Simon.

22

It's the day of the operation to remove the tumor and I've hardly slept. Shasta takes me to the hospital early before Aunt Rosa is prepared for theatre. When someone's life is in danger it makes you appreciate how precious every little moment is, and all those moments that have gone undervalued can't be gotten back.

"I just want this thing removed so that I can get home," she says buoyantly.

"It'll be over before you know it. Hudson is missing you. He's been taking your gardening sweater into his bed with him," I tell Aunt Rosa, omitting that he is also off his food and pining for her.

"Aw, has he really? I miss him too."

"I wonder if I could sneak him in here?" I whisper, well away from the nurse's hearing range.

"No!" we both titter at the same time.

The nurse advises me not to stay around the hospital as they don't know how long the operation will take, and she promises to call when Aunt Rosa comes round from the anaesthetic. I give Aunt Rosa a tight hug and she pats me on the back, telling me not to worry.

"Do you want me to bring you anything from the store?"

"Chocolate donuts. I'd love some chocolate donuts. The hospital food isn't great. Sorry Doc!" she smiles at a passing doctor.

I kiss her hand as she is wheeled off on a trolley.

"I love you," I call after her, not knowing if she has heard me.

"You too," she answers, and waves her hand as they take her away.

I wander aimlessly around the nearby shops, window shopping to fill in the time. I'm jellified with nerves and might as well be in the hospital rather than worrying what's going on there. I buy a bumper selection of donuts and return to the hospital. I keep watching the clock, nursing the plastic cup of watery coffee that has long since gone cold. Shasta comes into the waiting area carrying a bunch of pink roses for Aunt Rosa and patiently sits with me for a while.

Several hours after the surgery has begun Aunt Rosa is brought back to her room, still drowsy from the anaesthetic. The relief is served on a double edged sword – now we have to wait for the prognosis.

"I'll go for a walk and give you guys some space. I won't be far away," says Shasta thoughtfully.

The duty nurse tells me the doctor is on his way to see Rosa, but as far as she knew the operation had gone well.

"Oh, is this your daughter?" asks the nurse enthusiastically.

"No. I'm her niece," I correct.

The nurse looks at Rosa and then back at me.

"Oh...it's just...people say all sorts of funny things when they're coming round from anaesthetic," says the nurse, and she leaves the room.

I wrinkle up my nose and shrug off the comment. I remember my mom used to tell me not to wrinkle my nose like that, because one day I'd have lines there. So far she's been wrong about that, although Aunt Rosa has the same habit and right now she looks much older than usual. She is grey and drawn after the operation.

A new doctor comes in and eyes me suspiciously, then checks with Aunt Rosa if she would prefer privacy, but she declines it. The doctor explains that they have successfully removed the tumor and depending on the lab results they will decide whether or not she needs further treatment.

"It was a very large tumor. In order to get it all we had to make a substantial incision on your abdomen. You need to be careful not to re–open the wound. Unfortunately because you already have a cesarean incision there is more risk involved."

What the hell is he talking about? Caesarean incision indeed! I draw back in horror. This guy doesn't know his ass from his elbow. She's never had kids. My faith in him vanishes.

"I think you've made a mistake," I interrupt. "She has never had a cesarean. She doesn't have children." I roll my eyes to Aunt Rosa expecting validation. She is staring blankly straight ahead, saying nothing.

The doctor doesn't answer me.

"I'll be back later to see how you are. We might need to adjust your pain meds." The doctor looks from me to her and takes his leave.

"What is he talking about? Shit! Is he even sure it was you he operated on?!"

Aunt Rosa rolls her head back on the pillow, raising her eyes to the ceiling. Her previously grey pallor is changing from red through to white every few seconds.

"You need to get a new surgeon!"

"Tara."

"I've got private medical. I'll take care of it."

"Tara!"

I go silent. Something very important is coming.

"I did have a baby."

I clutch the side of the bed. The world just tilted.

"What?" I mutter in a shocked whisper. I feel like a great big ball of string is unravelling.

"I've wanted to tell you for a very long time. I've just never found the right moment."

"Umm...that's kind of a big secret to keep," I shake my head.

"When I was young I had a boyfriend my parents disapproved of. My father banned me from seeing him because his family were...unsuitable. I had to do what my father said, so I stopped seeing him. Then I discovered I was pregnant," a dry sob chokes her.

"Oh my God. So you did have a baby?" I swallow hard and put my hand on hers, squeezing her fingers tight, shaking my head because this is unbelievable. I can imagine how it must have been for her back then. She squeezes my hand back before she takes a visibly deep breath and carries on.

"I was sent away to have the baby, and have it adopted, so no–one would know. My parents arranged everything. I came back to Big Spruce and right away my father pressurized me into marrying Charlie."

"Did you get to choose the baby's parents? Did you see the baby? Do you know where it is now?"

"Frank and Honour were told they were infertile. I begged my parents to let my brother bring up my baby. It was the best solution I could think of, because that way I'd get to see her. That was the only thing they conceded on."

"I don't understand..." I shake my head. This doesn't make sense. How can my parents have adopted a daughter and I not know about it?

"Tara, I'm so sorry. That baby was you," her voice shakes so badly I can hardly make out the words. "You are my daughter."

I reel backwards in shock.

I can't even start to process this. Everything has turned upside down. My life is suddenly unrecognisable. I'm not who I thought. My very foundations are false.

"You are my mother? Frank and Honour weren't my parents?" my voice is pinched with emotion.

"I'm sorry." Aunt Rosa is gripping my hand hard.

"Anthony isn't even my brother?" I ask. This explains a lot. I have never felt like I truly belonged in the family, and that there was something different about me. I'm looking for something solid to focus on.

"I'm so sorry darling. I never wanted to give you up, but I couldn't keep you. Do you see?"

I nod, staring into the face of my mom. Where are the words?

"I do see. Now it makes sense," I mutter.

"I'm so sorry. Are you mad at me? I'm so sorry. You have every right to be angry." She squeezes my hand harder.

"No...all this time I thought I had no parents and there you were. All that time wasted," I tell her, feeling like I've both lost and received something special.

"I never stopped loving you. I watched you grow and thought of you every hour of every day. Not a day went past when I didn't blame myself for being so weak and pathetic. I wish I'd been stronger. I wish I'd said no to my family. Not long after you were born Honour found out she was pregnant with Anthony. It surprised everyone, and proved the doctors wrong."

"I see."

"I love you Tara. I don't expect you to ever forgive me." Her blue eyes are pleading and tender.

"I do forgive you," I tell her and then the tears come. "I just wish I'd known sooner."

I bring my tear–stained face to hers and gently hug her. I ponder the word mother, but it doesn't fit, not yet anyway.

"I'm so sorry. I'm so sorry," she murmurs repeatedly while we both sit crying. I'm close enough to hear her breath catch in her chest.

"Are you OK?" I ask, thinking it must be stress from the emotion. She puts her hand to her chest, inhales and opens her mouth wide.

"Do you want some water?" I ask reaching for the jug, but it's empty. "I'll just go refill this. "

"No. Stay," her voice is croaky and weak. She drops my hand, clutches her chest, and cries out in pain.

"Nurse!" I yell.

Aunt Rosa is struggling to breathe.

"Nurse!" I scream louder.

She stares at me, unblinking, taking in everything about my face.

"I love you, Tara. Be brave," she says, her voice barely audible.

Nurses appear and push me aside. "Stand back."

"No! That's my mom," I'm crying and sobbing. I get close to the top of the bed, giving them sufficient room. Aunt Rosa's face is contorted with pain. I want them to do all they can to make it stop.

"Help her! She can't breathe!"

I hear many voices, but I see only one face. The voices aren't talking to me. They are talking about a cardiac arrest, but it's of no meaning to me. Only one thing matters – they have to save my mother's life. The medics are working quickly and I bend my head to her, whispering determinedly for her not to go.

"Look at me," I tell her, pointing to my eyes. "Look at

me," I demand, trying to force her to stay conscious. She does as I ask and turns her head to me.

"Please don't go. Not now," I beg her. "You can't go. I won't let you!"

Aunt Rosa's beautiful blue eyes are looking at me, but I don't think she can see. She is straining. Quiet shunts of breath are leaving her body. There is another rattling breath. Her eyes rise skyward then drop. Her pupils fix straight ahead under her falling eyelids. Her body relaxes, as she passes. The unthinkable has happened.

I scream in anguish, hopelessly holding on to what is left of her. My legs give way and I collapse forward. Shasta appears and catches me. My family life is slipping into the past. They shock her and try to bring her back, but it's too late for that.

Her body lies vacant.

Aunt Rosa is dead.

23

The world didn't stop when Aunt Rosa died. That in itself is a miracle. I can barely remember arranging her funeral. In an automated, practical state I'd organized what was necessary to lay her to rest. Many people I've never met before have been calling at the house: bringing food and paying tribute to Rosa. I've not slept, nor have I been awake. I've drifted around in a fog, simply functioning, but I've found great comfort in the hum drum of the visitors, and the community she loved has shown great warmth and companionship.

So many people turned out in their droves. The church was full and overflowed with mourners, who had to stand where they could. They even lined the sides of the church, spilling outside. I'm not the only one who has lost someone special and I treasure the fact that she touched so many lives. This may sound warped, but in a weird way I sort of enjoyed the funeral. Not the part where they lowered her into the ground – I cried with such aching sorrow that I could have caved in – it was after that.

At one point I noticed Shasta approach Cain Shimlow as he got into his car. Shasta leaned in the window at him. I held my breath for a few moments, fearing trouble, and then my view was obscured by a lady who offered her condolences. The next thing I saw was Simon wide–eyed and looking around as Shasta seemed to throw something, but everything passed off without incident.

After the burial we had a gathering back at Evergreen which would have been what she wanted: sharing her home and hospitality with dozens of her friends and acquaintances. It's ironic the house name suggests something which doesn't change with the seasons, something which is eternal and there we were celebrating Aunt Rosa's life. Small quiet clusters of people sat around sharing stories about her. Knowing she brought joy to the lives of so many extinguished some sadness, and I felt less alone in the midst of her friends. I didn't want to let go of them, or the memories they keep alive.

Now it's the end of the day and everyone, bar Shasta and Simon, have left. I sigh with tiredness but my mind is still active.

"I don't know what happened to Cain Shimlow. I was sure he would turn up here; not that I wanted him to."

Simon suddenly looks alert and glances at Shasta, who doesn't respond to Simon's prompting furtive look. Simon has always been rubbish at keeping secrets.

"What did you do?" I direct the question to Shasta.

"You should have seen him. I would have wet my pants if it'd been me. He was like Liam Neeson in *Taken*. 'I will kill you!'" Simon spills the beans with great enthusiasm.

"Simon. Zip it," Shasta is hiding a grin behind a look of concern as he stares at me, clearly not wanting this incident made known to me.

"You didn't?" I can't stifle my giggle, and the tension of the day turns into gales of laughter and tears as Simon describes Shasta leaning in the car window, threatening Cain Shimlow and removing the car keys which he then threw into the lake. I love how Shasta tackled him so discreetly and stopped him coming near the house – I'm also relieved no-one else saw what happened.

"I want to stay here tonight and make sure you're alright," says Shasta.

"I'd like that." I lean against him, but I don't feel needy, nor did I feel crowded. I don't feel much at all at the moment, but it's good to have Shasta with me regardless.

Hudson climbs on the bed beside me. I turn on my side nestling into the thick fur, stroking and comforting the dog who is mourning the loss of his mistress. There isn't much space, but Shasta lies down behind me and drapes his arm protectively over me and I fall asleep.

I awaken in the night with the feeling that someone is standing at the side of the bed, trying to make their presence felt. Hudson has also woken up. He is pointing his nose at the space and is looking back at me, excitedly beating his tail on the bed. I don't know whether to be scared or cry. Then I feel soothed, feeling Aunt Rosa's presence in the cool, statically charged air around me. I whisper out loud to her.

"Are you safe? We miss you," I whisper.

The static increases and my whole body prickles as her energy intensifies. I can even smell her. '*Love you, I'm sorry.*' I hear the words in my head and I have a vision of her, smiling in the tranquillity of a flower–filled garden. I know she has found peace and doesn't want me to be upset. She's in that infinitely familiar place called home. Nevertheless, I can't stop the tears flowing.

Her energy evaporates. I know she's fine and I'm not fretful for her. My grief is a selfish one, for what I no longer have. I'm mourning 'my' loss. But even so the vast cavern of emptiness within me remains. I urge myself to get it together, but a tiny part of me stomps in misery that I'd only just found my mother, then she left.

Shasta is lying awake with this hand propping up his head.

"It was her, it was Aunt Rosa."

"I know" he replies as though it was the most normal thing in the world.

"You go back to sleep, I'm going downstairs."

I leave him slumbering in bed. I wrap my dressing gown around me and smile as I pass the old writing table which Aunt Rosa bought from the auction only weeks before. I guess she now knows I've kept the amulet. The thought makes me smile. I take the amulet out of the drawer and go downstairs.

I finish a glass of water, still standing in the dark, looking out of the window to the shining silver and green of the moonlit garden and the huge sequoia trees, majestic and proud, in the heart of it.

The amulet in my palm begins to get warm as I toy with it. It's beginning to gently glow a beautiful, pinkish–red light, silhouetting the golden symbols in front of the ruby. I feel it gently pulsing; it's faint, but it's alive in my hand. I look up again at the sequoia trees. They are motionless like before, but now the trees are humming a rhythmic deep base sound, which is pulsing and vibrating up through my feet.

My body absorbs the simultaneous vibrations from the trees and the amulet. I'm barely aware of myself and I can feel only one vibration. I'm indistinguishable from the humming and pulsing through and around me. I feel the oneness and unity as my awareness expands way beyond myself. Exhilarated by the rhythmic pulsing I feel like an inexplicable harmonization is happening. I'm humbled and privileged. Some might say I'm delirious with grief, but they can say what they like. This is real. The humming is growing stronger.

I walk outside and look up at the sky, where a myriad

of colors are sweeping and mixing in the air. A beam of light is shining up from every tree in the forest, collecting in a central point. A wider and brighter beam of light is shining from the top of the two giant sequoia trees, shooting up into star–like sparks, within an enormous portal of light and color. I'm rapt as though I'm looking into the eyes of God.

It's luring me in. I want to be in that space. It has an infinite, powerful, magic which radiates through me, lifting my energy. The portal is a gateway, a shared connection between the cosmos and the earth. The trees look to be collaborating; the conical, spear–shaped fir trees are drawing and sending light through the portal. The trees have a unique and magnificent vocation – I could never have imagined this.

These spears of light are conducting high frequency energy between heaven and earth. The trees unite the energy delivering it through roots and tips. They are powerful conductors of energy. The pulsing light is passing through the portals, ebbing and flowing with the energy of the universe.

It feels like a direct connection with an infinite mass of energy – the vibration is euphoric and calming. I feel bright, wispy and gossamer thin, as though I could drift on a breeze.

The amulet is growing warmer. The humming vibration from it increases while I watch the gathering of lights in the sky. I imagine myself in the portal, to this other dimension. I see quick fire messages and codes which I can't comprehend, but they are being infused into the light, ready to pass on. It feels like it's there for anyone to clear and raise their vibration – the coded light pulses are increasing the incoming light even further.

I'm beginning to feel more conscious of my body again. The humming and pulsing is subsiding as I detach from it. I know it's still there, but I can't sustain the vision any longer. My mind whirls with altered perceptions. I push my feet into the ground, feeling my foundation on the earth again, instinctively thanking it. *Wow. Who is going to believe this?*

I have to tell Shasta. I go back into the kitchen just as Shasta arrives in the room.

"I've just had a vivid dream. I know what the Hermetic Seal on the amulet is for," his eyes are glittering as he pauses for breath.

I raise my eyebrows and grin at him.

"The geometry represents creation and the ruby represents the life force. Together they represent new creation from the source power. Everything there is Quintessence."

I nod then shake my head. "I don't get it."

"The Hermetic Seal can clear the grid–lines and portals by clearing negative resistance."

"That ties in with what I've just seen."

Shasta's brow furrows questioningly.

"I saw the fir trees conducting light between heaven and earth – I mean I actually saw it with my own eyes. It was the most spectacular thing I've ever seen. The trees hold frequencies and pulse energy through the portals. The light passing through was swirling with colors. It was magnificent. The light is filtering in to recalibrate everything. The portals are in constant motion – the amulet resonates with it. I felt everything connected by a network, like every other living thing on the planet already knows this. We're the last to understand." I already know I sound like a lunatic.

"Trees have always been important. Shamans say they connected heaven and earth. They called them 'the standing people' who guarded humanity. But this? This is another level."

"You're making me sound sane." But I'm glad of his acceptance.

"There are fewer trees on the planet now than when changes happened in the past. It limits how much energy can get through to unblock the earth's subtle energy grid. We can try clearing the blocks using the Hermetic symbol."

"I want to plant a forest. It would draw new energy in – kind of like paying it forward." I'm sounding like an activist. I open my mouth and a hippy speaks. Giselle would be proud.

"The hundredth monkey," says Shasta.

"I don't know what that is."

"It's a known phenomenon where thoughts and ideas instantly spread from a group to the remainder of the population once a critical number is reached. A group of monkeys on an island learned to wash sweet potatoes and the younger ones learned to do it from observing. Once a certain number of monkeys started doing it, the behaviour was noticed in other monkey groups on other islands. Hence 'the hundredth monkey'," we finish the sentence together.

"It's the tipping point."

"Ha, amazing. If worldwide everybody planted one tree, the energy generated from that would add more light and so on. I'm going to plant a tree for Aunt Rosa."

"I can't think of anything more fitting," Shasta nods at me.

"It could be a new tradition. When someone dies, instead of flowers, a tree gets planted. Nice symbolism too."

I make us some coffee and we sit talking through the night.

Shasta tells me more about his lucid dream. How he saw the Hermetic Seal or Quintessence symbol in Egyptian times and I tell him what I had found out online – that the symbol was used in alchemy to transform metal into gold. Although it's likely a metaphor for personal change.

I make the decision to start with me and use the Hermetic Seal to transform myself. I visualize the symbol on my heart, seeing the golden rays shining through the symbol. I feel peaceful and trusting.

Just before dawn I visualize the Hermetic Seal on my heart, seeing the golden rays shining through the symbol. Crimson streaks light up the violet sky as dawn breaks. I feel positive and alive. It crosses my mind that it's almost disrespectful of Aunt Rosa's passing over, but I don't feel guilty that I'm not curled up with a box of tissues in a dark room. I feel inspired and ready for anything. I want to let more light in and whether Aunt Rosa knew it or not, she herself was a luminaire for she shone light into the lives of so many people.

Shasta takes a phone call and he looks tense. He shakes his head as he rings off.

"There's been another arson attack on the reservation."

"Your family?"

"No. Someone set fire to Michael's stable. It's more intimidation. His dog raised the alarm and they managed to set the horses loose."

"Do they know who did it?"

Shasta's lip curls and he shrugs.

"No. Crime on the reservation is a low priority for the police. I've got to go. Do you want to come with me?"

If there is trouble I would rather be with Shasta than anyone; that way I also know he's safe. It hardly seems credible to me that anyone I know could have been behind the attack; but then I think of Tray's words and Shimlow's threats and the possibilities seem endless.

24

Even this early in the morning it's warm and there's a bright, blue sky overhead – it's becoming a regular thing in Big Spruce. Simon is still asleep when we drive out to the reservation. I know not to expect wig–wams and tee–pees, although I was hoping for something more cultural and authentic – this isn't it. The modest homes are basic and lived in, though they are set in a lovely landscape.

Shasta describes how many of the family homes are overcrowded as they have long waiting lists for subsidized housing on the reservation. Poverty and unemployment are rife, which contributes to the high suicide rate. The drug and alcohol problems are well known.

"Would you ever want to go back to the old ways: living off the land, before the reservations?" I ask.

"In a heart–beat I would. Some of the problems on the Rez are because we've lost our cultural identity and the way of life which supports it. Some of our traditions have been forgotten. In the old times there was dignity and independence, strength and spirit. Some try to keep the customs alive. The old ways: honor, nature and responsibility. The Sacred Hoop, which keeps everything on the earth intertwined, depends on balance for survival; helping each other keeps the hoop intact. It was a simple life – not without its hardships, but the spirit of my people thrived back then."

"Are things hard for your family?"

"I take care of them as best I can, but they don't like change. I have to abide by their wishes. It's been a problem, but they have free will. I honor that."

We pull alongside what was, until a few hours ago, a

barn. It is now a charred mass of smoking embers. The house belongs to Michael, a proud looking man with a leathery, weathered face who looks vaguely suspicious of me. He's an elder in the tribe. Shasta introduces the man, who speaks without anger – yet his chin defiantly juts out as he reminds Shasta he isn't going to roll over for anyone. We stand talking, leaning on the corral fence while Shasta checks over the horses.

"You're a friend of Shasta's?" Michael asks making an obvious appraisal of me.

I nod, thinking that was already apparent.

"He doesn't normally bring anyone out here – people from town don't usually come this way," Michael looks like he is waiting for a reaction.

"I've not been before – just driven past." I feel awkward, unsure if I'm welcome or not.

Michael doesn't take his eyes off me for a second.

"Where did you get that?" Michael asks, looking pointedly at the amulet, mostly obscured by the edge of my shirt. I'd forgotten it was there.

"It was a gift," I reluctantly reply, not sure what business it is of his but not wanting to be rude.

"That belonged to my friend."

"Blanche Whitelaw?"

Michael nods and his face relaxes. "You must have known her well."

"I'm sorry to say I never met her," I reply and Michael looks suspicious again.

I explain how I came to have the amulet, emphasizing that Barnaby had given it to me – just to clear up any doubt that I may be a thief.

"How did you know Blanche?"

Michael's face breaks into a gummy grin with spaces where teeth had been, yet the kindness in his smile seems all the more sincere.

"Blanche used to visit a friend of mine here. He was a shaman. We got to know each other well. She learned much from my friend and they used to collect herbs to make medicines. Blanche was one of the few people he trusted to pass on his knowledge to."

"I'd love to meet him."

"That'd be hard. He's been dead for years," Michael grins mischievously and his eyes crinkle up until his pupils look like raisins.

"What else did he teach her?"

Michael shrugs. "There were many things he didn't tell anyone else – not even me. They did rituals together. He used to call her the Shadow Chaser. The old ones used to swear she kept our land safe."

"Do you think she did?"

"Maybe. We didn't have trouble back then like we do now," he looks at the charred ruins of the barn.

"So, you saw her wear the amulet?"

"I never saw her without it. She believed it kept her safe."

"Long after the shaman died my wife got sick. She had a fever so bad I thought she might die. She wouldn't see a doctor, but she let Blanche come. She gave her medicine and stayed with her all night – Blanche kept death from the door that night," Michael nods to himself, his black eyes look sad and wistful.

"And now...your wife?" His face is appealing me to ask.

"Oh, she's alive alright. But a man can hope," he laughs uproariously at himself for luring me in. An elderly woman's face appears at the window to see what the noise is. Michael gives her a cheery wave and a lingering look of pure love.

Shasta comes over, stands next to me and puts his arm around my back.

"What are you two up to?" Shasta smiles at Michael's infectious laugh.

"I was just telling Tara about old Lehman."

"Who?"

"The old shaman. Old as the hills he was. You may be too young to remember him," says Michael.

"Lehman? That was his name?" I ask, hardly believing what I'm hearing.

Michael nods and turns his attention to Shasta; they start discussing the horses, leaving me with my thoughts for a few moments. It's too much of a coincidence. Could it really have been the guy in the near death experience? It's not a common name. I have to admit it's all very close to home, and the fact I've now got Blanche's amulet, it can't be a coincidence. It's like there's a conspiracy in another world, but why would I get Blanche Whitelaw's talisman? Why me?

Shasta reassures Michael about the horses and apart from being spooked and restless they're physically fine. We leave Michael's and set off for Shasta's place. He wants to check on the contractors who are working on his house – it's almost completely finished now. To me his house is a piece of art.

I stroll through the empty interior, imagining where I would put the furniture. I'm racing ahead of myself, imagining myself living there with Shasta: getting out of bed and looking across the lake, eating breakfast by the water's edge. When I realise what I'm doing, I stop my thoughts instantly. I can't think like that. I may have to leave soon, and the longer I stay, the more I know I won't want to go.

I wander down to the rocky outcrop at the lakeside, lost in my thoughts of what I should do next. Now Aunt Rosa is gone, and so is my reason for being in Big Spruce. Patricia wants me back at work, and soon.

"Are you thinking of leaving?" asks Shasta who could have been there for a while. He sits down beside me and we are there in that beautiful fizzing space again.

"Leave? Oh, you mean–"

"You know what I mean. Back to New York." I'm so uneasy with this conversation because I haven't organised my thoughts yet. "I don't want to go back, but I've got to go back to work. It's where I earn my living,"

"And that's what you want?" asks Shasta.

"No, but I don't have a choice," I reply.

"There are always choices," he is staring intently at me, making me squirm. I close my eyes and drop down into my heart. I can feel him gently touch my fingers. I look up at him with clarity and certainty.

"I love you," I tell him honestly.

"I know," he says with that straight smile.

"You know?" I giggle but I'm actually thrown.

"I knew it before you did." He pulls my face towards him and our lips touch. My heart palpates every time.

"I won't keep you caged, Tara. You're like a wild horse trying not to get caught."

Shasta looks out across the lake, rubbing my hand in his palm.

"I won't try and stop you from doing what you want to do," he says.

"You won't?" I'm taking this as a bad thing for some reason.

"No. You're free to live the way you chose. I want things to be good for you, whatever that is." His expression is unreadable.

I know he's letting me make my decision unhindered; which is admirable, but part of me wants him to declare his undying love and tell me to stay – even if I say no. *Dear God, what is wrong with me?* The word fickle doesn't even cover it. I'm concerned. After my declaration he hasn't even said he loves me back. Maybe he's changed his mind about that.

"A lot transpired to bring you here. Do you think there may have been a higher reason?"

"I definitely do but..." But if that reason isn't him, then perhaps there isn't one.

"Then don't decide yet. Just ask to see the way ahead."

"OK," I say, happy to defer the matter. I put my hands on his chest and rest my forehead on him when he wraps his arms tightly around me. I breathe in his fresh, manly scent.

Shasta drives me home before he goes to work and we kiss in full view of the neighbors. I don't care. I like that he publicly stakes his claim on me. I expect they've seen Shasta's jeep parked outside overnight too.

Pandora and Errol had been to Aunt Rosa's funeral and were perfectly polite and formal, which was fine by me. I wave Shasta off, feeling a little confused about our relationship. I'm used to possessiveness and restriction; this is open space and freedom – I'm feeling a bit agoraphobic.

I open the front door and pick up the mail from the floor. It's all for Aunt Rosa, apart from one white envelope which is addressed to me. I still automatically think of her as Aunt Rosa. I can't get used to referring to her as my mother. Simon has been really getting into the swing of things this week and has been out a lot. I'm glad he's keeping occupied. I start to open the letter when a cab pulls up outside the house. The driver opens the trunk and takes out a bag. The door opens and I recognize the long, wavy, auburn hair. It's Giselle. I bounce down the steps and fling my arms around her.

"What are you doing here?"

"I'm sorry I didn't get here in time for the funeral. I came as soon as I could get away. I'm so sorry about Aunt Rosa. I know she meant a lot to you." She is hugging me as tightly as she can, suffocating me in her thick hair.

Apart from Shasta and Simon, I haven't told anyone about Aunt Rosa's revelation that she is, or rather was, my mother. I guess if she hadn't told people in life she wouldn't want it broadcasted in death either. I'll obviously tell Giselle though.

It feels like ages since I've seen her and we are overdue one of our marathon chats. Giselle can read me so well that I generally don't get anything past her. Not that I want to, but sometimes I like to process my thoughts before I talk about them.

Simon comes in after being at the spa. He is equally surprised to see Giselle. Now our trio is complete: Simon opens a bottle of red wine and I make dinner for us all. We leave the dishes, curl up on the sofa, relax and catch up. My jaw aches from talking. It's a great relief to get some perspective on what's been happening. Giselle doesn't hold pity parties. She's matter of fact about everything. To her everything is surmountable and she listens without criticism when I tell her that Aunt Rosa was in fact my mother. By now Simon has fallen asleep in the chair, which is no wonder because he's already heard it all.

"Are you angry about it?" asks Giselle.

"No. But I'm disappointed she didn't have the courage to go against her family and bring me up."

"But it wouldn't have been common then, especially around here and in a strict authoritarian family, it must have been very difficult for her. At least the way it was done meant she was still a part of your life," Giselle replies diplomatically.

"I know, and I'm grateful for that. But why didn't she tell me earlier? She could have done it after Frank and Honour died. That would have been appropriate."

"I guess she had her reasons. Does your brother...er cousin I suppose, know yet?"

"Jeez, no. I don't think there is any reason for him to know. I'll need to let the dust settle a while."

"Aunt Rosa lost the love of her life. Now I'd like to find out who he is; I want to find out who my father is. He may still be out there somewhere."

"You could be opening a whole can of worms there. He could be married with grown up children, and maybe even grandchildren now."

"I could be, but I need to know. I'm just not sure where to start looking."

"You could start discretely asking around Rosa's old friends and start looking for suspects."

"Suspects!" I laugh.

"Things have a way of coming out," says Giselle, upending her glass of Shiraz.

"Anyway, let me tell you what happened last night," I say, attempting to top up Giselle's glass; but only a trickle comes out of the empty bottle.

I update her on the mystical adventures of the previous night. She isn't at all surprised by the visitation from Aunt Rosa, but it really fires her up when I tell her about seeing the trees channelling energy. I tell her as much as I know and explain Shasta's vision about how the Hermetic Seal of Light can be used. I've never seen her so excited.

"Wow. We've got to do something with this. This could be why you're here, and maybe even why I'm here?"

"Anyway, do you want a coffee now?" I ask, needing something other than wine.

"Sure. Go ahead."

"Aw, look at sleeping beauty." I take Simon's empty glass from him while he sleeps in the chair, drooling onto the hand which is holding his head up.

On the way to the kitchen I pass through the hallway just as the front door bursts open. Startled, I skitter to the side before I even see who it is.

"Anthony! Nice of you to knock!" I lower my voice instinctively to counteract the fury coming in my direction. He weaves unsteadily towards me, brandishing a piece of paper. His face is purple, his lips are pared back in menace, and from the reek of alcohol I guess he's been on a drinking binge.

"Hello, Sis! You weren't going to tell me, were you?" he is slurring and spitting his words.

My stomach flips over. *Does he know?*

I need to stay calm and not enter the ring with him.

"Or should I say cousin!" he spews.

He knows alright. But how? My mind races.

"Anthony, I think you need to calm down and explain to me what's going on."

"Pah! Don't you think you can tell me what to do, princess. Just because you're used to getting what you want. You always get everything. Literally! She left it all to you...the house...the cash. She tossed the leftovers to me and the boys. Are you happy now?"

"How do you know this? I haven't a clue what you're talking about."

"It's all here in her Will. You've got a copy too so don't play dumb with me. What a nice surprise it was when I got it in the mail today."

It dawns on me that I hadn't opened the letter that had arrived earlier.

"And the biggest surprise is...you're not even my sister! Did you know all along? Is that why you didn't want to know us? You had it all mapped out didn't you? Come and stay, butter her up, get on her good side before she croaks it. Then suddenly she's dead. Or did you arrange that too?"

"That's enough," I snap.

"Did I hit a nerve?"

"You bastard!"

"Say it like it is, bitch!"

"I only found out she was my birth mother just before she died. How dare you insinuate I had anything to do with that," I shout. So much for not getting in the ring with him.

"Liar!" shouts Anthony swaying on the spot. He probably won't even remember this in the morning.

"That's enough Anthony," says Giselle who has now

entered the drama, drawing herself up to full height and folding her arms like a referee.

"You need to leave and come back when you're sober, then we can talk about this," I tell him.

"So now I'm drunk am I? You should try it sometime Miss Goody Two–shoes. That's you. Always looking down on people."

"I want to help you Anthony, but I don't know how."

"Don't start now."

"I have tried, but you reject any kind of love or affection I've offered."

He doesn't even seem to hear my last sentence as he looks towards the floor, swaying and repeating the words 'you never did' to himself over and over. He looks up with renewed hate and lurches towards me, his shoulders swing round as his right fist curls up. I duck out of the way and he loses impetus barely managing to stay on his feet.

"It's time for you to leave Anthony. I'll call you a cab."

He topples into the wall. "Idiot. Sit down before you fall down!" I grab his arm and shove him into the nearest chair as I reach for my cell phone

"I fall asleep and World War III breaks out! What did I miss?" Simon appears looking befuddled, bleary eyed and barely awake. He pulls a puzzled face at Anthony who is now falling asleep in the chair. While waiting for the cab to turn up, Shasta arrives and gives Anthony a hard look.

"He's just leaving. There's the cab now."

Shasta and I put Anthony's arms over our shoulders and half carry his limp weight down the porch steps, and into the cab giving the driver his address before returning inside. I introduce Giselle and Shasta while in a trance and I walk to the table where I'd thrown the mail and pick up the white envelope which is addressed to me. The letter is from Rosa's lawyer and contains the Last Will and Testament of Rosa May Cummings. I read it twice, then lay it on the kitchen table and put my head in my hands. I don't know what to feel.

Anthony was right. Apart from a small amount of cash everything else has been left to me. The will states '... and to my daughter, Tara Elizabeth North, I bequeath everything else.'

Stunned, I shake my head. In the end Rosa did announce me as her daughter. She must have intended to tell me after all. It looks like she really just hadn't found the right time. My thoughts have jammed. I'm hugely grateful for what she has given me, and I deeply appreciate that she has formally proclaimed who I actually am. I smile, but I've such a longing to see Rosa right now and hold her close. Giselle is asking me questions, but I need some time to think. Shasta just puts his arm on my shoulder. I show them Rosa's Will underlining that it names me as her daughter. Giselle sits down heavily in the chair and stares at me open mouthed.

"I'm glad she made it formal," she murmurs, finally closing her mouth.

Shasta strokes my hand supportively. "I know how much that means to you," he says quietly.

"I need to take this in. I can't think right now," I reply, wanting to divert the attention from me. Giselle makes tea for everyone and we sit around the kitchen table talking for a while. I notice how fraught and tired Shasta looks.

"Is everything alright?" I ask, glancing at the furrowed lines of tension on his brow.

"Just one of those days. Tempers on the reservation

are at boiling point. There was a break in at the Native American History Centre last night; nothing was stolen, just vandalism and some artefacts and documents were destroyed," says Shasta, his voice unusually brittle.

"Silly question, but do they know who did it?"

"A couple of teenagers from the reservation are suspected. They were seen causing a disturbance and fighting in the town."

"Why would they vandalize a place like that?"

"I don't think they would, but they're the obvious suspects."

"It's more intimidation isn't it?"

Shasta shrugs.

"It could be. What's frustrating is the authorities say it's just 'in fighting' and leave us to take care of it. Anyway, never mind that now," says Shasta.

Giselle is keen to get to know Shasta and I'm barely able to get a word in because she is enthusiastically picking Shasta's brains about the Hermetic Seal. Simon is bored stiff and decides to go to bed. Giselle is exuberant, although Shasta seems quiet and reluctant; I'm not surprised after the day he's had. I sit listening intently to their discussions until I feel myself nodding off. A plan seems to be coming together to do some geopathic energy clearing and combine it with camping. We're all utterly exhausted and call it a night shortly after 2:00 a.m.

25

Simon has taken Hudson for an early morning walk. It's extraordinary how easily he seems to have kicked back into the slower pace of life in Big Spruce, and formed such a strong bond with the dog. However, when Simon gets back from his walk he's horrified to discover that plans for a camping trip are beginning to take shape. Giselle, Shasta and I are sitting at the kitchen table scoffing scrambled eggs on toast, and washing it down with fresh coffee while Giselle looks at a map.

"Look, it's a stretch for me to be out of the big city and in the countryside, but camping...that really is the limit. I'm not going," Simon sounds adamant.

"Don't be such a drama queen. What are you scared of?" asks Giselle.

"Oh, just the dark, the snakes, the bears, the insects and anyone who wants to stab me through a tent," Simon moans, while buttering toast.

"You don't have to come," says Shasta casually.

"*Hmph*. So are you all going?" asks Simon.

"Yes. I'd like you to come but you can stay at home if you'd rather," I tell him.

"Is Hudson going too?" asks Simon hesitantly.

"Yes, Hudson is going too." I can't hide my grin.

He looks down at Hudson who is intently watching Simon's toast and drooling on the floor. He pats the dog on the head and gives him half.

"OK then I'll come," says Simon.

That was a remarkable turnaround.

"Good. Your incessant noise will keep the bears away. But you will need to be quiet occasionally," says Giselle.

Simon looks at me, pulls a face and salutes Giselle behind her back.

"Giselle you ask a lot of a guy. Will there be somewhere I can charge my cell phone?" Simon asks seriously.

Shasta straightens up and looks formidably at Simon.

"Maybe we should leave him at home," says Shasta.

"Simon, stop winding Shasta up! This trip does have a purpose. The idea is to clear geopathic stress to bring more energy in. We'll be using symbols, and doing whatever we need to do to disperse negative energy. There's magic out there," says Giselle.

"I'll go along with it, but you guys have seriously lost your minds. I think you might need looking after," says Simon; Giselle snorts back at him.

"Here, memorize this symbol. This is what you'll need to visualize and contribute your energy," says Giselle, passing him a picture.

"So are you saying that just by visualizing it, something magic is going to happen?" asks Simon grimacing.

"You create with your mind. What you focus on, you create more of, so use your thoughts wisely," says Giselle.

"Be mindful of your–"

"No *Star Wars* quotes!" says Shasta putting his hands up, interrupting Simon.

The group dynamic is intense and I'm having my doubts about the cohesiveness of our little alliance because the personalities are so contrasting. I've already spoken to Svetlana and she's keen to come along; she's bringing her husband James who also happens to be a friend of Shasta's. Apparently James is an experienced climber and an outdoorsman who has great local knowledge and all the best equipment anyone could ask for.

Our little adventure feels like its gaining momentum, which makes me a little apprehensive and I'm having doubts about what we'll achieve. At best we will clear old stagnant energies and increase the light flow. The worst–case scenario is that nothing happens, and we look like a bunch of tree–hugging hippies. But I'm buoyed by the prospect of a camping trip with good company in beautiful surroundings. This could be an opportunity to make memories to laugh at later. I haven't had much space to mourn Aunt Rosa. My time has been filled, which has been a welcome distraction. I know I can't by–pass the pain forever, and I don't expect to; I feel she's around me and closer than ever. I just wish I could see her.

Giselle and I are in charge of getting the food supplies for the trip, so I drive us to the supermarket in town where I bump into Roger Walsh from next door.

"Feeding the masses?" he asks.

"A few of us are going for a camping trip. Why don't you come with us? The more the merrier and all that," I ask, really hoping he can join us because he was such good company at his parent's dinner party, and we made a good connection.

"I haven't been camping since I was a Boy Scout. I don't know if it's for me really. I like my home comforts," Roger hesitates.

"Come on, you great boiled lettuce," Giselle breezes amiably past him on her way to the car. Roger looks astounded.

"Oh, she's coming too. That's Giselle."

And as if by magic Roger decides to come along.

"It's an eclectic gathering, but they won't eat you. I'm not sure about Giselle though," I add.

Back at the house we re–group and start sorting out what we need for the trip. Between Shasta, James and Roger we have plenty of tents and equipment to choose from. Laughter and excitement is filling the house – Aunt Rosa would have loved it. We gather everything together and it feels like we were going on vacation instead of camping. We load the truck and Shasta's jeep with what we can, so we can leave fairly early the next morning.

Shasta has chosen the camping location, near to a place he recently worked on to clear energies; but it wasn't that successful. He tells us about a great natural camping spot where we can get fresh water, and it isn't far from the place where he'd found a geopathic anomaly; a blocked energy drain.

We rummage in the shed for the spare tent and sleeping bag which is here somewhere. I pass Shasta an old worn cooking pot which may come in useful. Simon is looking on and supervising, or so he thinks.

"So it's not even a campsite! Where are we supposed to go to the bathroom?" howls Simon.

"Here. You'll be needing this," says Shasta, and tosses Simon an old yellow children's spade he found lying in the shed.

Simon catches it and curls up his lip. "For making sandcastles?"

"For your bathroom needs. You'll need to dig a hole so we don't all stand in it," replies Shasta.

"Urgh," mutters Simon, apparently affronted. He tosses the spade back into the shed. This is going to be fun.

The next morning we wake up to another blue sky, which is ideal for camping. It's never usually this dry around here and some of the stunted grass is tinder dry and yellowing.

Roger piles out of his house with a surprisingly large supply of camping gear. It looks like he is absconding with us, which amuses me no end.

Svetlana and James check in at the house and we're ready to go. Seven people, two dogs and three vehicles set off in a small convoy, heading out of town. We're following Shasta and it's not long until he pulls over in a quiet valley not far from Fort Jarvis.

We can only take the vehicles so far, so we park them in a fenced off clearing made for the job. We make our way through the conifers, managing to take most of our equipment on the first run. Shasta leads the way to the pretty camping spot, where the trees thin out and the short grass is ideal for pitching the tents. Beside us is a rocky riverbank with a small pebbled cove. Campers have left behind a mound of blackened stones, which is all that remains from their fire and close by there are a couple of fallen logs which can be used for seats. A narrow rocky bluff rises up behind us as the mountain elevation soars from here. The river bubbling quietly past is rhythmic and soothing.

Spirits are high in the camp, and as the tents are set up there is a strong sense of camaraderie with everyone working together. The four tents are pitched in a circle with the entrances facing each other and we build a fire in the centre, dragging in logs for seating. The ground has that wonderful hollow, soft, springy feel underfoot, created by layers of pine needles and moss.

James uses some dried leaves as kindling for the fire, which he sets within a stony surround. He is taking the camp organisation very seriously, giving advice to anyone who stands still and scratches their head for more than a second, whether they needed it or not. Simon has tried admirably to put up the tent he is sharing with Giselle, but he's struggling and getting frustrated. James doesn't waste any time diving in to show Simon how it's done, but there is no indication of impatience or irritation with Simon. In a few moves James has the tent up.

"I can put the tent pegs in," says Simon competently.

"OK. Just make sure you have the awning pulled tight. You don't want to be blown away if the wind gets up. Here's a mallet. Drive the pegs well into the ground so no–one trips over them," says James, and Simon pulls a sarcastic face.

"I know that," he replies defensively then looks away and flicks his eyebrows up.

James smiles at Simon. "I'll let you get on with it then."

I had instantly liked James, who is very much a man's man. He's stocky and rugged: ex–military, cropped light brown hair, a square face and a stubbly jaw. He's completely at ease out here and radiates that confidence to everyone, but I wonder how he feels about the earth healing aspect of the trip. He could always decline to be part of it, which is fair enough. Svetlana meditates so it wouldn't be totally unfamiliar to him. I mention it to Shasta.

"The guy is a nature lover. That's all it takes. Someone's presence is enough to add more energy."

"So what do you want us to do for the earthwork?"

"It'll be an intuitive ceremony."

"I'm glad witch hunts died out!" says Giselle, overhearing us as she comes back from collecting water from the river.

Shasta has already put up the tent we're sharing. I unpack the food and Svetlana naturally gravitates to the role of chief cook and starts preparing lunch. We settle around the campfire and eat heartily, savoring the food, which tastes better in the open air.

The discussion quickly turns to the tree energies and portals. Now that we're all together in this environment we've definitely bonded together. Shasta passes around a picture of the Hermetic Seal of Light, which he plans on using to raise the energy, in whatever way becomes apparent.

"You know this is similar to some of the markings in the cave paintings I've seen," says James.

"Where?" asks Shasta.

"There's a well–hidden cave at a place where I climb. There are a few ancient cave paintings there. They're mostly what you'd normally expect, but there are other unusual markings too. I think the symbol is there, or something very similar at least. I remember it because it's so striking," says James.

"If that's right then the original earth keepers must have been using it in their ceremonies. Why have I never heard of this?" Shasta looks perplexed and slightly irritated.

"Maybe it's been kept hidden to prevent against misuse. It would pre–date the time when the Native American land was plundered for all it's worth. They may have known it was coming, and wanted to protect the symbol in case it fell into the wrong hands. It can't have been the right time. If it's being revealed now it must be part of the plan," chips in Giselle.

"I'm sure it's only to be used with integrity, not for manipulation or control," says Svetlana.

From my pocket I remove a piece of red cloth and unwrap it to reveal the ruby amulet and hold it up for the others to see. "Here's another way the symbol has been used. It's also called Quintessence. It symbolizes creation of all things from energy."

"How did you get that?" asks Svetlana, reaching over and touching the amulet and I tell them the story of how it used to belong to Blanche Whitelaw before it came to me.

"It's a transformative symbol – like a mandala, a symbol of self and the universe," says Shasta.

"So could you do something bad with it? Or maybe you could magic me up a Ferrari?" asks Simon.

"Is that for the highest purpose of good?" asks Giselle.

"Certainly be for my good. I don't know what you mean by that so I better not use it. Could be like passing a baby a loaded gun!" Simon deprecates.

"That's why the symbol has been hidden. In all likelihood the motivation would have been destructive. It's prevented the symbol being misused," says Shasta.

"But if there is no right or wrong anyway, then how can it be wrong to ask for something material?" asks Giselle.

"It's not. But it might distract you from finding real purpose and meaning. If you're completely self–responsible, you don't misuse power anyway – you know it will come back on you. If you do something harmful unwittingly, that's one thing, but if you do it with full awareness and intention, it's more consequential," remarks Svetlana.

"Simon, just visualize the symbol and ask that the highest good be done," clarifies Shasta. "I keep hearing about how the earth's energy network is being upgraded to a crystalline grid network, from the magnetic one. It'll take years for the changes to totally integrate."

"Sounds like broadband," says Simon.

"With earth healing I've found vortexes of dark, low

vibration energy. They're basically blocked energy drains that hold old stagnant energies. The vortexes are a kind of sub–portal on the network. They're power nodes. Some of them are resistant because they're so blocked and they can't function properly. That's why I want to try using the Hermetic Seal, with added intention from all of us," says Shasta.

"In acupuncture there's a treatment to clear 'aggressive energy' and it's one of the first things I do on a new client. Old tainted energies don't always shift themselves. People can have a remarkable shift, physically and emotionally, once it's removed. I've known big life changes to occur after that's been done," explains Svetlana.

"That's what happens with the earth healing too. The old stagnant energies shift and it allows fresh light to come in. The energy enters, through portals and power nodes, connecting to other dimensions along the crystalline grid. If we focus our thoughts on releasing the old out–dated energies using the Hermetic Seal, we can help shift things along."

"Maybe new super conductor communities will evolve to show how it's done," says Simon sarcastically. We look at each other, like he might have a point there.

"I don't have the answers, I don't think anyone has, and that's the point. We need to clear the vortexes to help integrate the new paradigm; which is happening, it's already happening all over the world. There's a divine plan in operation. We can welcome it or resist it, but it's not a foregone conclusion. It could still go either way if we're complacent," says Shasta.

We talk at length and I tell them about the vision I had, about the trees bringing in energy and illuminating everything with the light they hold, passing through their root system into the ground. I look around at Roger and Simon, both of whom seem to be listening or maybe Simon has just gone into a trance.

"This is where we come in. The more people that focus on drawing light through the Hermetic Seal, the more that we'll clear energetic debris, especially this stagnant vortex, and turn it into a power spot," says Shasta.

"So what do you want us to do? I'm not going to dance naked in the pale moonlight; I've a reputation to live up to," says James.

"No you haven't," Svetlana sniggers.

"Glad to hear that!" smirks Shasta. "Let's see how it unfolds. Keep the intention to harmonize and remember the symbol because that's the main thing you'll need to use. There'll be a reason why each of us is here. It's likely that each of our unique vibrations amounts to exactly what is needed. None of this is coincidence."

The blue sky of this morning has long since disappeared and dark thundery clouds are gathering overhead. We secure the camp then follow Shasta and James, who are walking and talking up ahead. The rest of us walk pensively behind.

"Oh I love silence!" says Simon, then he gives us a running commentary on every rock and tree we pass. Shasta and James stop. It looks like we've reached the right place. It looks innocent enough but it feels ugly. There's a humid background heat which makes me feel irritable and claustrophobic. I have the brief thought that we should just go home. The ground here is oddly soggy and tugs underfoot. There is absolutely no undergrowth. There are fewer trees than the rest of the surrounding countryside, and even these few trees are scraggy and look half dead.

Roger comments on the heavy, bog–like feel of the ground and I get the impression that Simon and Svetlana are nervous and talking rapidly to soothe themselves, but then none of us really know what to expect. I look to Shasta for a signal as to what to do, but he is quiet and still, so I don't disturb him. He is tuning in to the life force of the surroundings, connecting with the hidden energies.

"OK. Seven. We need all seven of us."

Shasta walks a little way from our group.

"Here. This is the spot," he says reaching into his pocket and taking out several pieces of quartz. We watch while he places them on the ground, marking out three points of a triangle and four corners of a square within it, then he directs us to form a circle. He says a blessing in Salish, his own native language which I don't understand, but I recognize he's attuning and seeking guidance and protection for us. He then states the intention of the group: to relinquish stagnant energy in the vortex, to release it to the universe for transformation, and to allow clear energy to flow.

I feel safe, joined by our hands in the circle, but wonder what would happen if the circle was broken?

"Tara, you need to go into the center," says Shasta.

"Why?" I ask, not keen to find out.

"Because that's what I'm being shown. You have the amulet and you need to stand in the centre. You're safe in the circle. We'll hold it around you," says Shasta. I'm marginally re–assured.

I touch the amulet which hangs around my neck and step forward into the center. The sudden fear that the earth will somehow swallow me up like quicksand flits through my mind. I step into the middle of the circle and try to silence the fearful commentary before it grows. Instead I imagine myself clear and full of light then anchor my energy down through my feet, bringing it back up again and out through the top of my head to connect with the universe. This was one of the things I'd been shown in my meditation class in New York; I never imagined I'd be using it for this.

"Now hold the light and visualize the Hermetic Seal," says Shasta.

I close my eyes and everyone is silent while they quietly go within themselves. Gentle warmth emanates from the amulet, and my hand automatically clasps it. I visualize the Hermetic Seal of Light hovering above the ground; I strongly state my intention for the energy of the vortex to be cleared and refreshed, and that the sub–portal be energised.

A flickering sensation starts around my legs, working its way up over my body. I'm tingling from the energy which is moving around me. The soles of my feet begin to tug as energy pulses through and around me, yet I remain motionless, like a compass needle in a small tornado. I begin to hear a high pitched whistling sound, as though air is being sucked out. The thick, cloying atmosphere is moving and being dredged up from the ground as it is being filtered. The swamp–like feel of the air is beginning to change. Something is whistling past my ears. All the while I keep strengthening the symbol. Am I moving? I open my eyes and I can see dark shapes in the air, moving skywards.

"You OK, Tara?" asks Svetlana. Her voice is terse and seems to be a long way off.

I nod, but don't answer. I don't want to break the focus.

"She's fine," says Shasta sounding brusque. "Focus on the symbol."

An even greater surge of energy passes around me, triggered by the change in amplitude of the group's focus. My lungs struggle to inhale air. I feel like something is dying and a great sadness rips through my chest. The hideous, musty, rotting odor of decay stings my nostrils as the energy is released. I exhale with a wheeze, as years of misery, disease and disorder pass through the vortex, finally being relinquished.

The smell of decay lifts and my breathing becomes easy again. A cool fresh breeze drifts past my face and the heavy atmosphere has lightened. I can smell pure clear ozone. Everything is silent again. I'm spellbound by the pristine atmosphere in the forest. Filaments of light are shining in the trees, moving in regular pulsing movements from their roots as light channels upwards to the heavens. The effervescent beauty of pearlised twigs and bark, shimmering pink, blue and indigo, is illuminating the dark sky with an enchanting eerie glow. A wave of communication from the trees passes to the group and a shudder passes through me. I feel tremendous gratitude from the spears of light for our intervention. I take a clean, inspirational breath in awe of their blessing. I feel higher than high, and anchored with peace.

"It's done," says Shasta.

I re–join the circle then Shasta makes another incantation in his native tongue, blessing and closing the ritual.

"Amazing," says Giselle, clasping her hands and shaking her head.

"I can honestly say I've never felt anything like that before, but can we go now?" asks Simon.

"I'm no expert, but that was powerful stuff. This place feels better now," says Roger.

"What the heck just happened to Tara?" asks Svetlana "Am I the only one who saw that?" Her face is stern and she fixes her eyes on Shasta.

"Saw what?" I ask.

"You were disappearing. You began to flicker, then I could barely see you!"

"What?" I look between Shasta and Svetlana.

"You were there and you were safe. It was the dark energy being drawn out that obscured our view of you. You were completely protected. How are you feeling?" he asks.

"Overwhelmed, but in a good way. That was out of this world," I reply, blinking in disbelief.

"I've never seen or felt anything like that. That was incredible. I'm not going to lie, but it has spooked me," says Svetlana.

"But you feel the change?" asks Shasta.

"Yes. I'm just shocked to have seen all the whirling dark energy. For the first time I have actually seen what it looks like. I've used acupuncture for years to clear people's tainted energy, but I've never seen anything like that," says Svetlana.

"That was the greatest experience ever. The trees lit up and shone when the shift was complete," I tell them, also validating it to myself.

"I saw that too," says Shasta.

"Let's get back to camp," says James, looking up at the sky and putting his arm protectively around Svetlana.

"I'm glad someone is talking sense," says Simon looking around unsurely, ready for someone to lead the way.

"It's this way," says Roger, nodding in the direction we came in.

"Are you sure? I thought we came from that direction," says Simon looking suspiciously at Roger, "but I'd get lost in my own closet." He cheerily follows him anyhow.

26

We set off back to camp and I glance back over my shoulder at where we've just been. The energy feels fresh and clear but there's something else too – a heightened electrified atmosphere, the air feels stimulated, as though a thunder storm is brewing.

Roger and Simon are deep in conversation in front of us. We've only been walking for a few minutes when Roger stops dead in his tracks and stares straight ahead, silently watching something. Simon continues talking, oblivious. Within a few strides we've caught up with them.

"It's a burning bush," Roger mutters, his jaw slack, looking utterly bewildered. We follow his gaze to a faint, ghostly light coming from a fir tree, then stop and stare for a few seconds – trying to take in exactly what we are seeing. An eerie glow is cast in the air, from what looks like lighted tapers extending off the tips of the tree in a luminous display of violet–blue flames. Sparks are travelling along the extremities of branches, darting upwards and disappearing at the tip. It looks like the tree is on fire but there's no sign of burning. There is silence apart from a hissing crackling noise coming from the flames.

"It's St. Elmo's Fire," says James, stepping closer to the tree and reaching up to touch the phenomenon, but he can't.

"What? Do you mean like the movie?" asks Svetlana incredulously.

"It's not a real fire. By another name, it's a coronal discharge. It's a weather phenomenon. Amazing isn't it? It's attracted to pointed objects. The charged air in the clouds is trying to discharge through a conductor on earth," says James, very matter–of–factly.

Shasta picks up a long broken branch and reaches up to the flames. They suddenly appear on the end of the piece of wood. We look around at each other, grinning in awe.

"It can mean there's going to be a lightning strike. Be worried if your hair starts to rise up," remarks James, although I can't tell if he's joking or not.

"So, aren't we standing in a bad place if there is?" Simon's nose twitches.

"Don't worry. It'll strike the tallest first. You'll be fine," Giselle aims a sisterly wise–crack at him.

We stand in awe, admiring the show and the fire continues to play around on the tree, which has no heat coming from it. Something catches my attention and I glance at Simon standing beside me. His hair is, as always, meticulously spiked but it doesn't usually have tufts of bright blue light coming off it. I don't know whether to tell him or not. He could start hyperventilating.

"Shasta," I murmur quietly, trying to get his attention.

He looks round and I nod towards Simon's head. Giselle turns around and catches the gesture.

"Oh my God! Look at your hair!" she points at Simon and erupts into laughter.

Simon's hands shoot to his head. He inadvertently runs his fingers through the flames, and shakes his head as though he's expecting an insect to fall out. He brings his hand down; small blue flames are dancing off his fingers. He yells at the top of his voice, and rubs his hand, trying to put out the flames. They stay for a couple more seconds then vanish.

"Is it gone now?" Simon asks Shasta, showing him the top of his head.

"Ah...yeah. It's gone," he tells a white lie, and pats

Simon's thickly gelled hair, flicking his thumb up when a flame jumps onto it.

"We have to go!" says James sharply, startling us with his abrupt tone.

"What's up?" asks Svetlana.

"Your hair is rising," he replies, grasping her arm and striding forward.

I gawp at Svetlana and Giselle and start giggling. Their statically charged hair is lifting up.

"Look at yourself!" says Giselle.

Simon shouts expletives and takes off at speed in front of James. No one waits for direction; we all follow James's example and start to run. So he wasn't joking after all.

"Quickly," he orders. My grin vanishes. Shasta grabs my hand and pulls me in front of him. Adrenaline charged, we start running for safety; crashing through the undergrowth, blood pumping hard, pounding in my temples. The sound of our getaway is broken by a groundbreaking thud like the boom of cannon fire. The ground reverberates. Simon flings his arms up in the air, covers his head and yelps.

"What the hell was that?" asks Roger, his eyes darting to James.

I stumble the last few metres into camp and look back at where we've come from. A plume of dust and smoke is rising into the grey sky.

"Lightning strike," says Shasta, head high as though he can see above the forest.

"That was lucky," Giselle, puts her hands on her red cheeks, her eyes glittering with excitement.

"That was fun," I reply, thrilled by all the excitement.

"James, let's go back. A fire could have started. Then we

really would be in trouble," directs Shasta, a clear steel streak in his voice.

The wind strengthens and the electrified atmosphere disperses as the dark clouds overhead have been blown away. The thunder doesn't come. A short while later James and Shasta return to camp, reassured that the lightning strike hasn't started a forest fire. Svetlana stokes the diminishing fire and warms water for coffee. The thrill of the afternoon's adventures evident in the happy hum of conversation. The group is unified and excited by what happened – each of us seems to have our own perception and understanding of it but it's abundantly clear that a profound and positive change occurred.

Svetlana cooks up dinner and we ravenously tuck in – lunchtime seems like a long time ago now. She serves up copious portions of fried chicken, steak and burgers, with nut cutlets for the vegetarians. The smell of sweet, buttery corn on the cob roasting on the fire is divine.

As it begins to get dark, the mood around the campfire mellows. James is deep in conversation with Svetlana. Giselle folds her arms around herself for warmth, which doesn't go unnoticed by Roger, who obligingly gives her his coat. He sits shyly down beside her and awkwardly uses the opportunity to get to talk to her. I know Giselle and I can tell from her body language that Roger is firmly in the friend zone and might as well be chasing his own tail.

"You were great today," whispers Shasta, pushing my hair back from my face and kissing my head.

"Would it have worked without the symbol?"

He shrugs. "The symbol definitely gave it extra power."

"Barnaby Whitelaw's mother was quite an enigma. What a coincidence that I found the amulet."

"That was no coincidence," Shasta sounds emphatic. "She didn't just dish out advice and herbs. She paved the way for a new wave."

"Break it up you two" says Simon, throwing himself down beside Shasta and I.

I give Simon a hug and make room for him.

"I know this wasn't exactly your thing, but thanks for what you did," I tell Simon, genuinely impressed he even came camping, let alone took part in the earthwork.

"Don't put this in the papers, but I even slightly enjoyed it. I was sceptical, but it's like there's a web holding everything together," says Simon.

"They say you can't find magic if you don't believe it exists," Shasta comments, then tosses a twig into the fire.

"What's going on over there?" Simon asks, nodding in the direction of Giselle and Roger.

"I think Giselle has an admirer."

"Jeez. Lucky Giselle. He's a keeper that one."

Simon pulls his sweater tighter around himself and folds his arms. He makes a fuss about the cold wind, but then he isn't exactly dressed appropriately. He's getting into one of his moan–a–thons, which usually results in misery for everyone who has to listen. I offer him a blanket to put around himself but he refuses, so I don't indulge him any further.

"I didn't come prepared for this! I don't even own arctic wear," he complains.

"It's just a bit of wind," says Shasta, suggesting that Simon comes nearer to the fire. He does, but then complains his face is burning and his back is cold. Simon is on a one–way track to despair central, getting himself in a tizzy and he decides to get ready for bed. I think it's not helping that his new love interest is heterosexual.

"Do you want the spade?" asks Shasta nonchalantly.

"You know where you can stick your spade! I've got to pee though. Keep me covered." Simon takes a lantern and stumbles out of sight, with the lantern bobbing around – we can still see it lurching and swinging to and fro as he relieves himself. I giggle at the sight and Giselle sniggers too. The lantern hits the ground and it goes dark. Next comes the sound of Simon swearing profusely as he throws a tantrum about his feet getting wet. Giselle and I break into howls of raucous laughter and it sets everyone off.

"Hmph. I don't know what you find so funny," moans Simon, unzipping his tent, and placing his shoes under the canopy as he climbs in.

"Goodnight!" calls Simon.

"Someone's coming," alerts James.

"Yeah, right," replies Simon, thinking he is being teased. However, he pokes his head out from the tent.

Shasta stands up and follows the direction of James's gaze. The dogs have been quiet and content all night but they are suddenly alert. Scout has jumped up and is beside Shasta, barking insistently with her hackles up.

My heart is hammering. What the hell is out there? Who would be out here at this time of night?

"Who's there?" shouts Shasta into the darkness.

There is no reply.

"I just saw a torch. There it is again," says James, pointing.

The hollow thud of heavy feet on the ground signals someone's arrival.

"Hello!" a voice comes out of the darkness, but its owner is still unseen.

"Who's there?" calls Shasta irritably.

Two men in uniforms step out from the darkness into the firelight. I breathe a sigh of relief.

"Sheriff Whitelaw. What are you doing here?" asks Shasta.

Barnaby and his colleague Patrick appear, followed by a group of six or seven others who are dressed in ordinary clothes, wearing serious expressions and carrying guns and torches.

"Pastor," says Roger, nodding to a man in a wide-brimmed waxed hat, whose face I can't see.

"This is a surprise!" says Cain Shimlow.

"This looks serious. What's the posse for?" asks James, his eyes narrowing to a hard, triangular profile.

"We saw your lights. What's your purpose here?" asks Barnaby Whitelaw, sounding officious.

"We're camping. That's alright isn't it?" asks Shasta.

"We're searching for a young child who's gone missing. He was last seen on a picnic with his family at Silver Creek this afternoon. Have you seen anything?" says Patrick.

"Nothing," replies James.

"The boy is three years old. His name is Toby. He wandered off from his family and hasn't been seen since. That was around 4 p.m. this afternoon, so he's already been out on his own for several hours. As you can appreciate, we urgently need to find this child," Barnaby sounds forthright and not in the mood for frivolity.

"Oh my God! Anything could have happened to the little guy!" says Svetlana.

"How far do you think he has gone?" asks James.

"We've got officers and helpers out looking for him within a two mile radius of where he was last seen. A child that age can't have gone too far. We don't think he's been abducted, but we're not ruling anything out. We can only hope he is still alive, but we need to be realistic about his chances of survival on his own. We're not ruling out the possibility that the rogue bear which has been seen in town has attacked him. It is a very real and distinct possibility," says Barnaby, looking grim.

"I don't think that's likely," contradicts Shasta, his face hard as flint

"And you'd know that would you?" replies Barnaby.

"We'll join the search and do whatever we can," I intervene in the bizarre tension which has erupted between Barnaby and Shasta.

"We'd hate to disturb your little camping trip though," a nasty snarl from a voice I recognize comes from the back of the group. I'm sure he wasn't there a moment ago. Even in the gloom I would have noticed Anthony with his gun casually over his shoulder.

"Anthony. I didn't see you there," I squint at him in the darkness.

"Let's not waste time here talking. Let's go back to the clearing and disperse from there. We have got every available man out looking. We have plenty of officers combing the area where Toby was last seen, so you would be better searching close to the perimeter of the search radius. You guys know the area. Report in if you find anything," instructs Barnaby. He motions for the others to follow, and they hurriedly leave our camp.

Barnaby Whitelaw's usual hearty friendliness is absent tonight, although it's hardly surprising, given the serious circumstances. The wind blusters against the tents and I wish for the rain to stay away. Shasta and James huddle over maps in fervent discussion about the possible whereabouts of the missing child.

"His parents must be going out of their minds. Let's get out there, right now," says Giselle, "we're wasting time here."

"We need a plan first," says Shasta who manages to hear Giselle despite being in deep discussion with James. His hearing ability is uncanny.

"He's right. Give them a minute to come up with something, then we'll set off," I tell Giselle.

"Let's secure the camp then we're ready to go," says Roger practically.

"This is a nightmare! How is anyone going to find a child alone out in this wilderness? And the bear...!" Simon whines, taking a puff of his asthma inhaler.

"Someone needs to stay in camp in case the child turns up here," says Roger. We all turn to look at Simon.

"No way am I staying here on my own!" says Simon, vigorously shaking his inhaler and trying to take another puff.

Giselle stiffly raises her eyebrows at him.

"I've run out, and my spare is at the house!" says Simon, sounding desperate.

"It's obvious you should stay. You don't have to do anything, just keep the fire burning and make sure the lanterns stay lit," says Giselle.

"You could go back to the house: get your inhaler, grab some all weather gear and some extra batteries. While you're there tell my dad about the search in case he hasn't already joined in. It won't take long and you have a phone." Roger is duly stepping up to the plate.

Simon gives in reluctantly.

"If these weren't extreme circumstances I would just go

home," he says, his voice wobbles with fear and I feel sorry for him, but this is important.

"Right this is what we're going to do," says James taking the lead. "We need to split into two groups. Tara and Giselle, you go with Shasta. Roger, you come with Svetlana and I. Simon you can go home and get extra supplies then return to camp as quickly as you can. We need you here, just in case."

"If I have to." Simon wilts in defeat.

"We will search a place near Shadow Gorge, close to where I sometimes climb. It's not far from where the child went missing. I know it pretty well. There are caves there that he could be in," says James.

Duly briefed, we take the minimum necessary supplies so we aren't weighed down and leave one lantern at the camp.

"Simon, you can take my car." I pass him the keys when we get to the parking area where we left the vehicles. He's anxious, but I admire him all the more because I know it's difficult for him.

"Just get all the batteries you can and see if you can round up anyone else to help," Shasta tells Simon, slinging a rucksack onto his shoulder.

"Make sure your cell phones are on loud," says Simon.

"Be brave," I mutter to Simon and climb in the jeep with Shasta and Giselle.

Simon climbs into the truck but doesn't reply. We pull quickly away, following after James. I've a twinge of guilt about Simon going off on his own but it's probably good for him, and he is an adult. Right now the objective is to find Toby as quickly as possible – if it's not already too late.

27

The rising wind and falling temperature signals deteriorating weather. What a night for a child to go missing. Toby is alone and probably scared stiff in the dark and cold when he should be tucked up safe and cosy at home. I didn't know how he got separated from his family, but I'm sure no amount of recriminations from anyone else will compare to the suffering they are going through right now. Adrenaline courses through me and I want to be out of the vehicle and doing something constructive.

We pass several police blocks on the way, where passing motorists are being stopped. We follow James up a dirt track road. An improvised gate in the form of a tree trunk discourages anyone from getting past. It seems to indicate that this area is closed off. The trees are particularly crowded and dense here, so access is more difficult. No wonder this place isn't frequented much.

We abandon the vehicles, grabbing the torches and lanterns. James straps on a backpack and leads us through the undergrowth. I have the sensation that we are gaining altitude because my toes are being pressed upward and I have to shift my weight forward to balance, but the light isn't sufficient to see how far we are climbing, only the earth beneath my feet becomes more uneven and disconcerting. I want to straighten up but I can't.

Trudging in silence, we don't seem to be making much progress.

"It'll thin out in a few minutes. Then we can spread out," says James.

"Is that wise?" asks Giselle. "You're the only one who knows where we are going."

"I can get us back if that's what you're worried about," remarks Shasta.

"I don't like it. I think we should all stick together. What if someone gets injured?"

"I agree. I don't think we should split up," I add.

"But we can cover a greater area that way," reasons James.

"That won't be much use if one of us disappears down a ravine," I argue.

"Do you want to find this kid or not?" snaps James, losing patience with our resistance.

"We don't want any dead heroes," says Giselle.

There is a yell up ahead which is followed by the sound of branches snapping.

"Svetlana!" shouts James.

Svetlana has lost her footing on the rocky ground. She slips down into the bushes. James lurches forward, grabs her arm and stops her sliding any further.

"This is so dangerous!" shouts Svetlana, clearly rattled.

"Let's stay together. It might improve further on," Shasta's voice is carried away on the wind, and I can hardly hear him.

We press on further. The driving wind is slowing our progress.

"Stop! I see something." Shasta is bending down and stretching between branches to pick something up.

"What is it?" asks James.

"It's a child's shoe," Shasta sounds abrupt.

"So Toby has been this way..." says James.

I breathe out between my teeth and look Shasta in the eye. "This isn't good is it?"

"It means we might be close," is all he says, not disclosing his thoughts.

I look at Giselle and Svetlana's strained faces, which are etched with fear. Svetlana's eyes look red and I suspect she's crying.

"Toby!" Giselle and Svetlana call in unison.

"No! Don't call him. He might be somewhere safe. We don't want him trying to find us in the dark," Shasta instructs.

The howl of a wolf penetrates the air, adding to the escalating anxiety. In reflex, I shine my torch deeper into the trees, but there is nothing there. I look back in the direction we've just come. There looks to be a couple of torches below, which are somewhat closer than the road. I wonder if other searchers are following us.

"Stay close to me everyone. There's a sheer drop a few metres to your right. You'll be fine. Just no fast moves," instructs James.

"And he wanted us to split up?" I hear Giselle mutter to herself.

"Come on, we've got to stay positive," I tell her, trying to revive her moral.

In all the drama I hadn't even thought to ask for help from the spirit realm. I begin to pray that we find Toby soon. I repeat the request then affirm it aloud – the strength of sound has to be stronger than thought. I shine my torch left and right as we walk in convoy. To the left there is a steep cliff–face, to the right is shrubbery and presumably a sheer drop. Shasta calls Scout and Hudson back from the front of our procession. He holds Toby's tiny shoe for Scout to smell.

"Where is he, girl?" Shasta asks Scout. The wind is swirling and the dog whines in response, pacing in circles, apparently frustrated.

"We're nearly there. There is a hidden cave behind some of the trees, but it's well camouflaged," says James.

We push past the tree branches and shrubbery, only to find the craggy cliff wall.

"Are you sure this is the right place?" asks Roger.

"Damn sure! Just keep looking," says James.

We spread out in a line a few feet apart, moving parallel with the rock face, checking our own area before we move on to the next spot.

"I hear dogs," says Shasta on alert.

"I can't hear anything," I say, straining to hear; but I trust his superior sense.

"Hudson and Scout are in front of us, so it's not them," I tell him, and I'm thankful to have dogs with us, although I'm nervous for their safety.

"Anything?" calls James.

The response is negative. The landscape is changing and becoming more expansive. The rocky escarpment looks to be lower here, with a slope on the opposite side and I relax slightly, now that the imminent danger of falling down the gorge has passed.

Out of the corner of my eye I glimpse something which is now familiar to me. A pale blue oval light is levitating in front of a tree. I turn to look at it square on and this time, unlike the others, I continue to see the light guarding the spot. I'm sure I can make out the shape of a man within the orb.

"Shasta! Over here!" I call.

He turns towards me, calling out directions to James, but I don't know if he has heard. Scout runs in front of me whining, with Hudson following behind.

"Where is he?" I ask the dogs, sensing their mounting

enthusiasm. I shine my torch towards the tree and the dogs vanish behind it.

I push back a couple of tree branches which are completely obscuring a rocky outline. This must be the cave entrance.

"Don't go in there," warns Shasta. He gets ahead of me to the cave mouth and shines the torch on the opposite wall, lighting up the ancient cave paintings.

"That's the cave I told you about," says James, pushing past with a lantern held up, about to go in; but a high pitched yelp startles him and Scout is racing out of the cave barking. She hurtles into James, sending him reeling backwards and she skids to a stop in front of Shasta, barking frantically at him. With lightning reaction Shasta twists around, and pulls me backwards.

"Get back!" he yells to the others. Panic stricken, we look for whatever danger he's reacting to. Everyone shines their torches and lanterns in the direction of the cave. I'm rooted to the spot, unsure what to do because Hudson hasn't come out of the cave.

"Hudson!" I scream and lunge forward, but Shasta is holding my arm.

A fearsome roar echoes out of the cave and instinctively we move back a few steps. From the blackness, the dark hulking shape of a bear comes charging out of the cave, stopping at the entrance. The bear stops and rears up. Nobody moves. We are thunderstruck. We should run – but we don't. Scout frantically hurls herself towards the bear, barking viciously yet staying out of reach. It looks like she is goading the bear, luring her out. Seconds tick past and the bear defensively holds her ground, warning us not to come any further.

"She isn't coming out. She's protecting something. Cubs?" whispers Shasta.

"A child?" I whisper back, only moving my eyes. He has understood.

"Everyone just back up slowly," says Shasta in a hushed tone.

We retreat very slowly, moving fractionally backwards, being careful not to make any sudden moves. The bear is silent, but stands upright watching us. She is defensive, but not actively seeking confrontation. I feel a surge of immense love for this magnificently powerful animal. We're in her territory and a threat to her; she could kill any one of us with a strike of her paw, but her reluctance is apparent. There is a pleading look in her intelligent eyes, imploring us to leave her in peace. I can't look away from her, bewitched by her raw power and grace.

A crazed shout from behind us shatters the silence and angry voices converge from the darkness. Shasta leaps toward the noise. The bear roars in response. A single gunshot rings out.

"No!" I scream.

The bear is struck down. She falls softly onto her paws, then her glorious, powerful body hits the ground with a thud. Despite her strength they killed her with a single bullet.

There is silence.

Violent tears of rage blind me as I scan for the gunman among the band of men. I'm incensed beyond reason, and ready to turn the gun on the hunter.

"Shimlow!" I yell in disbelief at him as he slowly, and smugly, lowers his rifle, savoring the kill.

"I just saved your life," Shimlow drawls, not taking his eyes off the prize as she lies there, robbed of her life.

"What the hell Tara!" Anthony's voice sounds shocked and he's staring crazily at me, like he has seen a ghost. I ignore him and turn back to where the bear is lying on the ground. Shasta is kneeling reverently beside the bear with his hand on her. He talks to her, in soft tuneful tones, speaking blessings which are unfamiliar to me. I'm moved beyond words and I too kneel beside the bear, placing my fingers in her thick fur. Her plump body is warm, but lifeless. I look up and watch the diamond particles ascending as she leaves her body.

James is tentatively entering the cave. I've almost forgotten the point of our search in the first place. I stand up and follow behind him into the darkness. The black and ochre figures of the cave paintings, depicting people, animals, shapes and symbols, mark most of one wall.

"Hudson!" I call into the darkness.

"Look," says James and he lifts the lantern higher.

Curled up asleep on the floor of the cave, amongst a large divot of dried leaves, is a tiny blonde–haired boy in a red sweatshirt. His breathing is obliviously deep and rhythmic. Hudson is dutifully lying beside him, guarding the vulnerable, sleeping child. My heart surges with love at the sight.

James drapes a blanket around Toby, and I scoop his light body into my arms. He stirs and opens his eyes. Upon seeing me, a stranger, he begins to cry.

"I'll carry him back down," says Shasta, picking the child up and holding him tight against his shoulder. The little boy quickly falls asleep again. Svetlana starts to cry with relief. We're all shocked, in disbelief and awe that the toddler had shared the cave with the bear. I wonder who found who. Had she lost a cub, or was her instinct to nurture greater than her need to hunt? There are no witnesses to the bear and boy's story, but the magic was evident. We can only wonder why the bear had shared her cave and protected him, but I guess, species aside, nurturing isn't conditional.

James calls ahead to say that Toby had been found. When we reach the access point an ambulance is waiting, ready to check Toby over but he seems completely unharmed.

"I don't know about you, but I'd like to go home to my own bed," I say to Giselle who is rubbing off dried blood from scratches on her hands.

"Aren't you forgetting something?" she asks.

"What?"

"Simon. He'll be back at camp. We can pick him up on the way."

"Oh God! I hope he's alright."

"I'll get him. You guys go home," says James, and we don't argue.

Roger joins us in the jeep. The roads are virtually empty, clear of the earlier police blockades. Blue and white flashing lights from behind alert us to another ambulance. We slow and allow it to overtake. Rounding the bend Shasta has to brake to avoid the ambulance which has stopped beside a police car.

"Someone's had an accident," says Giselle with faint alarm.

The road has a deep verge on either side, adjacent to fields. Someone has gone quite a way off the road and overturned their vehicle in a field. I blink hard, unable to comprehend the scene.

Aunt Rosa's truck is lying in the field on its roof.

"Simon!"

28

It was a mistake to let Simon go off like that. Judging by the state of the pick–up truck, which is balancing precariously on its roof, he may not even be alive. Shasta stops the jeep and Giselle is bolting out of the door before it reaches a standstill.

"Simon!" Giselle calls. "He might be trapped inside."

There are no street lights on this stretch of road; only the headlights from the police car and the ambulance provide any light.

The paramedics are walking to the police car. They open the rear door and speak to the occupants.

"That's my truck! My friend was driving!" I shout ahead to the paramedics while running to the police car. The paramedic looks over his shoulder at us.

"Is this your friend?" says one paramedic, moving back to let me see the passenger in the back of the police car.

Simon's tousled head appears from the back of the car, sporting a small abrasion to his forehead.

"Sorry about the pick–up," says Simon miserably.

"Never mind the damn pick–up. You're alive!" I tell him, attempting to hug him and getting pushed out by the paramedics.

"We need to check him over," says the paramedic, ushering Simon into the back of the ambulance. "I'm sure he'll be fine but we'll just take him in for assessment."

The paramedic questions him about what happened and gives him a quick inspection.

"He must have been in there for ages because he set off hours ago," I tell the paramedic.

"I'm frozen stiff," says Simon wringing his hands. They wrap him in a silver foil blanket.

"I'll go with him," says Giselle, getting into the ambulance without waiting for a reply.

"Only one of you." The paramedic blocks the door and prevents me from also getting into the ambulance.

I watch as the red glow of the ambulance's tail lights disappear. What do I do now? A policeman takes some details and advises us to go home as the truck won't be retrieved until daylight.

The house is eerily quiet when we get home, especially after all the drama. I'm restless and potter around: tidying up and collecting my thoughts. Shasta makes a chamomile tea for us both and we sit waiting on news of Simon. Giselle and Simon come in a short while later, having had the all clear from the hospital.

Finally, with everyone safely home and accounted for, I can go to sleep. I slide into bed beside Shasta who is already fast asleep, his face peaceful, his breath deep and fast with exhaustion. I smile and watch him sleep for a while, studying every angle and hollow of his proud, peaceful face. Something is telling me I need to enjoy our time together now as the future is uncertain.

When I wake in the morning I reach out for Shasta, only to find that there is an empty space next to me. A chink of golden sunlight pools on my face through a gap in the curtains and I look around using my hand as a visor. I didn't even hear Shasta get up. It's already 9:40 a.m., which is a ridiculously late time to wake up. I can't help but feel disappointed. Not only have I over–slept, but Shasta isn't here to slumber with me. It's such a precious start to the day to wake up with him. I stretch and push back the duvet. I pull back the curtains, unveiling a brilliant blue sky and a world bathed in sunshine. The bedroom door opens and Shasta comes in carrying toast and orange juice.

"Don't get up," he says, placing the tray on the bedside table. "I want you to myself."

His arms reach round my waist, pulling me backwards and I tumble back onto the bed. He grabs both my hands, pins them above my head and stops me from going anywhere. He lowers his face so close, without letting his mouth touch mine. The space between us fizzes. I reach up and trace the line of his jaw with my finger, and draw him towards me. I part my lips and his mouth covers mine.

"I like it when it's just us," Shasta presses against me.

The doorbell interrupts our intimacy.

"Let someone else get it."

"They're asleep." I get out of bed and look out of the window. "It's the police."

Shasta groans, then effortlessly glides off the bed and out the bedroom door, dressed only in a pair of jeans. I'm not oblivious to the levity of the police being at the door, but I can't help admire the fluid movements and the tanned muscles on his torso and the low slung jeans, which are resting on his narrow hips. I grab my robe, drape it over my shoulders and follow him downstairs.

Shasta has already let the two police officers in and they're standing in the hallway. I recognise one of the policemen from last night.

"I'm Shasta King, Tara's boyfriend," Shasta introduces himself. My cheeks bloom pink with pride, that this strikingly beautiful man with the naked torso identifies himself with me.

"Miss North, we'd like to talk to you about last night's accident involving Simon Miller."

"I think Simon is still asleep, but I can wake him for you?" I offer.

"We can speak to him later, but right now it's you we want to speak to."

My stomach lurches and I tighten my robe around me.

"That sounds ominous."

"Are you the owner of the vehicle involved in the accident last night?"

"Yes. It was my, um... aunt's truck, but I've inherited it."

"Does Simon usually drive it?"

"No. We joined in the search party last night, so I loaned the car to Simon to go home and get supplies."

"When did you last drive the vehicle?"

"Yesterday. Why?"

"Was there a problem with the vehicle then?"

"No. We were camping so I parked up nearby. Did you find a problem with the truck?"

"The brake cables had been tampered with," the officer watches my reaction intently.

I shake my head at him. "That can't be. It was fine when I left it," I reply, looking him dead in the eye, returning the stare.

"Were you with the group the whole time?" he asks, pushing this impromptu interview along.

"I don't like where this is going," I reply flatly.

"Tara was with us the whole time. I can vouch for that," says Shasta with an impudent tone

"Are you sure about that?" asks the policeman.

Shasta bristles, gains height and juts his chin out further.

"Once we unloaded the camping equipment I didn't go back to the truck. I wouldn't know how to cut brakes anyway!" I'm feeling defensive now.

"So are you saying that someone tampered with the brakes while you were camping? Why would someone do that Miss North?"

"I don't know," I shrug at the policeman.

"What she's saying is that the vehicle was fine when she left it. It's beginning to sound like you're putting words in her mouth," says Shasta, his eyes narrow and direct.

"We will obviously want to corroborate your story with your friends, but if what you say is true, it looks like someone wanted to hurt you," the officer looks me up and down, as though he's looking for the reason why.

"You need to find out who did this! This is attempted murder. Can't you get fingerprints from the vehicle?" asks Shasta, his brow creases and he's looking increasingly intimidating.

"We're aware of that," says the policeman sarcastically. "Forensics are already looking into it."

"By the sound of things you guys are actually going to do your job this time. I'm glad about that. The spate of crimes around here have gone unnoticed long enough," says Shasta.

"Mr King, I don't care for your aspersions, and I'm not aware of a 'spate of crimes'," dismisses the officer.

"There have been attacks on the homes of people on the Reservation: vandalism, arson and now an attempt on the life of a loved one," Shasta continues unperturbed.

"We have no evidence, but in my opinion it's just in–fighting and retaliation," says the officer.

"Have you looked for any evidence?" asks Shasta.

"Mr King, if you have a problem with the way your community is being policed, there are proper channels to address the issue. I'm not here to discuss that now. I'm not trying to frighten you Miss North, but you need to be on your guard. We'll be in touch," the officer says and flicks a sideways glance at Shasta.

"I'll show you out," Shasta says.

I wander into the lounge and flop on the sofa with the plump, oversized, cushions which, in contrast to the discussions, are reassuring. Shasta comes in and stands in front of the fireplace, still and poised; ready to strike. He's antagonised from the confrontation with the policeman.

"This could be because you're with me. This could be more intimidation to pressurise us to relinquish the land. I don't want you caught up in this."

"It might not be. Maybe the police are wrong and it was just an accident. The truck wasn't well maintained. It's old and Rosa ran it into the ground. Anthony used to do work on it only if it was needed, but never before."

"Tara, I'm all for positive thinking, but you need to be realistic."

I feel slightly nauseous and trace back through the events of last night. It must have happened while we were in the campsite. We did have visitors; Barnaby Whitelaw and the rest of the search party had shown up, but it wouldn't be credible to consider blame could lie there when a lawman was present. Or maybe that was it. Perhaps someone in the group used the opportunity knowing they would have a strong alibi – being in the company of the Sheriff.

"Shasta, do you remember last night when the search party showed up?"

"Yep." He is pacing around, eyes darting and lost in thought.

"Do you remember that Anthony didn't make himself known until minutes after they had arrived in our camp?"

"Mmm. Vaguely." He's not paying much attention.

"That could be because he wasn't there, not to start with anyway. He could have held back at the parking lot then quietly caught up and slipped in with the rest of the search party. But...this is ridiculous. I can't believe I'm even thinking this."

Shasta looks back at me, his stony face communicating nothing. "It's possible. His fingerprints would already be on the truck too, so it would be almost impossible to prove."

"It's a ridiculous thought. He wouldn't do that. I know he doesn't like me, but he wouldn't stoop to that." I feel slightly ashamed that the idea even came to me.

Shasta raises his eyebrows.

"People aren't themselves when hatred takes over."

"Maybe I should talk to him about it?" Although I don't relish the idea, I feel I should do something.

"Not on your own you won't. Anyway, if he did do it, if he's lost his way that badly, then he's beyond your reach for now. It could spur him into taking more extreme action. You can't fix him, only he can do that. He's letting jealousy push him over the edge."

"Maybe I can calm things."

"Maybe you'll inflame things. This wouldn't be the right time to speak to him. If you go voicing your suspicions you'll antagonize him. He sees you as being isolated but he needs to know you're not an easy target. He needs a shot across his bows. Don't go there, Tara. Promise me you're not going to do anything stupid."

"He's alienating himself and I don't want to be his enemy. I'm on his side. He's family." I could be completely wrong on this one, and Anthony would never forgive me for suspecting him of having anything to do with it. But if I'm right...I don't want to create bigger problems for him. He isn't my biological brother, but we've been brought up as such. It hurts to think he could want to harm me, but I still feel protective of him, motherly almost. His vulnerability is equal to his angst. He's hell–bent on destruction and harming himself.

"Good morning. You two look intense for this time of day," Giselle yawns, as she pads past the doorway, in her pyjamas, on her way to the kitchen.

The doorbell rings again.

Shasta grimaces.

"It would be nice to have some peace and quiet round here," he says going to get the door while I race upstairs and throw some clothes on.

This time it's James and Svetlana with the camping equipment which they retrieved from the night before. Although Shasta had called them last night and told them what had happened to Simon, they need to be brought up to speed on this morning's police visit and the brake–tampering revelation. Unable to sleep through all the commotion, Simon comes into the kitchen; rubbing his eyes he pulls up a chair.

"I need a drink," he motions to Giselle who is the nearest person to the coffee pot.

"How are you feeling?" ask Svetlana sympathetically.

"Never better," answers Simon, holding his head in his hands. Then he spots his reflection on the side of the coffee pot and tenderly pats the wound dressing on his head.

"You need acupuncture for the shock," says Svetlana.

"The shock was lying in the car in the dark and not

being able to get out. I was terrified. I had to wait for the police to find me."

"It sounds awful. Traumas like that can stay in your system for years. I get clients who have never felt well since an injury, and it's often shock. If you come over to the clinic later I'll do you a treatment," Svetlana gives him much more sympathy than he's had from anybody else. The difference is that we know how much he can milk it.

Simon looks at her suspiciously. "But you use needles, right?"

"Yes, but for you I'll only be using my thickest knitting needles!" Svetlana teases him.

"I expected more from you. I get no sympathy from this lot!" retorts Simon.

Simon attracts so much teasing, and it even happens with those who don't know him well. There's an undercurrent of comedy in everything he says.

While the others chat Giselle catches my eye and glances to the back door, silently motioning for me to follow her, away from the others. I top up my tea with hot water and can feel Shasta watching me as I meander casually outside. I sit down beside Giselle on the top step and mentally send a greeting to the two giant sequoia trees.

"When are you going to tell him?" she asks.

"Tell who what?"

"Tell Shasta that you're going back to New York."

"Am I?"

"Oh come on Tara. The longer you leave it, the worse it'll get; or are you trying to break both your hearts?"

"Why are you bringing this up now?"

"You haven't checked your emails this morning, have you?"

"No. Why?" A feeling of foreboding is creeping up on me. *Oh God, what's going on?*

Giselle scrolls through her phone, opens an email, and passes it to me.

"Patricia copied me in on this email this morning," says Giselle, who sighs and looks out across the garden.

A lump rises in my throat and I swallow hard, but I can't release it. This is the moment I've been dreading. I knew that sooner or later I would have to go back to work, though I prayed it would be as late as possible.

The email is addressed to me and copied to Giselle because she works in Human Resources. My eyes skip the formalities and pick out the important words, quickly assimilating them.

"She wants me to return to work next week...or give notice to terminate my contract," my voice falters when I read the ultimatum. I stare at Giselle who is looking at me wide-eyed, waiting for my response.

I feel myself wither as though the vitality I've accumulated from being in Big Spruce is leaching out.

"I can't go back," is my honest, rapid response to the panic splicing through me.

"But New York is where you live. Everything you've worked for is there. I know you Tara, and I think you need more than this town has to offer. Don't get me wrong it's a great place, but don't you need more than this?"

"Maybe you don't know me as well as you think. Just because that's the way I was doesn't mean that's the way I have to stay. People change. That's a good thing. A snapshot doesn't tell you the whole story. I left when I needed to shed a skin. Please don't judge me based on an outmoded idea of who you think I am."

"I just don't think this is enough for you. Tara, you're a go–getter, you need the challenge that city life offers you. Shasta is a great guy, but you always go for business types. It's such a huge swing for you."

"But every day in New York has been a repeat of the last: same routine, same stress, same kind of guy and the same outcome. You know the phrase 'lightning never strikes in the same place twice'? Well what if it does? Do you not question the statement because someone told you it was true? Do you hold onto it because it may just have been an exception, or do you choose something different? Just because you believe it doesn't make it true."

Giselle looks at me with utter sincerity.

"You're right. I should know that more than most people. If you want something different, you've got to do something different. Change is good, right?" she asks unsurely.

"What if the things I want aren't compatible? My career, it's my identity, it's who I am, I can't just give up my security for anything. I don't know if I can just change what I believe either." I play devil's advocate, arguing with Giselle and myself simultaneously.

"It's your 'perception' of your identity. It's one of the many aspects of you. It's all about perspectives. You just shift your position to get a new view. We make decisions based on what we believe to be right and true at that time. It's not right or wrong, it just is. What do you want, Tara?" she asks.

I shrug. "I've got the material stuff, thanks to Rosa. It makes life easier and gives me choices. I'm grateful for that. I've always had a plan that fits in with my projected ideal. Being back here wasn't part of that plan. I want something, but...perhaps I'll know when I find it."

"You've had fun looking!"

"You know when I came here I was desperate to belong to something safe, secure and real. I wanted to be part of a family. I had that with Rosa…or rather my mother. It doesn't really matter what her title was – the love was real. I wish she was still here. I miss her terribly. On Rosa's last day on this earth she gave me the gift of her motherhood, but it was snatched away so quickly. Since then all the labels have changed and I'm still figuring out where I belong. I gained a mother and lost a brother. In some ways I feel utterly lost Giselle, and yet in other ways I have the feeling that things are coming together."

"I've always considered you my family," says Giselle tenderly.

"And I have too. We've always had that bond. But blood ties, they matter too. That unconditional love for another that no matter what, the bond of blood can't be broken."

"So you can inherit their crazy foibles?"

"But you can also inherit their gifts."

Giselle nods. "You know familial beliefs and inherited emotions get passed down the line. Trauma experienced by a pregnant mother can lodge in the tissues of the foetus. It's programmed into us before we're born, then we get our own stuff to deal with too."

"I know. I take full responsibility for my stuff. All the clearing and improvements I do benefits the ancestral line past, present and future. But who the heck am I if I don't even know who half of my ancestors were? I don't want a family of my own until I've taken care of my own issues."

"What's been the benefit of being in Big Spruce?" probes Giselle.

"I guess it's given me the chance to step back and re–focus."

"So maybe going back to New York with a fresh perspective and greater insight is what you've been seeking?" suggests Giselle.

"I know I can't use Shasta as a crutch to make me happy, nor would he let me. Perhaps I just needed a leg up to find happiness where I already was?"

"Perhaps. You're my best friend Tara, and I want you to stay in New York because I'd miss you terribly..." says Giselle.

"You see that's the thing, everyone has an opinion of what is best. I don't know if I've ever made decisions based on what *I* want I've usually asked someone else to find out how I feel."

"I'm sorry. I'm not trying to sway you. Whatever you decide, I'll be happy for you."

"It's easier just to go with the consensus."

"Patricia is pushing you for a decision either way. It's your call."

"I've meditated, gone inside and asked my heart what it wants, but I'm just not hearing it."

"Maybe you're just having trouble interpreting it."

"It needs to be more obvious,"

"Ha. I just hope you don't get a brutal push in the right direction, that you get the message before the stakes are raised and..." Giselle trails off, interrupted by the back door opening.

"There you are! Sorry, am I interrupting something? Just saying goodbye, James and I are leaving," says Svetlana.

"No. We're just coming in now anyway," replies Giselle getting up off the step, following Svetlana indoors to join the others; but my mind is still on Giselle's comment about the stakes being raised for me to get the message. I truly hope she's wrong.

29

Just as Svetlana and James are leaving a temporary hire car arrives as a replacement for the truck.

"I've got things to do at home. Do you want to come with me?" asks Shasta.

Giselle looks up at me from under her eyelashes and gives me a subtle nod.

"Simon recommends the hot spring spa, so I fancy doing that this morning. You go ahead and we'll catch up later," she says diplomatically, giving me the opportunity to talk to Shasta.

I leave the hire car for Giselle and Simon to use, and head for the peace and tranquillity of the lakeside lodge. I need to decompress, and the lake retreat is the perfect place for that. I also need to find a way of bringing up the subject of me going back to New York. I'm not looking forward to that conversation much. As we drive to Shasta's place I think of all the simple things I will miss. It distracts me from thinking of the bigger issue. Anxiety is unfurling in my stomach. *Hello, it's been a while.*

I can hardly bring myself to think about leaving Shasta, and returning to my life in New York is taking up ample headspace, so I can avoid it a while longer. What I feel for him is raw and instinctive, without logic or reason. It makes me skittish, because I doubt this degree of love and passion can actually be a good thing. There's danger in that; but as I see it, there's heartache either way.

I've heard that people can build up a mental image of their ideal partner: what they would look like, the job they do, their background, and that subconsciously we're all working towards that match. Was that my problem? Had the seed I planted years ago grown into a cedar instead of the oak I had expected?

Aunt Rosa used to joke that she planted so many random seeds that one day she would end up with a tuna tree. Was Shasta my tuna tree? I'd been known to build all sorts of walls around my heart before and it made my heart a safer, but lonelier, place. There is also the drawback that it makes it difficult to express, or even know, what I truly feel. I've tried to push through that, but I guess I still have work to do.

I love that Shasta and I can enjoy silence together, and yet the raging chemistry can make me squirm in my seat. He isn't always easy to read but I'm improving at getting the essence of his thoughts. He's better at reading me, but sometimes I can hear him in my mind. Can I imagine Shasta moving to New York? No. I can't envisage that at all. The magical life force of this place is his foundation. He could live anywhere, but he wouldn't thrive. He has chosen to make his life here, and he has responsibilities and family here.

We turn off the main highway onto the track road which leads past the sequoia grove, through the forest to the lodge and house by the lakeshore. The house looks striking in the bright sunlight. The triangular roof peaks majestically over the lake a few metres away. It feels proud, like its owner. The striking symmetry, natural materials and earthy colors, blend beauty with integrity into the lakeside landscape. The prism–like reflections in the glass give it a cryptic, other–worldly feel as though there is another dimension within.

Shasta walks into the house and makes his presence felt by inspecting the work. He questions the foreman on several points and I decide it's best if I leave him to it. I stroll through the spacious rooms, admiring the way each window frames a beautiful aspect of nature.

"Do you like it?" asks Shasta coming up behind me.

"*Like?* Seriously? It's beautiful."

"Come on, let me show you something," says Shasta.

Behind the lodge is a wooden four–stall stable. I notice the fencing of a new larger corral. The one I'd seen before was rough and make–shift, and only used for keeping the horses he was working on inside, or for the occasional training session.

"There's someone here I want you to meet," says Shasta looking into one of the stables.

"Huh?"

The pale gold head of a pretty palomino horse appears as she lifts her head above the door. She's shy but curious. Her warm brown eyes have a silver sheen to them and she seems not to make eye contact. There's a feeling of sadness about her.

"Oh you're beautiful," I tell the horse.

"This is Penny."

"Penny," I whisper to her as I stroke my hands over her thick blonde mane.

"She's virtually blind. This is her home now," says Shasta, quietly soothing the little horse with his voice.

I suddenly feel choked and tearful.

"She had another horse as a field companion, but he died recently. Her friend used to see for her. They were inseparable. The owners were going to put her to sleep, thinking it was the kindest thing to do, but I wouldn't let them do that to her," says Shasta.

Penny's ears flicker back and forward and I'm sure she

understands what he's saying. Her nose stretches towards me, her gentle mouth feeling over my neck and face.

"Won't she need some company?" I ask.

"She's still settling in, but I'll find a companion for her. I want to see how she gets on with visiting horses first. She has a warm spirit, but she's grieving for her lost pal. Scout seems to like her," says Shasta, opening the stable door and letting the dog in to join Penny. She lowers her head and they nuzzle each other.

I'm charmed by the good feelings around here. The wave of peace hits a counter current of fear, bringing emotions to the surface. I can't stand it any longer. I have to get it out. My heart begins to race and my hands shake in anxious anticipation.

"I need to talk to you," I blurt.

"No good conversation ever started like that," says Shasta levelly.

I walk over to the corral fence, and lean heavily on it for support. Tears already start to fall and I haven't even begun to speak.

"I'm sorry."

"Just say it."

"I've had an email from work. They want me to return next week...otherwise I'll have no job to return to."

"So...?" Shasta blanches despite his dark skin.

"I guess I have to go back."

"You don't have to do anything you don't want to."

"It's my livelihood."

"Is that what means the most to you?"

"I don't know what I think anymore, but I spent years focusing on my career, and security is everything I've worked for. I can't just let it go. I don't want to leave but–"

"Then don't."

He is standing close, but we aren't touching. That familiar frisson amplifies between us, charged by impending separation. I look up through the tears on my eyelashes into his chiselled face and his deep brown eyes interrogate mine.

"...I have to."

"Do you even know what love is? Tara, what we have isn't common. We're twin flames. What we have is so rare and astonishing that very few people get to experience it. We can have many soul mates, but only one twin flame. We're hued from the same spark. We're complete as individuals but when we join together it takes things to a new level. It takes lifetimes of learning for us to reach the resonance to be together."

"How do you know this, Shasta?"

"How do you not?" he snaps.

"I may not be as intuitive as you, but don't you dare put me down," I say, my voice lowers in threat.

"I'm not putting you down. You do that enough already. Perhaps it's just not the right time for us yet. If you feel you need to go back to New York, then you still need to work things out for yourself. Perhaps it's for the best that you go."

"What? So *I* can work it out? You've got it all sewn up have you? How come you know what's best for me? You don't get to make decisions for me. If I don't even have my own opinion then I have nothing."

"Where are you getting this from? I've given you your head and let you have all the space you need to make your decision without telling you what to do."

"You're keen for me to go though?"

"I can't win. I love you and that simple fact will always be true, no matter what."

And there it is, the emerging truth: Shasta is willing to throw the towel in. The proof of our value would be how much he wants us to be together, not how easily he will stand down. We just don't match up on this one. I step toward him and reach up to his chest, wanting him to close his arms around me, needing his reassurance.

"I'm sorry. I can't see a way forward for us. You have your life here. I can't gamble with mine – I can't stay and I can't ask you to leave," I mumble through the tears which are dropping off my top lip.

"Now who is making decisions for me? You're the one who's leaving, but I don't want you here under duress," he says coolly. "You've already made up your mind to go," he says, staring into the distance.

"I'm in turmoil, Shasta. I needed to tell you my dilemma because I thought maybe you would have the answer."

"Take the time you need. You know in your heart what to do. I'll be here for you, because I believe our future is together. I'm in for the long–haul, but if you go...I will let you."

We hug tightly and I fight the feeling that we are saying goodbye and cling to the reassurance of his words to avoid severance. I have never known anyone with more integrity. If what he is doing is putting my needs before his then I admire him for it, but I have no reference point, other than to compare to the questionable motives of old relationships. I've known plausible liars and cheaters before, and if history is repeating itself then perhaps this is his way of getting out.

I look up into his face, looking for some sort of truth. I

can find none. We kiss passionately, and I savor the soft strength and taste of his lips. He turns me round so I'm facing away from him, before putting his arms around me and together we stand quietly. In the silence my head and heart quit fighting with each other. In that moment it dawns on me that his feelings are true. It's me who has trust issues and it's me who has to resolve them.

"I'll take you home," says Shasta, his voice is indefinable. I don't argue and let him take me back to the house. He watches me from the jeep until I turn the key in the door.

I don't look back.

30

I put my back against the door and close it, breathing out long and slow, infinitely glad to have time to be with my thoughts in my own space.

Hudson comes to greet me, beating the wall with his tail. Thank God dogs don't speak. I'm sure I can feel my mother here in the house with me. There, I said it – *my mother*. That is what Rosa was and it's time to accept that. I wonder if Hudson misses her as much as I do; perhaps more so. He has her old, woollen gardening sweater in his bed and snuggles it constantly. She had been his world.

I plop down on the sofa and curl up in a nest of cushions, tucking one into my middle for comfort. I imagine Rosa sitting in her chair and us chattering as though she had never left. I'm running through recent events in my mind, telling her about Shasta, asking her advice and imagining her reply. I think of all the things I would have asked her if I'd known the truth sooner; not least the question of who my father is. All those times she sat there and all the things she never said. On the little side table there is a photo of her and Hudson together and she looks so hearty, with her round cheeks, warm smile and kindly eyes. It brings me comfort being in the house, like all will be well if I keep it the same.

I wander into her bedroom and sit on the bed, looking out of the window at the view she had woken to every morning, imagining the changing scene in rain, snow or sunshine. The room faces out to the back garden and the two sequoias that lead to the woods and lake beyond.

Dare I get rid of any of her clothes? I open the wardrobe and her scent engulfs me like a warm hug. I bury my nose in a chunky brown cardigan she used to wear and I'm flooded with happy memories and emotions. I'm not ready to get rid of any of her stuff. Not yet.

I feel like I'm facing goodbyes on so many levels. I wander around the house, lost in my thoughts of childhood. Years ago I had memorized the details of every nook and cranny, the way you do when you're a kid. The familiar pattern of wear on the wooden floor, the colored glass lampshades, the feel of the bathroom lino on my feet and the way I used to trace the outline of the tiles with my toes. The shape of the window fastenings, the different sounds each door made, the sound of activity in the kitchen, and the way the smell of baking bread drifted up the stairs.

I open the narrow door of the wooden staircase which leads to the attic. I haven't been up there since I was very young, and even then Rosa had discouraged me from going in because it was too dusty and would start me sneezing. Nonetheless my intrigue had gotten the better of me and I had snuck up on many occasions. I had tried on fancy hats and formal dresses which hadn't been worn since the occasion they were bought for.

There had been one particular dress which I had loved. Now it hangs from a peg covered in a garment bag. It is a simple long white dress of French lace with a round neckline. It was her wedding dress. I marvel at how neat a figure she must have had back then. Other dresses hang in an old oak wardrobe. The door no longer closes properly and it hangs invitingly open. Coats and dresses of various colors and patterns are hanging there, exposed and gathering dust. I start to sneeze.

One other dress looks neatly taken care of. It's a green satin gown with tiny pink flowers on a belt which hangs down the back. A matching green satin head–band is tucked into the top of the hanger. I don't know what occasion the dress had been bought for, but it looks like she wanted to preserve it.

Boxes of old ornaments have been wrapped in paper and put away. I smile to myself thinking that Rosa had tried to de–clutter. I don't think that she ever threw anything away. Stashing things in the attic was as close as she got. The attic holds a lifetime of memories, yet I don't know what stories are behind the old antiques and tacky ornaments. The framed pictures wrapped in newspaper may have been inherited from her parents, and never did find a home on these walls.

A purple chocolate box brims with old black and white photographs. Many of these people I don't know. I probably never will, because no names are written on them and there is no–one to ask. Nonetheless there is familiarity and love in those old pictures, and I embrace that.

I root around the old objects, connecting with everything and creating my own story behind its existence. I wonder if there is anything here to do with me, anything she didn't want anyone else to find. If there is such a thing, this is where she would put it. At first I feel I've intruded across an invisible line, but my curiosity is insatiable. I want to know more about myself and about where I came from.

I rummage inside boxes, move old furniture and pull out drawers in my quest. I search through boxes of letters, cards and old school reports. There are boxes with cuttings from newspapers and even more photographs, but there is nothing I can directly link with me.

I'm about to give up, when I turn to the monstrosity of

a wardrobe. How the heck did anyone get that up those narrow stairs? It looks like it separates into two halves, joined together with butterfly screws on the floor and top of the wardrobe. A subtle narrow drawer at the bottom of the wardrobe catches my attention, and I pull the small knob at the center of it. It doesn't budge. Clearly it hasn't been opened for years. Now I really want to know what's in that drawer. I pull and wiggle it from side to side until it gives way and comes completely off its runner.

The shallow drawer drops to the floor and a tiny bundle of paper wrapped in green ribbon falls at my feet. I crouch down and cross my legs to get comfortable. I pull the ribbon, releasing the neatly folded paper and envelopes which have been well concealed all this time.

"I'm sorry mom, but I have a right to know," I say out loud, in an attempt to ease my guilt about prying.

In one small envelope a tiny lock of fair curly hair is tied together with a piece of white thread. Is this my baby hair?

There are two other envelopes simply addressed *Rosa*. Each contains a love letter written by the same hand. The sentiment of each letter is the same – the writer asks if he has done something wrong, and tells Rosa that he would wait for her for as long as it took. It seems someone's love for Rosa was unrequited. The letters are signed off with one curvy squiggle which is completely illegible.

The last thing I unfold is a newspaper cutting in which Rosa has been photographed beside a slim handsome boy at the school prom. Both are formally dressed and look incredibly young, despite trying to appear grown up. I wouldn't have recognised Rosa except her name is on the cutting.

"Rosa North and Barnaby Whitelaw," I read out loud.

Barnaby? It couldn't be? I'm starting to make connections and draw conclusions. They were certainly old friends, but had they been more than that? Could it be that he was the man she was forbidden to see? Was he my father?

I shift my position on the floor and spot something I had missed. A tiny white, knitted, baby's bootee has fallen on the floor. I pick it up and squeeze it between my fingers and feel something stuffed inside the soft wool. I open it and pull out a piece of paper which has been folded over many times to fit inside the bootee. I unfold it over and over until the small piece of paper gives up its message.

My darling baby girl. If you are reading this you will probably already know the truth. I hope one day you can understand and forgive me. Please don't doubt my love for you, for giving you up was the hardest thing I've ever had to do. I will love you forever, Mommy xxx

The simple message awakens dormancy inside my heart. *Why did you hide it so well if you wanted me to find it?* Had her inner conflict been so great that it proved fatal? Had she lived a lie that had ultimately killed her? I feel no animosity towards my mother, but I feel peeved at the injustice; that any mother should be forced into giving up her own offspring, just because people were so caught up with how things looked with no regard for what really matters. Maybe they didn't grasp what really mattered. But aren't I also guilty of that?

I'm having a light bulb moment. Loving someone is what really matters, not exterior perceptions of reality. Actually, who really cares anyway? Acquaintances pay lip service, but they don't live your life; they're casual observers without understanding for what it feels like to own the experiences of others. Have I learned nothing from my time in Big Spruce? I know first-hand the powerlessness of people pleasing.

Issues are battling for processing space in my brain right now. I press my temples and try to focus on one thing at a time. Is Barnaby Whitelaw my father? How could I even broach that with him? He's still none the wiser that I'm Rosa's daughter, so he wouldn't even suspect. If he is, and it's a big IF, would he even want to know? Perhaps they had a teenage romance which fizzled out, never to be thought of again. But by the tone of the letters the writer was serious that he would wait for her – did Barnaby write the letters? As far as I knew he had never married.

Unrequited love had to be the worst kind. To never know what could have been. To perpetually hark back to the past, and 'the one who got away'. Perhaps everyone has one. I reckon it's only the lucky or the brave that get to be together forever. I'd heard friends talk about the 'one who got away' but I don't have such a person in my past.

In that moment something speaks to me so loudly, 'the answers to the future can be found in the past'. It's so clear it's as though I have just woken up from a lifelong trance. That person for me is Shasta. My chance to be with him is now and I stand on the cusp of messing that up and letting it go.

Finally I have clarity. I can see that I've been befuddled by my own stories, judgements and perceptions of how I expect life to be. What the hell had I been thinking? That is just it! That is all I have been doing – thinking! I have been living so much in my head that I couldn't hear my heart.

My spirit soars with sheer weightlessness. The dilemma is resolving and I see my future unfold before me, with the man I love, in a place so inspiringly beautiful. My heart swells with so much joy that it could split in two. I hadn't gotten it before, but everything I had wished for is right here. I didn't recognise the gift because of the packaging.

The only darkness is that I have already harmed my relationship with Shasta. I have to make amends, or is it already too late? I stand up quickly, and suddenly dizzy, I clutch the keepsake.

"Thank you. Thank you. Thank you for your guidance, Rosa. Still giving...always giving," I say loudly, my voice breaks the historic atmosphere of the attic and makes its own imprint in time.

The idea to place the letters back in the drawer crosses my mind. "No. It's time all secrets are out in the open."

I know what I have to do. I run downstairs to the study and fire up my laptop which has been relatively underused recently. I start to type the email response to Patricia Napier's 'return to work' ultimatum. Extreme heat flushes my cheeks as I type the polite, measured response; thanking her for being a wonderful mentor for the past seven years, but letting her know that I will NOT be returning, and giving notice to terminate my employment with immediate effect.

Am I really doing this? I'm jumping off a precipice, but damn it feels good. My heart pounds when my finger hovers over the keys. I feel like my future depends on one tiny strike of the keyboard. My finger drops. The email is sent.

I am burning hot with excitement and adrenaline. The boring, sensible part of me is reeling in horror that I've just jacked in my career at a top New York law firm. But I don't care. My singing spirit defeats the chattering teeth of my conscience. I print the email, ready to give to Shasta to show my commitment to our relationship. I fold it and place it in an envelope.

Suddenly the front door bursts open amid a clatter of footsteps.

"Tara!" shouts Giselle sounding hassled.

"Where's the fire?" I quip holding my hands up.

"Don't joke!" says Simon, following after Giselle.

"You know? So what the hell are you still doing here? We have to evacuate." She is actually serious.

"Why?"

"A wildfire has broken out. It's out of control and threatening the town. The fire department want all homes evacuated as a precaution."

"Like hell I'm evacuating! There is too much important stuff here."

"Don't be a martyr," says Giselle.

"A flaming burning martyr," says Simon.

A whiff of smoke hits my nostrils, and with it a primal instinct to run. Suddenly treasures from my past and my future look in jeopardy.

"Come on Hudson. Let's find Shasta."

31

"Hurry up! I don't know how much time we have. I heard the evacuation notice on the radio when we were in town. The stores are all closed up and the roads are busy with people trying to leave. The volunteer firemen are knocking on doors directing people to Fort Jarvis," says Giselle, hurrying me along.

My instinct is to grab as much stuff as I can, but instead I gather my bag and scoop in the contents of the paperwork drawer where important documents are kept. I've been wearing the amulet constantly, I feel for it around my neck and it's still there. I pull Hudson's lead off the hook, looping it around my neck, while I open the fridge and take out all the bottled water I can carry.

"Is it my imagination or is the smell of smoke getting stronger?" asks Simon, marching to the front door with his holdall already packed.

"I'm ready. Simon, take Hudson to the car with you. I just need to shut off the gas." I turn and go in the opposite direction. I find the gas shut–off tap and hope I've turned it off properly, but I don't hang around to check. The smell of smoke is already filtering into the house. There is a window open which I slam shut on the way through, then I lock the front door; truly expecting to return as soon as we get the all clear. I dump my meagre belongings into the trunk of the car as Giselle comes running down next door's path.

"There's no–one next door. I guess they've already gone," says Giselle.

I look up at Pandora and Errol's porch and notice the patio furniture has gone, presumably moved indoors.

"They could have let me know what's going on."

"They probably saw your car wasn't there and thought you were out," Giselle reasons.

She starts the engine and the radio blasts to life – I quickly turn it down. The radio presenter sounds direct but calm while repeating an evacuation notice. A couple of residents seem to be staying put. They stand in the street hosing down their property. I wonder if that actually works. Holding my cell phone to one ear and placing my hand over the other, I call Shasta. There is no answer. I try again. Still no answer. I quickly send him a text message.

At the end of the street two volunteer firemen are directing traffic towards Fort Jarvis. One of them holds his arm up, directing us to take a left turn. I'm not about to be directed just anywhere. I want to know how serious the fire is and make my own decision.

"Wait!" I call over to a volunteer who looks about nineteen years old. I get out of the car.

"What is she doing now?" I can hear Giselle say to Simon.

"Can you tell me where the fire actually is? I can't get hold of a friend who lives on the other side of Emerald Lake," I ask the volunteer fireman, trying to extract information from him by sounding meek and compliant. This measured approach defies my screaming instinct to just head towards Big Spruce.

"He's probably been evacuated already. We think the blaze started at a garage workshop east of the Langford Highway. It's spreading quickly because the strong winds are causing spot fires to break out on the southern slopes."

"Wow, you're really helpful. Thank you." I give him a lingering smile. The young volunteer puffs up, looking authoritative and pleased with himself.

"Is it likely to come further this way?"

"Yeah it is. Unless we get it under control or the wind changes, it's being driven this way. With it being afternoon it's harder to get it under control. We've a better chance at night, when the air is moist and the fire will burn slower."

"By then it would have spread far." My neck prickles with fear.

"At the moment the wind is blowing it uphill, so it's burning faster. We've got to be on the lookout for burning embers, or chunks of fuel rolling downhill starting new fires." The young volunteer is keen to impress with his knowledge, for which I'm grateful.

"I'm feeling better already," I anxiously turn away from him.

"Our crews are tackling it hard, ma'am," says the volunteer, backtracking as he tries to reassure. "Now go straight into Fort Jarvis and you'll be directed from there," he instructs.

"OK. Thanks." I confidently retreat with my mind made up.

He nods back at me as he returns to his colleague who is standing in the middle of the road directing traffic. I go back to the driver's side of the car.

"Finished flirting?" asks Simon flippantly.

"Giselle, let me drive." She looks at me warily and moves into the opposite seat, while I jump into the driver's side and take the wheel. As we approach the junction the young volunteer in the road automatically raises his arm, pointing to the left. I smile at him, wave, and accelerate quickly to the right, swerving around the volunteer in the road, leaving him shaking his head and Simon swearing as he slides in the back seat.

"Shasta's place is right in the path of the oncoming fire," I explain.

"Fair enough. We'll do what we have to do," says Giselle determinedly.

The road is clear because all the other traffic is heading in the opposite direction. I step on the accelerator, harder than I mean to.

"I think another car is about to be written off!" Simon warns.

A few people are still packing up their cars and being ushered out of town. We get to the far side of the Main Street when a burly deputy from the Sheriff's office stands in the middle of the road, blocking our way.

I stop dead, holding my hands up at him in anger and despair. I get out of the car to confront him.

"You can't go that way. The road is closed," he orders with not a trace of flexibility on his round face.

"Officer, my boyfriend is out there. He lives on the other side of Emerald Lake. If the fire is heading from Langford Highway it'll consume his place...if it hasn't already."

"The area has been evacuated. I'm sure he's out already. No–one is allowed through its too dangerous," he replies.

"That's why I need to find him. His place is isolated so maybe no–one has got to him!" I argue.

"I'm not letting you through," he insists, and I know negotiating with him isn't going to work.

I turn back to the car, hands on hips. My mind races through my options. I reckon I can get past the blockade, but that would mean putting Simon and Giselle's lives at risk. My fear for Shasta's safety is growing. I check my phone again. Still no call.

"Can you kindly turn your car around, ma'am?" commands the deputy.

I belligerently turn around to face him. "What would you do?" I raise my voice with exasperation, demanding an answer. From the corner of my eye I see another uniform approaching.

"What's the problem Tara?"

"Barnaby! At last someone who will talk sense."

"I don't know about that," says Barnaby, a twinkle in his serious eyes.

"Shasta is still out there, I'm sure of it. I can't reach him on his cell, and his house is under the ridge. The fire is heading that way. I need to get through," I implore.

"Shasta will know what to do. He'll be safe somewhere," replies Barnaby.

"So why isn't he answering his phone? His place is so cut–off, the fire marshals won't have gone there. Please Barnaby..."

Barnaby nods quietly in assessment.

"OK, I'll go and check on Shasta, but you have to stay here. Understand?"

"No, I have to come too."

"You're not! Take your friends and get out of here."

"I can't leave and not know what's happened to him. The entrance to his house is obscure, and I can lead you straight there. It'll be quicker if I come."

I'm glad to see Barnaby's expression change. He shakes his head and gives in. "Right, you can come but you do what I say."

"Yes, right," I toss the car keys to Giselle and tell her I'll meet them at the evacuation centre in Fort Jarvis. I have to run to catch up with the Sheriff who is already starting to drive off.

Helicopters are flying overhead, spreading water over the land. I still can't see any fire but there is plenty of smoke. The fear of the unseen danger is worse than knowing where the threat is. My imagination is telling me it could be anywhere because the tall pine trees on either side of the highway are masking the danger. Then we round a bend in the road and I see fire raging on the hillside. Flames are fanning sideways, directed by prevailing wind. There are still plenty of trees to fuel the fire on either side of the road. My anxiety escalates the closer we get to the burning hillside. My heart is thundering in my ears. Could Shasta already be caught in this?

"We can't go much further," warns Barnaby.

"We're nearly at the turning."

I'm so focused on scanning all around for danger that I vaguely notice the police radio. Barnaby speaks sharply to the other police officer on the radio.

"It's still out of control...a man has been pulled out of the garage workshop on Langley Highway–" says the voice. Barnaby abruptly ends the radio communication.

"What garage?" I turn and look Barnaby square in the face. I had heard the volunteer mention something about that, but it hadn't registered with me that it could be Anthony's garage.

"I don't know," dismisses Barnaby, his face is rigid and he is not making eye contact. We turn the final bend before the entrance to the track road and the view is obscured by smoke, but in the distance up ahead I can just make out the red of the fire engines in the distance.

"This road!" I point to the narrow track. Smoke drifts through the trees and for once I see the conifer trees and the sequoia grove as a threat to existence. I remember seeing something on the Discovery Channel about sequoias being more fire resistant than most trees, but perhaps that's just wishful thinking.

Barnaby drives hard over the uneven road. I hold on to stop myself becoming airborne because of the dips in the sloping road which leads down to the lakeshore.

We pull up at the cabin and I leap out of the Sheriff's car ahead of Barnaby and start calling Shasta's name. I'm relieved that the house is still standing, but it's tempered by the fact that Shasta's Toyota is parked outside. He couldn't have evacuated. I throw open the door to the wooden lodge shouting all the while. Suddenly I'm knocked off balance as Scout careers out the door. Why is Scout here and Shasta isn't? It doesn't make sense. There is no sign of him.

"He's got to be here. His car is here!" I shout to Barnaby, who is calling loudly now too. The contractors have also gone. I yell at the top of my voice, and take in a lungful of smoke which causes me to stop for a coughing fit. Barnaby runs round to the back of the lodge to the stables. He's pretty fast on his feet and determination makes up for his lack of fitness.

I catch up with Barnaby who is searching, breathlessly continuing to call for Shasta, but the exertion of running and inhaling smoke isn't doing him any good. I can hear banging and whinnying coming from Penny's stable. Scout is barking at the stable door. The horse's whinnying is getting more frantic and she's panicking.

"Penny," I lower my voice and call as soothingly as I can into the stable while her head swings back and forward above the stable door.

"It's OK. Everything will be alright," I try to reassure her.

Barnaby grabs a head–collar from the tack room. The smell of the smoke is terrifying the blind horse. She kicks and thrashes at the stable door. We nip in and close the half–door to prevent her bolting. I talk calmly to the horse while slipping the head–collar onto her.

My desperation to find Shasta is rising with every passing second of this futile search. Perhaps he's lying somewhere unconscious…or worse. My thoughts start to free–fall into overwhelming terror. Where the hell can he be?

I'll check the new house," shouts Barnaby, while I lead Penny out of the stable. Scout stays beside the horse, whining to her, clearly understanding her fear. Penny lowers her head and they communicate with snorts and whisker touching.

The door to the house has been left wide open and Barnaby is already in there. He comes out, red–faced and out of breath.

"He's not here, Tara."

"He can't be far. We've got to find him. He must be outside somewhere," I start coughing again and Barnaby grabs the horse's rope from me.

I level my mind. What is the best thing to do? We're all at risk. The smoke is thickening. I look up towards the glow on the ridge. Airborne sparks drift in the wind, heading in our direction. The fire is getting closer. I remember what the young fireman said about burning embers rolling downhill and igniting new areas. I realize that is now a very real threat. The lake will act as a natural fire break, but by the time it reaches there it would have consumed the lodge, the outbuilding and the lake house.

Part of the magic of this place is that it's surrounded by forest, but right now it's jeopardizing everything. The fire could spread around the perimeter of the lake to the town, and Aunt Rosa's house. Too many thoughts per second bombard me. The irony would be if Shasta is safe somewhere while we die looking for him. I can't risk something happening to Barnaby, I can't have that on my conscience. What would Shasta do? I stop in my tracks and take a deep breath, but there is too much smoke. I centre myself and try to get a mental connection with Shasta. Nothing. I fight the rising panic as gusts of smoke stream past. The inferno on the upper slopes continues its relentless threat.

My phone is vibrating in my pocket and I snatch it up thinking it must be Shasta, but the screen shows an incoming call from Svetlana.

"I can't get hold of James! He went to see Shasta about something and I've not heard from him since." Svetlana sounds fraught, but Barnaby also wants my attention.

"We have to take the animals and get out of here. I'll call for help" shouts Barnaby, and I wave, acknowledging that I've heard him.

"Svetlana, I'm at Shasta's house now and he's not here. There is no sign of either of them. The fire is close by. I can't speak now..."

I watch while Barnaby runs towards the car, holding Penny's collar. Suddenly Barnaby trips on a tree root and in a split second he's on the ground. He grunts and falls under Penny's hooves, letting go of the head–collar rope as he hits the ground. Penny wheels around in complete and utter terror, not knowing what has touched her. She rises up on her hind legs, skimming past Barnaby's head. In fear of her life Penny snorts and rolls her opaque, unseeing eyes, searching for an escape route from the madness around her. She bolts forward. I'm out of reach so I can't grab her and she starts to run in the direction of the forest. Scout barks and runs after her in pursuit.

Barnaby rolls onto his side and gets up, trying to bear weight on his leg, but his knee gives out beneath him. His face winces in pain and blood trickles from his nose. With a dismissive hand gesture he indicates he's fine, but red, breathless and now injured, he certainly isn't fine.

Scout is still barking as she peels off into the trees, chasing the fear-stricken horse, who looks to be heading towards the upper slopes. Barnaby hobbles to the car and is putting another call on the radio, updating whoever he is speaking to about our location. They report to him that the fire is already at the entrance to the access road we came down. We need a fire crew down here, now. There is a chance the track road could act as a natural fire-break, but the wind is continuing to push the flames inwards.

I wish I could turn back the clock. I wish Shasta and I hadn't parted company on uneasy terms and that we were just starting the day together all over again. Right now I can't see any way out apart from the possibility that we can escape by the lake. I run the idea past Barnaby but he says to stay here for now and wait for the fire crew. I know his knee is badly injured and that he's putting on a brave face.

"Stay here. I'm going after the animals," I shout and take off before Barnaby tries to talk me out of it. I can cover more ground on my own than I can with Barnaby. It's a cliché that you don't know what you've got until you lose it – well I don't intend to wait until then. I have to find Shasta and soon.

32

Penny and Scout have disappeared in entirely the wrong direction, away from the lakeshore. I follow the hoof prints and broken shrub foliage, hoping to find that the horse has either run out of steam or decided to stay where she is. But no such luck. Wisps of smoke stream past me and I duck low, looking for fresh air. I'm running uphill which is slowing my progress, but I have to find Scout and Penny. The air feels thicker and my lungs labor. I have to gasp for breath and I'm getting light headed.

I stop at a rocky stone pile around a wooden stick tied with white cloth. It is built in front of a small wooden shelter, which is little more than a peaked roof on top of four wooden posts, enclosed on three sides, with the opening facing out from the elevation, towards the lake. I know instantly that this is some sort of Native American shrine.

This must be the temple of the winds I'd heard Shasta speak off. It was made by his grandfather and he would take himself here sometimes to reconnect or perform a ceremony. It's humble to say the least. The grand name of temple is a vast exaggeration, but it's enchanting nonetheless. It's somewhere you can sit in retreat within nature, at one with it all. Inside a wide, flat stone has been used as an altar, complete with flowers, stones, a medicine wheel and feathers. If I ever get out of here alive I will come back to this place.

Close to the rock pile is what has once been a small stream, but is now little more than a trickle of water. I'm desperate for a drink. My mouth is so dry from the choking smoke, I can't swallow and my eyes sting. I lower my head to the stream, cupping the water with my hand and lifting it to my mouth. I slurp every little drop and give thanks for it.

And there, kneeling on the earth, I offer up a prayer that everyone is delivered safe from the fire. I invoke my birthright and talk to God and ask for help. I ask that the spirits of the wind, earth, water and fire conspire for the safety of all beings, and for Shasta's safe return. My amulet hangs around my neck and I feel its familiar hum when I state my prayer. I get a calm, clear response. The words 'sacrificing the old' come through clearly.

The dizziness is worsening. I think I'm going to pass out. I feel so weak. I need to rest to get my strength back, but my consciousness is dimming. I rest my head on the ground, giving in to it, I close my eyes.

I stir, not knowing how long I've been lying here. The familiar face of Lehman materializes in front of me, and I wonder if this time he will welcome me to the spirit world. His face ebbs in and out of my focus. But unlike the other times he's revealed himself, this time I feel him, and hear him louder and more forcefully than before. "Get up, get up," he is saying and I'm being pulled to my feet. I open my eyes to the blurry vision of a beautiful Indian face imploring me to move, but this is no vision – it's Shasta.

I hold on while he half drags, half carries me downhill towards the lakeshore where the air is less smoky. He pulls me into the shallow water, splashing it over my face and into my mouth, forcing my dry, burning throat to swallow and I choke. He keeps talking to me, keeping me alert. I hold onto him, unable to tell him how glad I am to see him. I do a double take and see Penny and Scout on the riverbank – I hope that everyone else is safe too. Gradually my head clears.

"You're safe now," he says, hugging me and smoothing the hair off my face.

"I thought something had happened to you," I mutter.

"What could happen to me?" he dismisses. "I know this place better than most. The wind has changed and the fire is retreating. It's going to be OK," he keeps repeating. I hug him with relief. The air is clearing as a fresh wind gusts across the lake, carrying the smoke away from us. We sit on the riverbank holding on to each other until all the danger has passed.

"Let's get you home," Shasta pulls me to my feet.

When we eventually get to the lodge Barnaby is impatiently sitting on the porch being attended to, and brushing off the fire service paramedic. The rest of the fire crew are looking around the property and checking for damage.

"Glad you're OK, Shasta. Tara wasn't going anywhere without you. You're as stubborn as your Aunt Rosa!" says Barnaby, gruffly waving the paramedic away. The thought to tell him the truth crosses my mind, but this isn't the time. The paramedic advises Barnaby to get his leg checked out at the hospital as soon as possible.

"I'll do that," dismisses Barnaby, paying no attention at all. We wait for a while to get the all-clear from the firemen that the fire is under control and we can now get through the access road. Barnaby limps off to the police car and heads back to town.

"Where did you get to? We searched everywhere for you," I ask Shasta, hugging him and not wanting to let go. He looks off into the distance, and doesn't answer me straight away.

"James and I went to speak to Anthony...about the brake tampering."

"You did what?"

"We couldn't just leave it. I wanted to put a shot across his bow before you spoke to him. He needed to know you've got back–up."

"I could handle it myself."

"I know you were. He just needed certain terms outlined to him. Anyway we didn't get to speak to him. When we got there the garage was already alight. Even the surrounding trees were well ablaze; we guess he must have had fuel stored somewhere. I knew Anthony could still be in there. We broke in and found him unconscious, so we carried him out."

"Is he alive?" I ask, already braced for the worst.

"Yes. I don't know how though. He was regaining consciousness when I left him with the paramedics at the garage, so he should be alright. He's a lucky man."

I sigh with relief. "How did the fire start?"

"Who knows?" Shasta gives a subtle shrug.

"Was it an accident?"

"Nothing is an accident around here. If the intention was to destroy the forest to get the protection order lifted, they didn't think it through."

"How come?"

"I'll show you later," Shasta replies secretively.

"How did you get back here? You didn't have your car?"

"I had to get Scout and Penny. The police wouldn't let anyone through, so I left James behind and got here on foot. That's why it took me so long."

"I was so scared something had happened to you."

"Like what?" he grins, making a joke of it as though he's immortal.

"Thank you," I mutter.

"For what?" Shasta looks perplexed.

"For Anthony's life – he could have been toast."

Shasta shakes his head in a dismissive gesture.

I remember the email which I printed off earlier, but now it seems like a lifetime ago. It's still stuffed in my pocket.

"I have something to show you." I hand him the crumpled paper.

He flicks his eyes over it and then fixes me with a gaze.

"Does this mean...?" Shasta asks slowly.

"I'm staying." I can hardly contain myself.

"Are you sure it's what you want?" he looks at me hard, as though he's daring me to back down.

"I finally figured it out," I smile up at him.

"I love you."

He inclines his head to me so we are face to face, noses touching, and he holds me like this, wrapped in his arms with my hand on his heart.

"And I love you."

We linger like this, soaking up the moment. Two sparks – one flame. I feel like we've accomplished a miracle.

"It's not just you that's making a fresh start. Let me show you," he smiles, and leads me by the hand down the track road towards the sequoia grove. There is something lying on the ground.

"This must be Barnaby's. It must have dropped out of his pocket when he fell," I pick up the wallet, rub the dust off it and check for ID. When I see the contents my mind briefly goes blank but is shocked back by an electrifying jolt in my heart.

"It does belong to Barnaby, but look at this." Bewildered, I show Shasta the old photograph of Rosa that was tucked into a side pouch. I stare at it feeling like I've imposed on an shrouded, intimate, romance. I piece together their history – re–kindling what I know of their past.

My instincts tell me the bond between Barnaby and Rosa was much deeper and stronger than anyone knew. Had he learned to accept he could only love her from a distance? He wouldn't be carrying a photograph around with him if he didn't have affection for her. This is the sign I've been looking for. It's the nudge I need to talk to Barnaby about my roots.

I gather the fragments of my mind that have been blown away by the possibility that my dad is not only alive and well – but that he could be the strong, affable character I'd already grown so fond of. I try not to let myself run away with the idea but I can't help it. I would love to have him as my father. It's a vacancy in my life that I've had for a long time.

The forest immediately around the house is unscathed, but a short distance away the fire has blown through the woods, destroying shrubs and razing vegetation to the ground. Yet from the burnt earth, the majestic redwoods trees are still standing proud, despite the fire–storm. The charred smell of the blackened earth is oddly reassuring.

"The fire has served the giant sequoias. The heat from it dries and opens the tree's cones, letting the seeds fall. The wildfire was Mother Earth's sacrifice for their sovereignty," says Shasta gazing up at the giant sequoias. "The sequoias are the shamans amongst trees. They're the kings of the forest."

I look up and tiny, papery, brown seeds fall on me, tickling my face. All around us there are quiet, fine, crackling noises, as thousands of tiny sequoia seeds fall with whispering lightness to the richly, renewed earth. It's a sight to behold and I outstretch my arms and gaze upward, enchanted by the tiny seeds cascading on and around us.

Shasta picks me up and spins me slowly around underneath the wispy, light seeds falling on us like confetti.

It feels like a blessing from nature in synchronicity with our new beginning. There are still points in life: defining moments where everything slows to a euphoric trance and true happiness is realised. Subtle feelings are magnified when you become acutely aware of everything in that moment. I will remember this still point for all eternity – my love for Shasta is engrained in my soul.

33

Life returned to normal very quickly in Big Spruce, and the town now bustles with a renewed sense of community from the shared experience.

Last night Shasta and I slept peacefully at my mother's house and in all my waking moments I felt gratitude for what I have. Giselle and Simon returned from the evacuation centre, full of tales of the exciting drama they'd been involved in. I told them I had quit my job and that I was starting a new life in Big Spruce – strangely, neither were surprised. Giselle asked the obvious question: why had it taken me so long to make the decision? Simon told me I couldn't get rid of him that easily, and I didn't doubt it.

Barnaby Whitelaw called me before I had the chance to call him. The levity in his voice was unmistakeable and I braced myself. He told me that although they initially suspected Anthony of setting fire to his garage while he was drunk, he denied it and the hospital found evidence that he had been deliberately knocked unconscious. So while the fire started at the garage, they suspected a third party, as yet unknown, was involved. Maybe now they'll start taking the criminal attacks seriously.

I winced with guilt that I hadn't gone to see Anthony. Perhaps I should have gone over there to build bridges with him. But he'd made his own choices, and choices have consequences. Forensics didn't come up with any evidence from Rosa's written–off truck. I didn't raise my suspicion that Anthony had tampered with the brakes. Punishment doesn't heal, but absolution might. I envision a sphere of light travelling from me to him, but he refuses it and I ask that it's held in the ether for when he's ready to receive it. That time is not now.

I told Barnaby that I'd found his wallet and suggested that I come over and return it to him. There was a pause, then he joked that I'd better not leave town with it, but he didn't commit to meeting up. I sensed his reluctance and let it go. I want to talk to him, but at the right time. He probably suspects I've seen the photograph of Rosa in his wallet, and he could be embarrassed. I look again at the newspaper cutting of the prom night, smiling at the youthful faces looking back at me, and carefully fold it away in my pocket, just in case the opportunity presents.

So I take Hudson for a walk, wandering down through the garden in all its familiarity, pausing to touch the magnificent sequoia trees. Everything seems bright and more luminous than usual, but perhaps I'm seeing things with fresh eyes. I follow the path feeling peaceful, but there is one small cloud of on the horizon. My origins are unclear. I can feel the weight of the issue. *In good time*, I tell myself. Hudson is bounding up ahead as usual, and keeps looking back at me with 'hurry up' eyebrows.

Despite seeking some quiet alone time I feel like I've even more company than usual. I watch travelling orbs moving at light speed through the forest. Transparent blue and violet spheres are hovering and moving in all directions. The minute I try to focus on them I lose them completely. It seems the guardians of the forest are vibrating at a faster tempo.

At the water's edge I toss a stick into the lake for Hudson then walk out onto the old wooden jetty and sprawl in the sun with the dog beside me, panting and drooling over chewed sticks.

A shadow is cast and the sunlight disappears. I open my eyes to find Barnaby on the jetty beside me.

"They said you were down here."

"Oh, I've left your wallet at the house,"

He smiles, looking distantly across the lake. As I watch him I feel his smile spread through me. This is the right time. Now I need the right words.

"I'm glad you came. I wanted to show you something." I pause and remove the cutting from my pocket. "I found this in the attic." I show Barnaby the newspaper cutting with the prom picture I've been carrying around with me. He looks down at the picture. Maybe I'm imagining it but I think he knows something is coming.

"I'm sorry, but I looked in your wallet. I found a photograph of Rosa. You loved her, didn't you?" I ask gently.

Barnaby softly traces his finger over the picture in his hand.

"I always have," he sighs.

"Why didn't you two get it together?" I ask, and see the wistful expression on Barnaby's face and cringe at my bluntness.

"She didn't want me," he says simply. "I fell in love with her when we were teenagers. I was sure she felt the same. We met behind her parents' back because they were so strict. They hated my mother, and what she did; they turned a lot of people against her. It was the stuff of fairytales until Rosa cut me off. She didn't want to see me. There were no arguments, no big fall outs. I didn't know what I'd done. Perhaps her parents twisted her opinion of my family..."

"I think that was the case. It wasn't her doing."

"I felt like she was hiding something. I hoped it was that she still had feelings for me. Then she went away and when she came back she seemed different. All grown up and mature. She didn't notice me anymore. She didn't seem to notice much of anything. She didn't go out, apart from to church. She seemed remote, like something was missing."

He takes a deep breath, sighs and looks out across the water. I smile and let the silence settle, encouraging him to finish. Eventually he looks back at me.

"I knew I'd never spend my life with anyone else. When you've known the best...well, it can't get any better. I had my memories."

"Didn't you ever want anyone else?" I ask him.

"There were others. No–one measured up. When she got married it nearly killed me. We got our friendship back, eventually. It was like nothing had happened. We never did talk about it," says Barnaby.

Everything is fitting into place but my stomach is somersaulting. My mouth is dry and I swallow hard. Unbidden tears well up and spill down my cheeks prompted by a sweeping sadness and anxiety about what I need to say. Barnaby looks awkward, unsure what to do.

"I miss her, Barnaby. Sometimes more than I think I can bear."

"I do too. I can't believe she's gone. When I walked down through the garden I expected to see her there. I don't want to upset you. Maybe it's best if I don't talk about her."

"No. Do talk about her. It keeps her alive," I sob, trying to get control of myself becoming overwhelmed by the strength of the emotions surging through me.

"She was one in a million your aunt," says Barnaby looking away but I've already seen the watery film in his eyes.

"Barnaby. There is something important I need to say."

His head swings round to face me, hearing the heavy tone in my voice. He looks at me hard, trying to figure out what the matter is. I'm going to have to blurt it out.

"Rosa had a baby."

Barnaby's face drains of all color and every muscle on his face goes slack. His eyes grow round and his lips part.

"She told me just before she died. Her parents sent her away because they found out she was pregnant. When the baby was born they forced her to give it up. She gave it to her brother and his wife to bring up as their own."

I can see his throat move as he listens, then his jaw flexes as he takes in every detail of what I'm telling him.

He stands up abruptly and takes a couple of strides away from me, holding his hands up in front of himself then he whirls back to face me. His warm brown eyes have taken on a harsher, hawk like appearance. I get to my feet.

"What are you saying? That I'm a father?" Barnaby stares at me.

"Is it possible?" I whisper.

"Of course it's possible!" he snaps.

This could go either way, but I can't go back now. I nod and can't speak because I've forgotten to breathe. I have to tell him.

"That prom photo was taken nine months before I was born," I nod, to the newspaper cutting. Barnaby's face lengthens and his mouth falls open. He stares at me. His brown eyes are blinking hard – realization is dawning.

"The last thing Rosa told me was...that I was her baby.

Rosa was my mother," I pause, hoping I've said enough for him to draw a conclusion.

Barnaby falls silent – his face pale and vacant. I'm thinking the worst, that I should never have told him. He looks catatonic. It is only brief and he regains some composure, but his lips move soundlessly at first

"I'm your father?" His voice is faint and barely a whisper. "Dear God. I don't believe it!" He paces back and forward, making a whistling sound between his teeth, then he seems to realize that his shock and distress is having an effect on me. He stops and looks at me, as though seeing me truly for the first time.

"This is a shock. Isn't it?" I feel foolish that I expected him to accept me – at least I had time to get used to the possibility of his paternity. I can feel myself draw back from him and the tears are drying. My heart is full of pride that he is my father, yet breaking at the same time.

"I'm not only a father? I'm your father!" he laughs nervously, bringing a finger to his nose, he sniffs and squints through moist, dewy eyelashes. His macho ego moves aside and his emotions surface.

"Is this for real?" he asks me. His brow is furrowed, but his mouth is curving at the corners. I nod and echo his smile.

"I think it's pretty conclusive. But we can have a test done." My voice is shuddering with emotion held back. Barnaby takes a step towards me; I take one towards him. Reading the myriad of emotions flicking through each other's faces, the distance between us closes and simultaneously we take one more step as our arms reach out to each other. We hug slightly awkwardly at first, then with more sincerity. The last piece of my past slots into place.

"Oh dear God. I never knew," says Barnaby patting my back.

"Neither of us did," I reply. "She nearly took her secret to the grave." I want to put my head on his chest the way I imagine a daughter would do with her father, the way I never had, but it feels too soon.

"All those empty years…and there you were. I'm shocked!" He looks up at the sky blinking rapidly to remove the tears welling up in his eyes. "Rosa, why didn't you tell me? We could have made it work."

"I lost my parents a long time ago. Now I find out my father is alive." The tears of my new joy spill out freely.

"There is a lot of time to make up for," says Barnaby as he awkwardly places his arm around my shoulder. He smiles kindly and I notice how similar our mouths are. Here I am with my dad. Who knew I would ever say that?

"Tara, I don't know how to be a dad, but I'd like to try; if you'd like that?" he adds quickly as though he has overstepped the mark.

I smile back at him, flooded with relief. "I'd like that. I can't think of anyone better."

"Shall we sit and talk a while?" he suggests. We sit quietly down on the jetty with so much to talk about, but unable to think of what to say. It'll take time to get to know each other, but already I feel a bond with him – I did when I first saw him.

"I don't like dark water," he says looking down into the lake.

"You never know what's hiding in there," I widen my eyes and concur wholeheartedly. I feel the gaps of those missing years begin to fill; my roots growing stronger as love flows through me, expanding outwards. The amulet around my neck glints in the bright sunlight, reminding me of its presence, like a wink from a loved one no longer present.

"I've got to ask. Do you think she knew?" I look from Barnaby to the pendant.

"I wouldn't put it past her. My mother always knew more than I did," he grins and holds my gaze. "Canny old girl, she was," he snorts and shakes his head.

That evening Giselle, Simon, Roger and I drive to Shasta's for a barbeque, which does seem ironic after the fire. We're celebrating the completion of Shasta's lake house. When we arrive there Michael, the elder from the reservation, is just leaving. I'm surprised but pleased to see him. Shasta asks him to stay for dinner but Michael politely excuses himself when we turn up. With the decibels Simon is clocking up it's hardly any wonder he doesn't stick around.

I feel like we arrived in the middle of something. Once Michael is gone I ask Shasta if everything is alright. He pulls me close to him draping his arm over me like a protective wing. I snuggle into him, happily at home there.

"They haven't given up," he replies with a peaceful inevitability I don't quite understand.

"Why?" I ask, not who.

"Michael saw someone leaving Anthony's garage, just before the fire."

"A witness. That's good."

There is only a flicker of wary acknowledgement in his intense beautiful eyes, but his mouth widens to a closed smile.

"Whatever it takes, I will look after you," Shasta replies.

I don't doubt him for a second.

Svetlana and James arrive in the fading light as the shifting, mauve, shadows of the forest move closer. The banter starts all over again and shrill laughter lilts in the air as stories are shared and teasing exchanges endorse the friendships.

"He wants me. He just doesn't know it yet," Simon's high pitched voice could well be heard in Canada.

"Dream on! Roger is all meat and potatoes but no mince," Giselle replies.

"I'll flip him. You wait and see," says Simon perkily and with utter certainty.

The delicious scorched smell from the barbeque stirs our appetites and the verbal ping pong dies down when the food is served.

After the barbeque I wander away from the lively chatter of the group to the water's edge and look back up at the house. The windows gently glow with reflected light from the dusky pink light of sundown. Shasta walks over and quietly takes my hand, looking up at his creation.

In the morning I get up at sunrise to plant the tree for Rosa. Letting the images of the past fade into the mellow morning light, I walk to the water's edge where the elements meet and feel the dynamic change where different harmonious frequencies connect. I wonder what that would look like in the world of pure light and sense fizzing, sparkling, colors dancing on the water. The strength and nobility of nature can never be matched.

I've infinite gratitude for the experiences that have led

me to my truth. I know not to regret my choices, or the opportunities I've missed. Sometimes they come around again. Like Shasta said 'truth is evolutionary'.

Rosa's tree has been sitting waiting in a terracotta pot, ready to be plugged into the earth. I pull off the clay container and tease its roots. I imagine the symbol of Quintessence in the ground and lovingly place the giant sequoia sapling into the earth, sealing it with the highest vibration I know.

I smooth the rich earth over its roots and look skywards, sending a blessing to all luminaires. In my mind's eye I see the world made of light and watch as a power boost echoes through the earth. A bright ripple of light goes around the planet, and around me the forest is alive: shining brightly, invigorated and humming a welcome.

Printed in Great Britain
by Amazon.co.uk, Ltd.,
Marston Gate.